## PRAISE FOR *RISING FAWN*

"Estelle Ford-Williamson's *Rising Fawn*, a novel of suspense Southern-style, is empowering and engrossing. . . . Williamson's treatment of Clare is hugely compassionate, and the novel's exploration of the north Georgia mountain where she comes to terms with herself is a beautiful meditation on place."

—VALERIE SAYERS, author of *The Age of Infidelity* and *The Powers*

"With characters and domestic life reminiscent of Lee Smith's classic *Calkwalk*, and Lawrence Naumoff's archetypal *Night of the Weeping Women*, Estelle Ford-Williamson crafts a gem of a story with Claire and Willie, whose marriage is about as compatible as their favorite magazines—*The New Yorker* and *Field & Stream*. Identify theft is the least of Claire's problems in this north Georgia saga. *Rising Fawn* is a winner from beginning to end."

—**William Walsh**, Director of MFA program, Reinhardt University

"Over a two-week span, readers are taken on a dizzying journey with sympathetic, lovable protagonist Clare Connor in Estelle Ford-Williamson's *Rising Fawn*. Anyone who's ever suffered from obsession and inner confusion will relate to this novel."

—GEORGE SINGLETON, author of *You Want More: Selected Stories*

"A routine case of identity fraud takes a young woman on a shocking journey of self-discovery, where she's forced to uncover a tangled skein of family secrets that will change the course of her life. Her journey, which begins in the modern world of corporate business, takes her deep into a wild and primitive landscape that carries its own mysteries and dark secrets. Rich in detail, poetic imagery, and fast-paced narrative, *Rising Fawn* is the kind of book that keeps you turning pages late into the night."

—CASSANDRA KING, author of *Tell Me a Story: My Life with Pat Conroy*

"In Estelle Ford-Williamson's riveting novel, *Rising Fawn*, she takes us on a journey as tumultuous as the rapids of a north Georgia river as Clare travels to the mountains while facing a series of life events that would make any woman lose her cool. Everyone who reads this well-written novel—and I know there will be many—will follow it to its very end, caught up in the thrall of one woman's tempestuous life."

—ROSEMARY DANIELL, award-winning author of *Secrets of the Zona Rosa: How Writing (and Sisterhood) Can Change Women's Lives*

# Rising Fawn

# Rising Fawn

ESTELLE FORD-WILLIAMSON

RESOURCE *Publications* · Eugene, Oregon

RISING FAWN

"Between, Georgia," a short story drawn from part of this book, selected as a
finalist for the Short Story America Prize, previously appeared in the anthology
Short Story America, Vol. 6 (Short Story America Press, 2018).

For information on speaking engagements, including online discussions, for
Rising Fawn, please go to http://www.estelleford-williamson.com. The website
contains additional information about the book and the geographic areas depicted
in the book.

Resource Publications
An Imprint of Wipf and Stock Publishers
199 W. 8th Ave., Suite 3
Eugene, OR 97401

www.wipfandstock.com

PAPERBACK ISBN: 978-1-7252-8003-8
HARDCOVER ISBN: 978-1-7252-8002-1
EBOOK ISBN: 978-1-7252-8004-5

Manufactured in the U.S.A.   09/29/20

To the music makers, the story tellers,
the natural and historical preservationists,
and the educators who help us know what it all means.

# Chapter 1

*Fraud.* The woman on the phone said call the fraud department of the bank. She couldn't be right. The woman also said that she, Clare Connor, owed ten thousand dollars from a series of Southern California cash advances, but Clare lived half a world away and hadn't travelled there lately.

She was here. Pine forests and hills of green and emerald-leaved trees outside the tall glass tower where she worked near the Chattahoochee River. Here, in her conference room where she helped professionals find their direction in life.

Clare felt lost, unable to think. She couldn't be a fraud. Someone was messing with her identity.

"Our records show you live in Tustin, California," the credit card company rep had said. "You visited several ATMs for cash advances in April." After Clare argued with her that she couldn't have done this, the woman told her to contact her bank and hung up. Clare felt the handset slip from the sweat on her hand.

"Not even 'goodbye,'" Clare told the walls. She didn't have another appointment for a couple of hours in this room where she met clients for coaching on lives and careers. She scrunched her shoulders to relax, felt her deep brown hair just brush the collar of her dress, and picked up the phone again. She looked at her organizer for a contact, punched in the numbers, waited for her bank to answer on the other end.

Young women dressed in fashionable short-skirted ensembles of white and black and pink and men in summer-weight suits passed by her window as she sat in the midst of the accounting section of the company. An outside consultant, she met with employees ranging from IT to field engineers

1

here. She turned to the wall as she grasped the handle of the phone there on the large table. She leaned forward in concentration, her brows joining in a frown.

*Where's Willie when I need him?* Clare thought. She considered calling him, but she decided she'd better get everything straight first. What could he do? This was hers to deal with. *Besides, he can't even make it home at a decent time.* She remembered looking for her last credit card statement the night before, after she'd tried to find out what was making him so late these days. She thought she owed a couple of hundred dollars on this low-interest card she got from a small bank in her neighborhood, but she couldn't find a current bill. Then it had occurred to her either she hadn't received one, or she'd misplaced it. Now she couldn't even find her balance, and the credit card company wouldn't talk to her. Embarrassing. More than embarrassing. She felt herself blurring, as if she were without substance, like the faint image in the glass.

The door opened and a tall, slender man looked in. It was Jeff Goodner, the human resources director.

"I hope you've got room in your schedule for a couple more tomorrow," he said.

Clare zoomed back to the present, all business.

"Sure." She stretched over the table, peered at her organizer. "Open at 10 and 11. I'm good."

"Great." Jeff smiled. "I'll send you an email." He closed the door.

Clare was calm for a moment, glad of more business. If there was doubt about her finances, more income would help.

But tiny shivers shot through her as she sat in the conference room. She glanced in the wall of windows again. The woman she saw—medium height, slender with light olive skin—belied the little girl she felt was inside. Right now, with fraud accusations coming from her credit card company, she felt like parts of her were strewn in the corners of a very large room, and she could not retrieve them to put herself back together again.

Clare reached for the phone and tapped in numbers to her bank, was routed to the fraud department, but no one was in. She left a voice mail with her information.

"I'm the one your records say lives somewhere other than where I know I live! You've got to straighten this out," she told the machine, using just enough humor to sound friendly as well as firm. The consumer guy she listened to on the radio said to go on the offense when there was a possible fraud involved. Banks had a way of making the one with the problem a victim.

A fearful thought: She didn't know when her bank would call her back. If she didn't report a lost or stolen card as soon as she knew about it, she'd be liable for the charges. However, if she did report it, she'd have to go through the tedious process of closing one account and opening another. For a moment she counted her one blessing: She and Willie kept their accounts separate, largely because he and his family had large holdings together. Fortunately, if something happened to her account, or vice versa, the other's accounts would not be affected.

She called the number for lost or stolen cards on the back of her card, and an automatic digital demon assured her it would close her account.

Clare thought back to her conversation with Willie last night. Many things about her husband—they'd been married five years—were a mystery. He seemed to deftly avoid questions about his whereabouts. Did she believe—as he told her—that he was having an after-hours drink with a guy from the brokerage? That fleeting, niggling question left her feeling a little lightheaded, and she grabbed the edge of the shiny mahogany table where she sat. The hard surface reassured her.

Willie usually had an early day, leaving soon after markets closed at four. What would take three hours or more to discuss?

"I'm meeting with one of the guys in the company who's explaining a new system to us," Willie had said last night. "I work better with people if I sit down *mano a mano* over a drink."

Okay, she'd bought that last night, but in the clear light of day, Clare had some questions. She didn't mention it to Willie last night, because it seemed so paranoid, but there was this phone call, a hang-up, about twenty minutes before he came in. It was probably a wrong number, but it was enough to make her wonder

Even her husband's name, Willie Clem, was a mystery. With the amazing wealth of his family, built up over years of buying and selling Georgia timberland, Clare was surprised his parents could not have picked out a more elegant name. Willie. It reminded her of the country singer with long braids and a taste for weed. Yet when she'd met Willie, his quirky good looks— he was a little pudgy looking, due to a round face—his engaging smile, and the subtle cool of someone with money had attracted her. It wasn't that she loved money, but a lot of her childhood had been spent wondering if her mother would bring home enough money from the family store to repair a roof leak or fix their car, prone to breakdowns. Her mother had taught her: Money beats poverty hands down. While his money couldn't hurt, Clare liked Willie for other reasons. He showed her caring and tenderness when she'd been injured. Best of all, he had a sense of fun that had somehow been bred out of Clare's gene pool.

"They could call him Bubba and I'd still have gone for him," she told her best friend, Helene. That was after her casual friendship with Willie turned more serious on a white-water paddling trip to the mountains. They went on to date for six months; Clare knew she was falling for him when she started giving up activities with her old friends to spend time with him and his pals.

The phone on the table in the conference room rang.

"Ms. Connor?" A cheerful representative called her back. "I've looked up your account, and according to your file, you sent us a fax telling us you were moving to California. That was several weeks ago. Then a week later, your husband sent a similar letter, and we, of course, sent your correspondence to the address he gave—"

"What?" Clare was shocked.

"It appears that you went to the ATMs out there quite a few times—"

"I wasn't *in* California."

"Well, it shows a couple of transactions almost every day—"

"How many times?" Clare interrupted.

"Oh, I'd say about twenty—"

"Between what dates?"

"April first to twentieth."

"Those are the dates we're busiest with our taxes. There's no way I'm going to be hitting ATMS in California at that time. For sure, I'm not going to be *moving* to California."

"Well, it appears you did make payments. I have a twenty-five-dollar money order—were you in Colorado at that time?"

Clare felt herself getting very warm and angry and scared. "I told you— I've been nowhere in those periods you mentioned!" She drew in a breath.

"Now I want you to send me all correspondence in my file. And please tell me why you made this change of address without contacting me? How long have I been your customer? Do I seem like the type—"

"W-well, just let me send you these documents, so maybe we can sort this out." The woman's voice quavered.

"What's the amount of the damage?" Clare asked.

"Well, there was a total of ten thousand dollars in cash advances at California ATMs."

"You're not going to hold me responsible for that!" Clare cried. "Please send me the copies of transactions including those faxes we supposedly sent you as soon as you can."

She hung up and went to stand by the fax in a nearby office. She felt herself shaking as she stood next to the machine, hoping those walking by didn't notice.

She checked her cell phone for client messages while she waited, and then a sheaf of slick papers came streaming out of the fax. There was a running tally showing someone had hit various ATMs in the LA area for three weeks, about every day, for six hundred dollars a day. There were neatly penned faxes requesting the address change—one in her name, one in her husband's, but both were in the same hand. Why couldn't a clerk see this clue? Did the small size of the bank mean the staff was less careful, less proficient at what banks do?

Clare looked at this strange handwriting of her name and raged. How could someone else take on her characteristics? The thief's handwriting was distinct, practiced. The person must have used a Sharpie pen because the words were dramatically black and even. The letters showed rounded, fat *e*'s and *l*'s. There was her name: The thief had created a flourish with the first letter of her name. Did that on both letters.

Clare cycled between manic questioning about how all this happened and deep concern about the hit to her credit. What if she had to live on her own? She couldn't buy a house. She couldn't even rent an apartment if they did a credit check and there was a fraud alert on her account. She'd absolutely have to fork out for a utility deposit.

Why are you going there, girl? She heard Helene scolding her. Where's your sense of yourself? How can you jump to living on your own from a financial hiccup like that? Clare was wonderfully lacking in self-confidence. Underneath the exterior of a thirty-year-old professional, she was like a bag lady, needy and not sure about tomorrow. Helene was always on her about it.

Her trust in her husband right now was shaky. When he found out about this, he'd be upset about possible damage to his own accounts. The hang-up the night before sprang into her mind again. Was that a call for him? Did it have anything to do with the fraud?

How did the thieves get their information? Okay, she had put credit card payments in the mailbox for pickup—she wouldn't anymore. So how did they come by her Social Security information and her birth date? And how in the hell did they come across her husband's ID? *We don't even have the same name. How could one person have access to his Social Security and his birthday and his full name? Even more mysterious—why didn't the company blink an eye in obeying the wishes of a person with a different name who says he's my husband, who says Clare's moved, so send Clare's credit card bills to this new California address?*

Clare returned to her conference room now, moving her purse to the locked credenza she'd had keys to but never used. She felt she had to keep things under guard so a worker or visitor in the office where she was working wouldn't walk in and swipe her ID. She went to the cafeteria for lunch, and she clenched her debit card in her fist so a techie wouldn't photo her private info while standing in line at the cafeteria and send it to God-knows-where.

Sitting at the conference room table again, she heard a buzzing near her and realized it was her cell phone set on silent. She grabbed in her purse for it and answered.

"Hi, honey," Willie said on the other end. Clare was glad to hear a friendly voice. But he never called her at work unless it was something really important; clients and the markets kept him busy. Why now?

"Just called to say hi. What's up?"

Clare felt torn. If she didn't tell him, it was dishonest, and this mess involved him, so he should know. But she dreaded the reaction.

"You won't believe this," she began her bad news.

"What's going on?"

"I just found out that someone hijacked my identity to take over my credit card account in California. Hit a slew of ATMs in the LA area, racked up thousands in cash withdrawals."

"Wow. That's bad. How much did they get?"

"Ten thousand—all of it bogus. Here's the worst part—they used my ID, Social Security, address, everything." She drew in a quick breath. "And they used your Social Security and ID, too. I don't know how they got it—"

"What?"

She imagined him exploding on the other end. "I have no idea how all this happened. Let's talk tonight."

Suddenly Willie was quiet.

"See you at home." He hung up.

Clare felt caught. Someone was fooling with her identity and no telling what they'd done with it. She was in a familiar place: financially frantic. The feeling returned like it had so many times: Something was wrong, she would not be safe. Clare felt her throat. It was its normal size, not shrunk down to the width of a soda straw like she thought it was. That person in the reflection still had face, hands, arms—but she felt like her body was disintegrating.

I'm panicking, she told herself. Get a grip.

A friend who was in a highly visible new-for-a-woman role in a corporation once shared what she did when she was confronted with something unsolvable. Lacking the mentors that men had, she'd had to figure out things as she went along. She told Clare her five-minute panic trick: For five minutes, she just let things go while she gave into feelings of inadequacy, stomping, singing, whatever she could do behind closed office doors to vent the scary feelings. Then she'd get down to business.

Clare wondered if she had five minutes to panic right now. She didn't. She went into her logical side to ward off her money-fear goblins. But she still thought about Willie. He was mad, she could tell. Was he cheating on her?

All the way home that night, Clare kept running possible scenarios of what had happened to kick off this identity theft and tried to anticipate Willie's words. She was delayed getting home. She'd taken time at work to phone a police report not only to the local police but to the Tustin, California police. Then she'd done some detective work on the Internet.

Willie was late, too. She pulled a steak from the freezer and put it on the Jenn-Air broiler.

She prepared a fresh salad with lots of vegetables and crunchy nuts, the way he liked it. She poured extra virgin olive oil into a sparkling decanter and took down a fresh bottle of tarragon vinegar from its shelf display. Baked potatoes steamed in the microwave, and multigrain bread was ready to go in the oven. She was taking a lot of care with dinner, but she winced as she cut Vidalia onions for the salad when she remembered she might be eating it alone. There was no message from Willie on the phone, so she had to assume he was with his "buddy" again as he'd been the night before.

She sensed a flash to her right. Light hit the oil decanter and bounced back in her face. Willie and the woman on the phone could be behind all this.

The phone rang, and she reached for the kitchen extension.

"Hello?"

A woman's voice snorted, as in a half-laugh, then clicked off.

This was a deliberate call, not a mistake. It was about the same time as the hang up the day before.

Clare felt blinded by the call—a voice was reaching her from some unknown place, pressing against her even through the windowed walls in her kitchen.

She went outside to the garden, closed her eyes, drew in the smells of the plants around her, and imagined herself as a blind person allowed only the scents of nature. She felt behind her, sat down on a bench, and breathed in slowly. She tried to imagine the plants as they were, but a spot above her breast hurt, and her body felt like it was wound tight like a spring. The phone call. A memory of a woman who'd stolen her boyfriend, Chad. He was her only other lover before Willie, back in her college days in Chicago. He'd dated another woman behind her back, then told Clare he was marrying Linda, a wealthy medical student. Hurt, and feelings of worthlessness, engulfed her for weeks after. Years after Chad and Linda, she still nursed a wound in her chest.

When she'd met Willie, she'd felt totally accepted for who she was. They met on a hiking and camping trip with mutual friends, part of an informal group of eco-minded mid-to-late twenties types. They had potlucks where they planned trips or shared pictures of past ventures hiking to Raven Cliffs, down into Providence Canyon in southwest Georgia or up Stone Mountain for a magnificent Sunday hike.

One September, the group signed up for a whitewater canoeing trip and started out on the upper Chattahoochee River. She ended up paired with Willie in a canoe. He wasn't super-muscular, as he seemed to carry some extra pounds, but he was competent with a paddle, and she was glad. But on the first run, she swerved off a rapid and snagged her hand between a rock and the side of the boat.

"Wow, let me see that," Willie said, taking her wet, bleeding fingers, hand hot with pain. He pulled their canoe onto a small beach, and they sat on the rocks above more rapids. Warm sun beat on their backs. The blond sun streaks in his brown hair looked like gold.

"Kinda makes you wonder if this is the sport to pursue," Willie laughed. Her fingers bled across her jeans and the bandana he brought out to stop the flow.

"At least I've still got fingers," she joked. "Did you see the missing fingertips on our leader's hands?" Now she surely knew how he got them.

Willie touched her fingers gently, then held them out to look closer.

"I don't think they're broken—they look mostly skinned and scraped, but you need to have it x-rayed for sure."

Her hand hurt, big time. But she watched how carefully Willie treated her, and she felt, well, cared for. He pulled her fingers together and wrapped his red bandana around them, then tied off the dressing with a small knot. The deep red soaked through the bright cloth. After a few minutes, the bleeding stopped. She was fixed, and she felt warm all over. Grateful. And something else.

Willie reached his hand to the back of her neck and pulled her face to his. Clare felt chills over her body, and excitement, a deep sexual yearning. He kissed her solidly, leaving no question he felt the same.

She stroked his face with her healthy hand and looked into his eyes.

"Thank you for helping me."

"Not a problem, ma'am," he smiled, and hugged her close. "Maybe you can give me a hand someday."

There was that twinkle in his eye.

That was a long time ago. How long was it since she'd felt that caring? Now she was scared about what was happening to her and how he might react. And what *was* that phone call?

Clare shuddered, kept her eyes closed, and concentrated more on her garden, on the smell of basil and the feel of air combing the hair on her arms. She could see the heavy hydrangeas raising their blue heads on strong stems above soft, dark green leaves. Everything outside smelled cool and earthy and pure and began to soothe her fears.

She heard the front door close and ducked into the kitchen in time to see Willie entering. He stood in the open doorway to the kitchen. He had his tie and sport coat off, his arm raised on the opening. He wore a quizzical look on his face. She remembered the woman on the hang-up. Her deep scare about others in Willie's life returned. The woman wanted Clare to know she was there.

"What's going on?" she asked, and immediately regretted it.

She saw his face crease in a frown and knew it was the wrong time to ask that.

What do you mean?" he asked. His blue eyes were shaded gray. His jaw moved as though he wanted to say more.

"I just got this phone call—"

"Are we going to talk about the identity theft?"

She should have waited to bring up the call. Her go-for-it attitude was great on the job, but it was a not such a good thing right now. She figured she'd already kicked off whatever she was starting, so she'd better keep at it.

"Not my identity, but maybe yours." That got his attention. He looked at her. His eyes shifted down, then up.

"Have you been seeing someone? I just got the second hang-up in as many days, timed just before you come home."

Willie was jingling change in his pocket. "Did you check the number?"

"We cancelled caller ID. Remember?"

Willie pulled his hand out of the pocket, put it on the doorframe.

"Well, I don't know anything about it." His face looked as though no one should have a care in the world. Then his face clouded. Hands now at his waist, elbows bent, he stood with his feet apart.

"What are you doing, Clare? What are you accusing me of? Is something going on with my accounts? I need you to tell me. I'm serious." He looked worried.

Clare's hands trembled. She couldn't let him see how rattled she was now that she'd put words to her fear. She needed to move.

"I'll get dinner on, it'll just take a few to put everything on the table." She moved past him.

"You *are* planning to talk about this and not some crazy fantasy of yours." His words hit her ears just as she moved past.

She felt the firm pressure of turned tables weighing on her. She would have to explain the credit issue—fast.

"Dinner in five," she said, turning to put the bread in the oven and ignoring him for the moment. The yeasty smell of the bake-it-yourself bread loaf turned her stomach. She didn't know why she told him about the woman's call at the very start. She just did it, so that she wouldn't chicken out and not bring it up tonight.

He squatted in front of the refrigerator to find a beer. His butt was cute, she'd always thought. Today it looked fat.

Willie ate his steak slowly, pushing it back and forth on his plate. He sorted the greens in the salad with his fork. He picked out the nuts she'd carefully put in it, a sure sign of pique.

She told him of the day's revelations. They both had accounts at that small bank in a shopping district not far away—they'd been enticed by five-hundred-dollar CDs in return for substantial deposits to open new accounts there. And Clare had signed up for a low-interest credit card. She'd found that most of the contacts were with the bank, not the credit card company. That was different from other credit cards she held.

"I'm just mystified," she said about the letters in their names the bank had faxed to her.

He looked at her as if she'd said something nasty.

"I don't think you're careful about where you put your ID," he said

Then he questioned her about leaving her ID first in one place and then in another. How many times had her purse or computer bag been left out in an office and not under lock and key? All that she could recall recently was a visit to the post office, where they both got passports—no trip planned, but fees were set to jump—and both gave their Social Security numbers, but no credit card numbers.

"If that's all you know, how did your ID and mine both get hijacked?" he asked. His change jingled in his pockets again. Food lay on his plate.

"True, but getting passports is the only time I can recall we did any-thing recently where people might link our names," Clare said. They focused on the clearest, most tangible threat, one simpler to deal with than the ac-cusation she'd made.

Clare put her knife and fork down on a plate of half-eaten food. The loaf of bread was untouched.

"All I know is you need to go to the police in the morning," he said. He got up, cleaned the food they hadn't eaten from their plates, and put them in the dishwasher. "This needs to be cleared up pronto. Fraud is like a Scud missile that takes out everything in sight. My family's business could be hit big time."

"I'll go see them as soon as a report is available."

"I wouldn't wait." With quick movements, he closed the dishwasher and moved toward the hallway. "I'm going downstairs to watch the news." He knew she didn't care for his TV news; she preferred newspapers.

Clare sat down in a chair in the dining room and emptied place mats and compelled crumbs to her with her napkin. She'd go get the police report tomorrow. She'd go early. Not wait.

She picked up the loaf of bread from its nesting spot in a basket. She brought it to her nose, feeling the weight of the crust. It smelled like a bakery, like the delicatessen bakery that delivered to her family's old store near Melanie Street in her old neighborhood. She licked the bread, tasting its salty skin. Then she wrapped it in aluminum foil for later heating and placed it in the refrigerator.

On her way upstairs to read the newspaper on the bed she looked from the doorway to downstairs and saw Willie was rigging some fishing lures.

After reading for a while, Clare felt distracted and put the paper aside. What a rollercoaster the day had been—the news about the credit card identity grab—and now her greatest fears about her husband were being realized. She glanced at her large ring. Sadness fell over her as she prepared for bed. The faxes she'd seen of the fake letters jumped into her head. Willie jangling change in his pocket, avoiding her question. The images followed each other like disjointed frames in a movie.

As she lay with the windows open to early summer cicadas and night calls of two owls, her mind went back to the white-water canoeing accident five years ago. That night, they'd stood in one of the bathrooms of the mountain cabin the group was staying in for the weekend. He tenderly and patiently rewrapped her hand, winding sterile gauze around her three injured fingers until she wore a slender white glove. While she'd been on trips with others—male and female— who were quick to analyze what went into such accidents, Willie was kinder. But he did say something curious. He was gently knotting the ends of gauze when the question came out.

"You Catholic?" he asked.

Clare's finger flashed again in pain.

"Why do you ask?" The pain went away, but the anger stayed.

He looked in her eyes.

"Tonight I want to love you," he said quietly, his fingers wrapped around her forearm, "in ways that don't have to do with fixing up your fingers." Her anger lifted. Prickles went up and down her arm, and other parts of her body grew warm.

"So you think I'll have religious scruples?" she asked. His eyes were so blue, set off by the sky-colored polo shirt he'd changed into after his shower.

"Maybe."

She shook her head. He hesitated for a moment, then drew her closer and hugged her. She hated being untruthful. It wasn't really a lie. She'd said no to the suggestion that it would get in their way. She'd been born Catholic, but that didn't mean she was one way or another when it came to loving someone. After her one other lover, Chad, she'd been reluctant to get so involved again. But Willy was caring, attractive, and here.

"This has nothing to do with my religion, but you do carry protection, right?"

They cuddled by a fire built in the cabin while the rest of their group swapped white-water paddling tales of near misses with rocks and hydraulics. He held her close, and the pain nearly went away. They'd only needed one of the sleeping rooms.

That cool, early fall evening, with the sound of the stream running over rocks just outside their windows and a fresh breeze filling the room, she learned what a terrific lover he was.

As she and Willie separated, she rolled over and placed her bandaged hand on his chest. He put one hand over hers and pulled his fingers through the ends of her hair with the other. He sighed deeply.

"You've got a marvelous body," he said, kissing her forehead.

"I have to say the same about you," she said. Moonlight was the only light, but she could see his eyes, and the shape of his body next to her. He got up to go to the bathroom, then came back and lay down beside her.

"You run into anybody?" she joked.

"Nope, but it's not much fun negotiating the shared bath because I had to use protection."

"I appreciate you using a condom," she said shyly. His eyes in the shadows appeared dark, shiny.

"You know there are some guys who wouldn't go along with the rubber stuff."

She was stung. Her body felt like a large stick had hit her in the chest. She moved away.

"That's a surprising thing to hear from someone who minutes ago was so thoughtful."

She shook the bed covers and pulled at them. He put his hand on her arm. His eyebrows wrinkled together.

"I get mixed up. I hear guys talking—locker room talk, I guess. Prevailing opinion is, guys don't like condoms. I'm sorry. I shouldn't—"

"Hey, I'm not some guy in a locker room." Across her front, she felt warm. She was trying to keep her voice low in case it carried.

Then she saw that his eyes were even darker, and they were wet. "You have to be careful," he said.

"Why?"

"I'm kind of a slob."

"I just want to be safe." She reached out and touched his hand on the bed between them.

"My old man. He calls me that."

"What? Slob?" She knew from what he'd told her that his father was very domineering.

"When you get an old man like Dan Clem, it's hard to do anything right," Willie said. "If I don't do enough to make money, he rides me. If I take the lead and go do some things, he turns sarcastic. 'Slob' is when I don't do things his way."

He stopped. She hesitated.

"But I thought you did well in your business."

"In my old man's book, it's never enough. Every deal I make, it's crap."

She thought as they talked about his father that there was a hint of whining in Willie's voice—it went a little higher when he talked about his dad—but she ignored that. Sounded like he had an older brother who was fond of liquor and often didn't show for work, and his father acted like that was perfectly okay. Willie dealt with it all by becoming a stockbroker rather than wobbling like a fifth wheel in the family real estate company. On the side, he had his own investments, but his father often tried to get him into some new deal. And so he went in with him on a few big projects.

"Sounds complicated," Clare said.

"I'll say," He kissed her softly, making her warm all over as he'd done before. "But let's not talk about him."

The next morning, Willie and Clare, with her hand carefully wrapped and awaiting a doctor's diagnosis about the bones, cut short the white-water canoeing, packed up, and drove back home together. It was the first time she recalled not completing an adventure weekend. Usually she was willing to try anything new if it didn't hurt or maim. For once, maybe it was time she chose her excitement more carefully.

But she wasn't careful about Willie. They spent the rest of the day in her bed.

Over the months they dated, Clare had found that their dinner dates stretched into languid lovemaking. So when her friends called for her to try the Ocoee or the New River white water, or even the tamer Nantahala, she declined. She settled for picnics by the Chattahoochee River with Willie and his friends. These outings were, she found, kind of an excuse for drinking a lot outdoors.

Now, lying in her big bed in Atlanta, Clare touched her right hand—it hadn't been broken, only badly bruised and cut. She was having trouble going back to sleep. In the mountains, she and Willie had broken through to a new level. She had sided with him in his ongoing conflict with his father, and he'd become her lover and friend and then husband. What happened? How could a man who was so tender in bed be such a puzzle?

Sometimes, reading in bed, she'd look over, amazed at the extreme sports and hunting and fishing magazines on his side, and then turn back to her own *New Yorker* or *Atlantic* and wonder at their differences. It wasn't that way when they began, was it? Of course, they hadn't spent much time reading in bed.

# Chapter 2

WEDNESDAY

Finally falling to sleep, Clare never heard Willie come to their king-sized bed. Wednesday morning, he was up early and showering when she woke. He didn't say much, grabbed an English muffin and coffee, and was off before she even got downstairs. Sometimes he left early, before her, but still she was put off that he was in such a rush.

Driving to her client's office, she tried to mentally put together all the signs of trouble bubbling up from Willie since the night she started looking for the missing credit card statement. Signs of a possible other person in his life? Maybe. Just clues that, a few years into the marriage, maybe they weren't compatible—she didn't know whether someone else was involved. The thought that their relationship might be in danger made her mouth feel like it was drawing down in one of those reverse smiley faces. She gripped the wheel of her bright yellow SUV.

Then there was the credit card mess.

It wasn't too long ago, when she was changing to her new career in coaching, before her business started off and before she met Willie, that she had wake-up-in-the-night fears about survival. She could get herself into a swivet of worry over whether the oak in her backyard would come crashing down on her house, as trees did in Atlanta storms. Or what if she couldn't make a mortgage payment and fell behind? Even today, when she wasn't quite sure about Willie, she could get herself into a frenzy of worry. Any media story about foreclosures jarred her and sent her into spirals of what ifs.

She was a contrast—on the one hand, Ms. Can Do with her clients, and, on the other, more like a young animal struggling to its feet after birth—unsure, testing the ground underneath for firmness and support. Right now she felt like that fawn.

Her cell phone rang, and Clare switched on Bluetooth, making sure she was hands-free to talk.

"How are you doing?" Helene asked.

"I'm crazy. I haven't caught you up to the latest! I'm actually on the way to work and I can't talk long. Let me call you when I can."

"Okay. Dodger treating you okay?"

"We'll talk later. 'Bye!"

She'd forgotten how much she had told Helene about Willie and his strange ways. She would have to catch her up to the latest.

Clare had told Helene about his tendency to be late and not tell her in advance. Sometimes he'd mention having a lot to do at work while they breakfasted. Then, that night, he'd show up way after dinner, never calling, just as she was putting his plate in the refrigerator. If it was one of her special meals, she'd be like a hot tea kettle boiling water by the time he got home. That was just one example of ways he confused her. Sometimes getting information out of him was a real tug-of-war.

"You ought to call him Dodger," Helene said. Then she began calling him that all the time, at least when it was just Clare and Helene.

Clare was really hurt not too many nights before when Willie seemed to become more like her enemy than her friend. They had a new couple from the neighborhood for dinner. At their gathering, Joe Shelton, the husband, had gotten in her face about her studiousness—and her religion—and Willie hadn't defended her, just let the guy run his mouth.

In fact, Willie had started the scene in the first place, laughing with Joe, while she sliced vegetables with a large chef's knife, about his wife being smart enough to get a full scholarship to St. John's in Chicago. Joe himself had quit college after two years and now made a bundle designing software. Willie barely slid through college. So Clare was definitely painted as the outlier.

Then Joe slammed his open palm down hard on the granite top in her kitchen and yelled, "You little saint! Where do you get off going to a place like that—you really did want to study if you went there!" Meanwhile, Willie just lifted his beer and smiled.

"That's really funny, Joe," she said, fake smiling. "But be careful I don't have a slip of the knife." She tipped the blade slightly. "So far you've dinged me for my college and for my religion!" They'd all laughed then, but Clare was furious. What kind of a husband treats his wife like that?

What would her mother tell her?

She pictured her mother, shanks of black and gray hair falling forward, drinking coffee at the dining room table, littered with forms for ordering groceries to stock their small store and Italian takeout market. She doubtless had learned her love of good food from her parents, but a lot of other things had been left out. There were stories about ancestors on her mother's side, an Italian fisherman who switched to coal mining there in the north Georgia mountains. On her father's side, she knew an Irish stonemason immigrated to the Tennessee River Valley. But her parents revealed no secrets about unfaithful spouses. Clare's father had died young and her mother never remarried, so little chance of cheating there.

Clare wondered about her mother, lying in a nursing home since a stroke six weeks ago. She knew she was all right, but were the nurses checking in on her to make sure she was alive? What would Frankie—her mother's original Italian name, Francesca, had been replaced long ago—make of all these questions about Willie? She liked Willie, her mother did. She almost heard her directing her to make nice with her husband, traditional Italian woman that she was.

That Thursday evening with the Sheltons, Willie teased her, too, about the tomatoes she splashed all over her apron front as she was cutting tomatoes for the salad as their company watched.

"You ought to wear hazmat gear," he teased her. He was so demeaning, with that and with the Joe Shelton comment. But later he'd wanted to make love like nothing had happened. As soon as she climbed between the soft sheets of the large bed, she felt his arms reaching around her.

She pulled herself back from him.

"Thanks for defending me against Joe. And what was that with the hazmat comment?"

"Wha—?"

"You said I should wear hazmat gear—"

"I didn't say that," he nuzzled her. "Aw, honey, let's be friends." He pulled her to him.

She was tired and decided the time for discussing wasn't now.

They snuggled and stroked each other, and before long she felt his muscles tighten. For just a moment, she hesitated. He *so conveniently* forgot his comment. But she slid under him, and she soon forgot her worries from dinner as he made love to her, calmly, sweetly, passionately.

This was the hard part to figure—no matter how distant she felt from Willie during many of her waking hours, she loved the good sex.

This morning, as Clare put away the questions about Willie and pulled into the parking lot at her client's building, she could still feel the loss of Willie's closeness. Sex made a big difference in their marriage. Was that all they had? She went on to think of the employee who would be waiting for her an elevator ride away, but a little memory of Willie's touch followed her up the walkway.

In the early afternoon, Clare signed in at police headquarters and asked the way to the detectives' area. Up the elevator and down a long hall, she came to a secured door. She punched in numbers that she'd been given and talked to a squawk box before the door released. She walked into an open room with a nest of cubicles winding around it. A conference table stood out like it was under a spotlight. Detective Maurice Scott was near the conference table, emerging from a gaggle of other officers—white and black—in street clothes. A tall, handsome Black man, he smiled and shook her hand. She was immediately glad she'd made an appointment. Scott made small talk about his just getting back to detecting after being a street cop for three years. He had her sit at the table—no privacy of cubicles.

"So you got, or you think you got, your identity hijacked; someone got a card in your name after filing for an address change and went to town."

"It was a total surprise. My husband and I were very busy during that time in April doing taxes. I didn't think about a missing credit card statement until the other day. And this is what I found out."

"Happens all the time. It's hard to know how it happens," Scott said, leaning back in his chair. He looked at her closely, as though sketching her for a drawing.

"Usually it's a gang—numbers of people involved. Nobody can trace the crooks because so many hands have had the goods." He told her about a case he'd solved where two roommates, one working for a politician, one a mortgage company, took out a mortgage on a vacant house owned by someone else in the politician's name using his ID and personal financial information. The politician was left owing hundreds of thousands of dollars until the fraud was discovered.

Clare was impressed. At least Scott knew the patterns.

"I got the bank's correspondence with the thief, the faxes they sent." Clare said. "Got the forwarding address and checked it out on the Internet. It came up as a drop box in California, one of those mailing centers with boxes for rent."

"Let me see what you got." She showed him the material she'd collected over the last day.

"Clever." His brown eyes scanned her printouts.

"Hey, Scott," one of the other detectives shouted. "You got a call—you're due in court. Right now!"

Scott looked up at the clock.

"They're calling now."

Scott's pleasant face frowned. He closed the file and unfolded from his chair. Clare looked up. "Are you leaving me in the middle of this?"

"Gotta go," Scott smiled. "You ever see a detective solve a case without a head?" He grabbed his hat and sport jacket and left.

Clare was wordless. Scott was already on the other side of the unit door.

Why did she feel as though she was a giant billiard ball on a pool table waiting to take a knock from a pool stick? Her hands shook as she pulled her computer bag onto her shoulder and left the secure area.

So much for her big ID theft. No one was going to help her.

Feeling hungry—she'd skipped lunch to go see Scott—Clare opened the mailbox at home to retrieve the day's mail. In the stack was an official-looking envelope from Tellum, Inc.—her credit report. She'd just requested Tellum issue a fraud alert on her account Tuesday morning.

That was fast, she thought—overnight service because the company was headquartered locally. She carried the thick white envelope inside with the magazines and put it on the table. Her stomach making odd noises, she ripped into the report: "Never late, never late," she repeated to herself as she scanned the sheets. Perfect credit report. It was also a history of her adult life—car purchases, retail spending with credit cards, mortgage with Willie, two-hundred-thousand-dollar home equity loan—wait, what home equity loan?

"Oh—my—God," she said aloud. She looked around to see if Willie had come in the house yet.

"A home equity line cashed out? A two-hundred-thousand-dollar loan, payments of seventeen hundred a month?" She felt her pulse race. Her face was becoming hot. "Overdue June tenth! I can't believe this! Shit!"

Clare left the table, set herself down on the staircase.

"We've been screwed—royally," she said to the floor.

"Hey." Willie found her there. "Are you going or coming?" She kept looking at the floor, not looking up at him.

"I've been hunting for you. What say let's eat out on the porch tonight. I'd like to go up to the lake, but it's too late. Whatcha got on for dinner?"

She looked up at him. He was smiling.

"Hadn't gotten to that point. I've got some deli chicken salad and some other things."

"Sounds good. Let's do it." He patted her shoulder as he walked past her up the stairs to change clothes in the bedroom.

He was awfully cheerful for a guy upset the night before about her prying questions and her credit card fraud. This morning, he'd hardly spoken, then he was gone to take a shower. Usually, after they made love, he would sing in the shower. "A Hard Day's Night," sung horribly off-key. But that didn't happen this morning. His jolly mood tonight was a bit confounding.

What if he was behind all this? Surely he wouldn't create a bogus loan in our name, too.

She followed him upstairs to change her clothes, thinking how she really did not want to fix dinner, dreading telling him the news in the Tellum envelope. He was at the top of the stairs, about to go in their room.

"Did you find out any more about the credit card fraud?" She was close to the rail at the top of the landing. His back was to their bedroom doorway.

"Dead end there," she said. "Police don't seem like they're going to do any investigating. Busy with life, seems like." She sounded casual, but she felt brittle.

She moved past him and went to the bed. She sat on the edge facing him as he pivoted in the doorway. Fear was raking over her. She tossed off her heels and pulled flat shoes from under the bed. She wiggled her feet in, not sure if she should say what she needed to say. He crossed the room.

She cleared her throat. "We got some bad news today."

He turned from the closet door. His blue eyes looked at her as though studying for a test. "What?"

"I got my credit report—it shows us owing a huge home equity loan I know nothing about."

He took in a breath. Then he just looked at her.

"First payment of seventeen hundred was overdue June tenth. It's a mix up." He seemed to be waiting. Now he was by the large armoire near the closet.

"I have no idea how this all happened."

"How much did you say it's for?"

"Two hundred thousand."

Willie's eyes narrowed, wrinkling the tan skin around them. She saw his mouth quiver, then it was back to normal. He looked over at the window, then back at her. He put his hands on his hips.

"Have you been doing something I don't know about?" He was not smiling at all. Clare felt caught, her chest tight like the knot in the tie he was now undoing. She said nothing. How could he accuse *her*? He's the one who probably got the loan—and the cash. She felt herself unable to move, as though struck by lightning and left in a vast, unreachable field all aglow with electricity.

"You need to think about moving out," Willie said suddenly.

"What?" Her empty stomach groaned. She felt the atmosphere charged, and light all around, blinding her, keeping her from seeing or hearing right. But Willie kept on talking, his tie draping his neck.

"That thing with the credit cards—now mortgage fraud. This gives me the creeps. How could you do such a thing?" He frowned deeply.

"What do you mean how could I do such a thing?"

Clare imagined giant hands pushing her away. "I had nothing to do with either one of them!"

"It just smells to high heaven to me. Haven't we had enough together that you didn't need to do that?" He stood next to the armoire. It was like two large, ominous figures towering over her. Her eye went to the replica of Rodin's *The Kiss*, a statue that sat in front of the mirror on their dresser. What passion they used to have. Where did it go?

"Willie, I have no idea what you're talking about!" Clare felt frantic. How could she stop him from talking, hurting her?

"I talked to my dad, and he says it'll ruin some of our deals if there's a question on my credit. And loan fraud, for God's sake!"

His father, scion of a family with money from generations of timbering. He did not like Clare. Willie defended his father at some times, railed against him at others. But right now he was on his father's side, and this was dangerous. She felt cast out, abandoned. She could hardly think what to say next. Surely this couldn't be. The heavy curtains on the windows seemed to close in on her.

"How do you know it's affecting your credit?"

"Dad just ran my credit report." Clare felt sadder than ever—his father was someone she couldn't compete with. "Said I've got a hell of a lot more debt than I should have. I can't risk this, Clare."

Willie's dad wasn't just competing. He was her enemy, and she was finished.

"What do you want? Why are you doing this, Willie?" She barely squeaked it out. Tears pulled at her throat, and she swallowed to keep her voice working.

"I don't know what's going on. I don't know why you did this. But I can't take a chance that my good credit is being sabotaged by yours. It's all I have. It's how my family and I do business."

Clare looked at Willie. His head was down, not looking at her, and his arm stretched out as though holding up the armoire. "I'll move out of the house," he said, "until you get your things together, find a place, and move."

Clare felt trapped, unable to breathe. She had to get away. She lifted up from the bed, walked, then ran to the door and down the stairs. Wide stairs, polished edges reflecting still strong afternoon sun, rushed up to her, held her up as she fled down them. He could not have said what he just said. She went out into the garden and softly touched, then picked, the red tomatoes she'd meant to have for dinner. Well, he could fix his own. He could just cram it. How could he leap from her credit card problems to their two-hundred-thousand-dollar problem and just say "Move out"? What in blazes was going on?

She looked at the earth around her plants. Mulch held the moisture in, cradled the spindly pale green plants that now grew nearly waist-high spreading foliage all over the sides of her tomato cages. The branches shook as though in a wind. She realized it was her hand, trembling as she reached for a tomato.

*Blood is blood.* The phrase kept running through her head. It was an old saying her mother had uttered frequently when she was growing up. It meant that alliances are inevitably drawn across bloodlines. In this case, that meant they excluded her. It would be hard to change Willie's mind.

He was in the kitchen standing near the counter when she emerged from the garden and the screened porch.

"You need to make plans to take care of yourself."

"What do you mean?" She put the tomatoes on the counter.

"You can do fine on your own." His words were precise.

"Wait a minute. I'm not prepared to go find a place to live. The first thing they'd ask for is a credit report. I'll look like I'm in over my head." Her house, not his. Her kitchen, not his.

"Not necessarily. You'd do okay. Overdue payments on a big home loan certainly explains why you're looking for a new place."

"But Willie—"

"Look," he said, glancing at her with eyes that were cool, unmoved. "You have resources of your own." He moved one shoulder as if shrugging her off. "Use them."

"Screw you!" she shouted. "You're not going to kick me out of this house! You leave. I'm not gonna leave."

"Clare, listen to me!" he said. His eyes were narrowed, his shoulders straight. "I've told you that I'll give you time to get your things together, find a place. If you make this difficult, I'll fight you—hard!"

"Then you find another place to sleep," she shouted. "And eat!"

She pushed past him, opened the refrigerator, and took out the chicken salad, a bottle of white wine, a plate, her tomatoes, a knife and fork, and walked out of the kitchen and up the stairs to their bedroom. She slammed the door, put her dinner down next to the Rodin, and flipped over on the bed.

She lay on her stomach, pulling herself up on her elbows, grabbing her head in her hands. He was kicking her out.

Divorce. She tried the word on in her mind, but it seemed like a foreign word. Willie was slipping from her, going away, really going away. Empty space would be left, whether she was at this house or another. When divorce happens, it's like death. The person is there, and then he isn't there. The toothbrush on the bathroom sink, the clothes in the closet, the other car in the driveway, Willie's smell—all gone. There would be no short notes by the phone, no cuddling, no sex, and being in each other's lives, no family birthdays at the lake.

Clare knew she was entitled to more than merely her possessions. But how much was her share of revenge, her price for being dumped?

She didn't have a family. Tonight she'd lost hers. He had a family—that was his power and he would use it. She sat on the bed, looking at the Rodin statue again. Clare moved it away from the mirror so there was no reflection, then turned the entangled bodies to the wall.

She felt like crying, but she couldn't. Her chest seemed bound with tight cloths. She heard the door downstairs slam and knew he was gone. Her tears finally came pushing up from within, shaking her body, spilling over her fingers like water seeping from a mountainside spring.

An image came to her mind, and there was a heaviness in her chest that drew her forward. She thought back to a cold, biting winter morning; she had awakened to see the outside veiled in a haze of gray. She must have been six, she was wearing new pink Strawberry Shortcake pajamas with feet in them, a Christmas gift. She padded into the dining room. Something was wrong.

There were no smells of bacon frying or coffee perking, smells that used to cling to the walls like humidity, and the warmth from the cooking was missing. In the dining room, where normally on a school day her father would be eating eggs, bacon, and biscuits her mother had made from scratch, there was no sign of either parent. She had entered the room, where one end of the table was heaped with newspapers and thick, stapled pastel ordering lists for food. The end closest to her was cleared for family meals. The room seemed tiny because of the large, dark wood cabinets on the side, all their top surfaces filled with angels and cherubs and other pieces of porcelain and china pottery.

Her sister Angela was eating a bowl of cereal. She must have been nearly twenty-one. She was wearing makeup that her mother claimed made her look like a gypsy, but Angela, bent on attracting a husband to transport her out of the small life of a grocer's daughter, had ignored her mother's complaint. Red lips and mascara dominated her sister's face.

"Where's Pop?" she asked Angela. "Where's Mom?"

Her sister looked up at her with what she thought was a sneer. Her red lips curled. "Jail." Clare felt a thud in her chest.

"In jail?" she asked, breathless.

"Not *in* the jail, precious," Angela laughed. "*At* the jail. Pop was robbed by a gunman and they're asking him questions."

Clare held her breath. Her father—in jail, at the jail. She didn't understand.

"What happened?"

"There was a stickup. They're just asking him about it."

"Where's Mom gone? Is she there, too?"

"No, she's at church. She's delivering the linens for Mass. I'm taking you to school. Get ready, Clare-bear. There's nothing to worry about."

But Clare did worry. All day at school she found it hard to do her work, thinking about her father in jail. What was he doing there? Were the police holding him? Would he be home when she came home?

Paul, her father, was standing in the living room when she arrived, and everything was okay. He was safe and unharmed. She hugged his long legs hard. He took her into his lap and held her in arms that seemed like they could encircle the world. His bushy eyebrows and kind eyes consoled her and took away her worries.

But the robbery was just the beginning. He collapsed in the market soon after, stricken with a fatal heart attack. The family shrank. In the years after that, Clare's mother and sister ran the store. When she would go there after school, Clare often heard them talking about the robbery.

"That was the beginning of the end for him," her mother would say. "They never caught the guy."

All through her younger years, Clare recalled having a fear about her mother's safety in the store and about having enough to live on. What if something happened to her mother? What if the same robber came back? She remembered a photograph of herself among friends in college; the others were laughing. But Clare had this scared look, as though anticipating danger, anxiety written all over her face in an unaware moment, fear her steady companion.

After her father's death, life for Clare turned lonely. Her fantasy life became one of creating small families with her dolls, dolls that would take trips, dolls that would picnic regularly.

Clare later reflected that the confusion about her father being at the jail, rather than in the jail, was typical of her young life. She didn't always get what was going on because her father was dead, and her mother was gone most of the time at the store.

Then one day Clare was at home with her sister and mother, who was trying to nap after work, following a night without sleep. The door to Angela's room flew open. With a sudden flouncing and flurry of clothes thrown into suitcases and angry shouts down the hall toward her mother, Angela left their home. She eventually called and said she wasn't coming back; she was in Florida and would look for work there. Gone. Done with her family.

After Angela abandoned the family, the family shrank again. Her mother and she were left, and it was very little of her mother, as she was either at the store or church.

Clare remembered once while in college, she consulted a therapist over her feelings of abandonment. The woman had asked at length about her mother. An Englishwoman, she sniffed and adjusted her plaid wool wrap and took a sip of her afternoon tea. She drank it by pouring milk first, then the brewed loose tea into her cup, Clare noted.

"Just tatters of a mother," the psychologist pronounced.

Here in her large, spacious home, Clare was being left again, this time by Willie and his family. Tears came again, and she reached for a Kleenex on her nightstand. Lying across the bed in a room she would sleep in alone, Clare thought about her mother. She needed her, that sliver of a mother. She would go to see her.

She looked at her watch and then out the window. Dark was still a couple of hours off. If she left now, she could make it to the nursing home and be back before nine.

At Angel's Arms, Clare walked down the hall, through the double doors, noting that the personnel she greeted were always different. Sometimes she worried about security, how they knew who was supposed to be there, but she kept going around the corner to the last room on the hall. Her mother's roommate seemed unconscious, as usual. Frankie was sleeping; still no change in six weeks. Her gown was loose and showing a bare porcelain shoulder. The French word *negligee*, in a neglectful state, popped into Clare's mind, and she drew her mother's gown closer to her neck. Her mother's thick, too long gray-streaked hair—no longer the dark brown Clare recalled from childhood—was neatly brushed back from her mother's face. She breathed evenly through her large nose. Her full lips were closed in quiet sleep. Someone had groomed Frankie, probably after a sponge bath, and she hadn't moved to disturb the effect.

Clare started for a moment as her mother's lips parted and began moving. At first Clare thought she was going to speak—no clear words had come from those lips since her stroke—but Frankie did not speak. Her lips moved quickly as though reciting a prayer.

*Hail, Mary, full of grace, the Lord is with thee Blessed art thou among women, and blessed is the fruit of thy womb,*

Clare sat tensely, waiting for what she thought might happen. Then she saw it.

*Jesus.*

Her mother nodded her head just at the moment of Christ's name in the Hail Mary. Then she rushed on, moving her mouth loosely, but quickly, saying the other words of the prayer.

Clare felt the depression she'd had since the hours before when Willie had laid the move-out demand on her. There was nothing else she could do. She began praying with her mother. She struggled to keep up, as her mother's rote prayer was faster than Clare could speak, even in a whisper.

Holy Mary, Mother of God, pray for us sinners, Now and at the hour of our death. Amen.

Why not pray? She had the name of a lawyer she'd gotten from an acquaintance whose divorce was very nasty.

"Get a good, strong female lawyer," her fellow life coach, Kitty Cramer, had said. "She'll scare the pants off the other side."

She was going to have to take action. It scared her. There were problems with Willie, but before he'd pushed her away, she really had not wanted a divorce. She would miss their times together, the meals at night, just that daily presence of another person, the familiar touch of his hand on hers. However, if she was being forced to separate, then she had to protect herself. She turned back to her mother and continued praying.

It had been a long time since she'd tried to connect with God or the Virgin Mary. Although they'd been almost constant companions in grade school through early college, she'd about lost her faith over the clergy scandals, and, before that, over the gory details of the Inquisition she'd studied in college.

Nonetheless, she found herself wanting to pray. How was she going to resolve this Willie Clem hurt? Could she get him back? At the same time, how could she ever sleep in the same house, let alone the same bed, with him?

Looking back at her mother's quiet form, the lips still moving quickly, Clare reached over and stroked her mother's hair and her face, smooth-skinned and attractive despite her eighty years. Why had she had her children so far apart—fifteen years between Angela and her? She was almost like an afterthought, or a late recognition of the waning opportunity to have more children. Why, as a good Catholic, had her mother not had more? Had she used birth control?

Her mother's generation of Catholics didn't do that, did they? If not, what accounted for the families of two and three children among her classmates in lower school and college? It was a mystery, just like the miracle she thought, in first and second grade, that had caused her nun teachers not to have children.

But what would she do for housing, now that Willie had told her to move out? And what would that do to the messy state of her financial affairs? How would that make *his* credit any safer, since the damage was already done? She moved her own lips in prayer and thought about options. An apartment? A house?

Clare shoved those thoughts aside as she looked at her poor mother's face and colorless, moving lips. She kissed her fingers and placed them on her mother's mouth. The parted lips paused for a second, then kept praying. Clare turned and left the room. Her body moved slowly as though weighed down with rocks.

# Chapter 3

Upstairs in her office at home, in a house that was stripped of any sound, Clare took a breath and punched the law firm's number.

"I was recommended by Kitty Cramer," she told the assistant on the line. "It's about a separation."

"Separation or divorce?" the woman inquired.

"I—I don't know."

A moment later, Sherry Goldstein was on the line.

"I'll be glad to meet with you" she said quickly. Her voice was surprisingly husky, like that of an older woman. "Bring financial statements."

"I don't know if I have anything like that—"

"Get them. I'm guessing if Kitty Cramer sent you, you're in deep trouble. You don't have a moment to lose with this."

"I don't know if I want to go for the jugular—"

"That's all I know to go for. I'm for you, kiddo, and if you don't want a fair settlement, you need to find another attorney." Clare felt pressure oozing from the woman's voice. Her words were sharp, seeming to give off sparks, like knives hitting a rolling tire rim.

"Maybe I'll do that."

"Look, honey," Sherry's voice softened, and she slowed down. The knife was off the tire rim. "I get calls all the time from women who want to divorce their husbands."

There was a pause, an intake of breath.

"I'm a breadwinner myself. I can't make a living with you ambivalent about what you want to do with your life."

"I guess it's hitting me a little hard what I need to do."

"You have a lot to think about." There was a hint of sympathy in Sherry's voice. A deep exhale. "I'm in business to help people. The way I help people is by going into a courtroom. It's nothing personal, but you need to think some more about what you really want to do here." Another exhale.

"If you want me to represent you, make an appointment. Wait—I see I have an opening at twelve-thirty today. If you want that, let my office know right away!"

Sherry Goldstein hung up, and Clare sat, feeling warm all over, looking at the phone. She was floored by the prickly, jabbing voice, the combativeness of the woman. Then she remembered Kitty Cramer's statement about getting a good, strong lawyer. Clare tried to picture who Willie would get. It would be someone who'd go for the jugular.

Clare's body shook as she approached the large entry hall in the offices of Sherry Goldstein. She walked slowly hoping she'd be able to stop her body from feeling it was flying down a wild ride at Six Flags. She'd brought some basic information—but nothing like financial statements. To get those, she would have had to go into Willie's office, and he had locked the door to that room.

She shivered as she recalled Willie's arctic manner the night before in their kitchen.

Now she tried to think of details of Willie's and his family's businesses. Did they sell their interest in the apartment complex in Norcross? They frequently talked about REITs and other investments, but she'd found it too complicated to keep up with. She did well just to make sure she kept up with the market with her own investments. Lost some, gained some. She didn't do badly.

Now it made sense, though, the dismissive way her father-in-law spoke to her the one time she attempted to find out more about their business.

"You don't need to worry your little head with this," Dan Clem had said. She had walked in on a conversation between him and Willie, and she asked about the REITs and how they worked. They were at a family party; Dan had smiled and pushed her onto Grace, her mother-in-law.

Grace had a grim look at the time. They were in Grace's large European-style kitchen, with gleaming stainless appliances and a wrought iron light fixture that was more like a heavy chandelier. Grace never spoke about financial matters. She laughed after a moment, shook her blond head, and said, "Too confusing for me!"

Now it was clear why her in-laws didn't want her to bother.

Clare was beginning to feel for the first time that she was a minicar after a wreck with a big rig truck. Post-impact, she now felt her arms broken, her hips dislocated, and bloody teeth falling onto the ground. Willie had her good, because she couldn't say for certain what he had. And that would be crucial in any proceedings—for separation or divorce. She should have been less trusting, less ignorant about what his resources were. She still wondered if his anger was about the credit mess or whether another woman, that mysterious, laughing phone caller, was to blame for the truck wreck.

Almost empty-handed in terms of what she figured a divorce attorney would be looking for, Clare sat waiting in a large conference room. She dreaded Sherry's scissor-like manner.

The real Sherry was a contrast to her picture on the website. There she'd dressed in a black suit with pearls and emphasized her law degree from the University of Virginia and her experience with a large downtown law firm before going solo.

Here she sported a purple suit that closely followed her curved figure. Her gold hair was not combed very well; it looked almost thoughtlessly arranged. Clare thought of the couple of female trial lawyers she'd met. They seemed like to favor the streaked or frosted hair of her sister's high school days, only now they called it highlights. All looked smashingly turned out, with just enough unkemptness, as Sherry displayed, to keep them from being confused with the corporate types. They definitely weren't Barbies, but it seemed that, along with using their obvious brains, it didn't hurt to wear long, red fingernails. After their greeting, Clare decided that Sherry's low voice was due to a smoking habit.

Sherry was more welcoming than Clare had thought she'd be.

"So he's kicking you out, huh?" She looked sympathetic.

"That's what he sounds like."

"We'll find you a suitable place. That's not the issue here. He can throw you out the door, but we'll find a door for you to come back through. We'll get you all you need and more. Where are the financial statements?"

"I don't have any statements—"

"If you decide to go ahead with this, bring checking account statements, tax returns—you name it. Before we get together again, write down everything that's happened. Oh, and who else is involved."

"I don't know how to get those. And all I have are mysterious phone calls where someone hangs up and a husband who suddenly wants me gone!" Clare found herself almost crying. She had nothing tangible to fight with.

"Get an appointment with me right away when you have some information. It'll be a retainer of four thousand dollars. I bill at four hundred an hour."

Clare swallowed hard. This was expensive.

"Can't get the documents, then we'll subpoena them. That'll up the costs, but we'll get what we need."

Clare felt bile swelling in her throat. Subpoena? This was real complicated.

Sherry looked into her eyes and put a hand over hers there on the conference room table.

"I know this is hard," she said steadily. Again sympathy. But nothing else.

Sherry got up and left the conference room.

Clare sat for a moment, dumb as a bird fallen from a nest. Financial statements? No chance. Other women? She just had suspicions.

She put a finger to her mouth and bit a fingernail. She hadn't done that in years. This was not going to be easy at all. What kind of a fix had Willie gotten her into? She had no idea what the first step was to get what she needed to support herself.

From her jarring meeting with Sherry, Clare went on to her least favorite chore—going by her old home to see about her mother's mail and home upkeep. Clare had power of attorney, and she knew the government would eventually swap her mother's home for her nursing home bills. She could really use money from the house now. But she shuddered at the thought of caring for her mother herself; she needed those round the clock workers at Angel's Arms.

As she drove on Cheshire Bridge Road to the old house on Melanie Street, Clare tried to calculate her own financial resources now. Her mainstay was her job. She didn't want to sell stocks that were her savings, at least not yet. The lengthy consulting contract she now held was about to expire, and though it had been renewed in the past—in fact it had been renewed twice— she was not expecting a third go at it. The company was in the midst of merger talks, and the hint of those talks three years ago were why she got the work in the first place. Her client, an unusual forward-thinking company, thought life coaching would help their talent stay put while they went through their discussions. Many did stay, but others had been so excited about their plans that they went ahead to other positions and careers, thanks to Clare's classes and one-on-ones.

Clare took a moment, bent her head slightly toward the steering wheel, taking a bow in front of her imagined clients.

Hey, Clare-bear, she chided herself. You also have two stops to make before your three o'clock appointment. Hello? Better be thinking about how you're going to get it all done!

Clare squeezed past her mother's compact Dodge, dust laying thick on the cover she'd put over it, parked in the narrow drive of her mother's house. She wondered how much money she could get for selling the car. As Clare opened the front door of the little house, she felt sadness creep through her chest. The mustiness of a home left unused for several weeks entered her nostrils, adding to the blue feeling. It was just a basic home, nothing fancy like the 1930s brick bungalows Atlanta's in-town area was known for. The 1940s square home was clapboard rather than brick, and it had been covered long ago with pale yellow vinyl that was now cream-colored and in bad need of pressure washing. Her eye went to the small dining room still piled with newspapers and even some left-over grocery store ordering lists from the business her mother had sold.

She felt sad for her mother, and she felt sad for herself. Frankie was at the end of her life. All of her familiar surroundings spoke of the meals she had prepared for herself and the many evenings with the TV for company or standing over the ironing board preparing the church's altar cloths. Now all that was over for Frankie. She couldn't say her mother had a good life. She'd seen the tragic early death of her husband, a daughter who deserted, and another whose life was falling apart. What had any of their lives come to?

With Sherry Goldstein's four grand retainer still nudging and bumping in her brain, Clare went through the mail that had settled on the floor under the mail drop in the front door. How many of these appeals did Frankie receive from Indian missions and Catholic hospital foundations? But there was one piece that caught her attention. The business envelope was hand-written and stamped—return address, Rising Fawn, Georgia—and bore a postmark from Trenton, Georgia. That had a familiar ring to it. She stuck that one in her purse and continued culling the mail, tossing most of it, pulling out bank statements and bills, collecting them to take with her.

She climbed in her small SUV, the color of a yellow traffic sign. She drove to Midtown Atlanta to meet Helene for a quick coffee at the cafe near her friend's office. On the drive, Clare found herself tuning out the traffic, even other drivers, and heard her mother's voice.

*"Povera bambina!"*

Frankie's voice said the same Italian accented phrase over and over in Clare's head. *Povera bambina.* That's what her sister had told her every time she went to her mother telling her what Angela had done to her. Her sister's cruel treatment of her stayed with her even today, years after her departure.

Here she was a poor baby facing fraudulent credit card charges, a near quarter million-dollar home equity loan she hadn't applied for, a husband wanting a divorce, and, instead of Helpful Harriet, a divorce lawyer who acted like bitch was a proper noun.

"*Aspire tua occhi!*" Angela would tell her to open her eyes around her. "You don't see things the way I see them. You like things done the way you like, but that's selfish. That's not how the world works. Where's your sense of family?" Angela at that time was clued into the past and their family traditions much more than she. But Clare was like the caboose in many families: the last to be part of the family, more like a grandchild than a child.

Clare recalled using her time with no other people around reading lots of books, *People* and *Elle* magazines, and watching soaps. She remembered the first time she came across a *Psychology Today* article tying achievement to desire and motivation more so than IQ. She ate cold dinners chewing on the magazine's tips for improving her life. She was attracted to creative people, but the starving artist life was not what she was after. She was after a better life than her mother's more-than-nodding acquaintance with poverty.

Often, even in the midst of the feeling of accomplishment, Clare felt like there was a dark cloud around her. She had trouble rousing herself to activity, frequently becoming unable to move because of what felt like a brick wall built up to her shoulders, confining her, keeping her from getting away. This was the downtime, as she called it. She used some of the techniques found in the magazines: make a plan, start a new project, set big goals and then little goals to get to a well-paying career.

When she did see her mother, she was preoccupied, trying to keep up with tasks for the market.

Her mother would ask her questions about school as if she were interested. Then she'd ask her why she didn't go out with other young girls, just like years before she wondered why Clare didn't play with other children in the neighborhood. She didn't seem to listen back when Clare told her she didn't know them. They went to the public school, not the Catholic school she did. Of course, her mother didn't socialize with the neighborhood mothers, so there was no link to any people on Melanie Street through them.

And what was it her mother would say about her?

"*No senso,*" her mother would say, shaking her head. She knew her mother thought her a bit unreliable and a profligate with money. But her mother also liked to tell her stories about her childhood and about growing up in Trenton in north Georgia. *That's why that envelope address was familiar.* Frankie told how the family scraped by with a small grocery store in the mountain town. They had kept a low profile, not drawing public attention to their Italian culture. That was about all Clare knew of the family there. They had died before she was born, those grandparents up there in the mountains.

Her father's people, too, were either dead or very feeble when she was a young child.

Because her father was so young when he died, her recollections of him warped with time. Did he ever have a mustache? She didn't know. His pictures, the several she used as a reference point to keep him in her mind, showed none, but she thought she remembered scratchy kisses. She no longer knew. If she recalled little of him, she knew much less of his family. She did recall that her father was very tall. She had a terribly faded color picture from before she was born that showed him and two brothers standing in Sunday clothes in a valley with a tall mountain in the rear, and all three were rangy.

But here she was thinking about stuff that wasn't going to help her now. *"No senso,"* she told herself.

"Shit," Clare cried. "It's all coming apart. *I'm* coming apart!"

Helene drank her favorite—iced latte, a color match to her skin—and listened to her friend's latest dilemma about Willie, about her mother's illness, and now the divorce lawyer.

Clare had called her—distraught, mumbling, needing to talk—from Sherry Goldstein's office lobby.

Clare felt a sudden coldness slice through her body there in the cafe. Then her chest began to cave inward. There was relief now that she could tell someone all that was going on. Like a sudden storm over the ocean, Clare felt shivers breaking over her. She grabbed her own drink and sipped through the straw. She shivered more. Now she felt tears gather in her eyelids.

"Willie wants me to move out—all our identity is circulating God knows where. His Social Security number, address, phones. Then someone took a huge *faux* home equity loan in our name—we're in real trouble. I'm so confused, I don't know which way is up."

"Why does he want you out? That doesn't make sense." Helene sat erect, not close. Her dark, doe eyes were intent.

"First of all, he said I should have known not to use a small bank credit card—it's cause they can't absorb a ten-thousand-dollar loss like a big bank can, so they're giving me a hard time. Then on the loan fraud thing, he thinks I'm up to something funny. I'm *not*! How can I help it if somebody targets us? We're helpless. He shouldn't be overreacting like this!"

"What did you do to him?" Her left eyebrow went up.

"Nothing." Great. Now her best friend was challenging her role in all this. Clare sniffed, reached for a Kleenex in her combined computer bag and purse.

"Has Dodger got a woman on the side?" Clare looked up, startled. Something told her not to mention the hang-up calls she'd received.

"I don't know." There was a chill on her shoulders.

"Your lawyer a good one?" Clare sensed Helene shifting from sympathy for Willie to siding with her in the likelihood Dodger had been unfaithful. There was that confounding habit of Helene's—taking both her and Willie's part at the same time.

"She'll be tough on him, but wait till you hear what she wants—all his financial statements—fat chance I'll be able to get within two feet of any paper he's got."

"You know what your real mortgage is. You know what you've got on your tax forms. How hard is it?" There was that arched eyebrow again.

"Sure, I know our taxes, but when it comes to his deals with his family—real estate, partnerships—no, I don't understand those forms at all."

Helene looked at Clare. It was one of those "Really, Clare, how stupid are you?" looks.

"Don't jump on me. He wants to play things close to the chest. I can't help it!" Clare cried. She quieted while the waitress checked to see if they needed anything else. Clare wondered what it would be like to wait tables for a living. It looked like a very young woman's job. It would take a long while to get four thousand dollars together doing that. Maybe bartending. . ..

She stopped rifling through her mental life coach catalog of options for others.

"This lawyer! I can't believe she's so unfeeling. She acts like she can't help me at all if I don't have statements. She says she'll have to subpoena his info. Can you imagine how tangled this is going to get?"

"You expected a therapist?" Helene's eyes were wide with the question. There was a hint of a smile, but Clare knew she was right. Helene was so practical and to the point. No bullshit here. She couldn't expect anything different.

Helene should have been a therapist. She was Clare's therapist, that was for sure.

Helene had been her friend ever since they'd been in the same group of redundant employees at their telecom company. Both had been in outside sales, making calls on corporations to get their lucrative office phone system business. But the shift to cell phones had caused the company to lose money. It was bought out by a larger telecom. Clare, Helene, and others went through outplacement classes to decide their new careers. Through their instructors, some of whom were certified life coaches, Clare began studies to become one herself. Helene, attracted by the commissions she was used to working for, had chosen mortgage originating, and she was very good at it, rarely looking for clients. Clare still thought she would have been a good counselor.

"Any bipolar disease in your family?" Helene asked.

Where did that question come from? Her mother was morose, mostly, although she occasionally showed some humor. She couldn't remember Frankie being excited about much in her life, outside of church. And her father—he was gone too soon from her life to remember. Now, the long-gone Angela? That was a possibility!

"Are you asking because you think I'm bipolar?"

Helene shrugged.

"You do seem up and down a lot. And you're really captured by Willie. If he's up, you're up. If he's down, you're down. And now he seems down on you, and you're pretty fragile."

"So you think I should see a therapist? I've done that in the past."

"Well, I'm not a therapist. But it might not be a bad idea."

"I'll have to think about it." Clare filed it away. She had too much going on right now. Here on the cafe patio, her friend was somber in her advice about the lawyer.

"Lawyers, female or not, are in the business of getting you a divorce," Helene said slowly, as though to make Clare understand something she found hard to grasp. She took another sip of the drink.

"If you're not prepared to bulldog it through, then she's wasting her time, giving up time she could bill working for angry, prepared clients who are ready to file, ready to claim a huge property settlement."

Clare's stomach cramped. Again, Helene was right on the money, but she didn't know if she was ready for the lawyer, didn't know if she could run as fast as Sherry was prepared to.

"I gotta go meet a client," Clare said slowly. "Then I need to start generating some money and figuring out where I'm gonna live."

She looked at Helene. Helene was smiling sympathetically.

"Not simple, is it?" Helene said, putting her hand over Clare's. Her hand was cool; Clare's was warm. But Clare felt better.

"On the credit card, remember what the consumer guru says. They messed it up, they gotta clean it up. Fax your bank a letter putting them on the defensive. How come they obeyed the fax from your husband when he's not even on the account?"

Clare smiled for the first time since the phone call to the bank's fraud department. Helene knew what to do. If she'd had her brains intact, she would have remembered some of the things Helene was pointing out.

"Why didn't they check out the address change with you?" Helene went on. "Even the post office sends you a notice when there's been a change, letting you know so you can catch it if it's not legitimate."

Helene rose, getting ready to go.

"And you're not responsible for the debt if you called them immediately. I can't believe the bank's not treating you better. Have you done something to make them suspicious of you?"

"No. Not before now," Clare replied.

"Well, you know those small banks—"

"Thanks for telling me what Willie told me. All I know is they weren't very nice to me. Acted like I deliberately tried to defraud them."

"When you get home, write them a long letter and send it certified mail asking them how they obeyed instructions from someone not on the account and why they didn't notify you of a change to your account."

Clare finally had something positive she could do.

"And Clare," Helene fixed her with a steady gaze. "Stop trying to do everything yourself. You should have called me. Pick up the phone, okay?"

"Okay."

Clare felt a little lighter as she walked out with Helene. At least some of the burden on her back was shifting.

Jason, her client, was struggling with the interview practice.

"Jason, we've done this 'tell me about yourself' thing a couple of times," Clare said, trying not to make him more nervous. She was on familiar ground, helping others with the tricks of her trade. She could do this and do it well. She felt calm.

Jason had not been able to answer when they role-played the classic interview question. She was surprised how often employers still used it and how hard it was for many people to answer. Jason had flubbed the answer, then called "cut" on himself a couple of times.

"You did it so well last time we met. Remember that your interviewer may be looking at all the peripheral stuff—do you take a while to answer, do you ramble, can you take charge of the question and show that you'll be able to be a leader on the team?"

Inside, she wondered at the strong, assured voice she was using. But she felt on firm ground. Most of the time she felt confident in her work, except of course when she did not. Right now, still a little flushed from her quick meeting with Helene, she was determined she would help the guy—her age, she guessed. Jason had the look and sensibilities of a young corporate type. He would be okay in an interview if he could get a better grip.

Jason looked disappointed, tucked his head some. Dark-eyed, with smooth brown hair cut close to a well-shaped head. He was attractive, tanned from a job that had a lot of outside fieldwork. He negotiated leases for cell tower land, but the potential merger partner had its own real estate staff, so probably wouldn't need him in the new corporation.

"Is there something on your mind?" she asked softly. Often there were personal things that came up in these sessions, and she tried to gently get problems out in order to boost the real interview.

Jason kept his head low, then shook it. Clare waited. He looked at the tanned fingers he spread out on the table in front of him, and then at Clare. His eyes were wet.

"My wife met some guy from England on the Internet!"

*God!* Clare thought. That's two of us with extra people in our marriages. Maybe Willie found someone on the Internet. Only he probably wouldn't have had to go that far. There are plenty of young women working at the stock brokerage. Would he want someone on his own level or someone lower, maybe an administrative assistant?

Clare caught herself mid-stitch in her own mental embroidery. She had to get real, focus first on her job right now and then on her own survival.

"I'm sorry, Jason," she said sympathetically. "How do you know about all this?"

"She told me. She said she's no longer in love with me, that this guy offers her everything—empathy, common interests. He likes theatre and I don't. She used to act in college. I don't like going out to clubs for music; she loves it."

"Gosh, I'm sorry to hear about this. You must feel really hurt. But let's look at what you really know. Have they actually met?"

"No, but he's planning a trip here next month."

"Well, if they've never met, maybe you've got a chance to retrieve your marriage. Are you seeing a counselor?"

Jason looked at her like she'd mooned him, and she thought of how she was resisting therapy for herself.

"I don't believe in all that stuff," he said with an accent that was decidedly southern something—Georgia or Alabama. "Some women go to therapists, but I don't. You've gotta be in or out of the marriage, and she's out."

Jason had fooled her with his outer appearance. He'd seemed hip, everything on the outside pointing to a truly with-it guy. But he was certainly not the sensitive-see-the-woman's-side-of-things, especially now that he'd been hurt. No, he was letting her know that therapy was sissy stuff.

"All I can tell you," she said, her voice low, "is that personal issues like that are pretty heavy. They can affect how you do in the job interview."

Jason's shoulders came up, and he looked like the quarterback about to go back in the game, his personal problems glossed over. Clare picked up the cue.

"You ready for the ninety-second drill?" She saw him moving impatiently, ready for the question.

"Remember I told you about the points of the compass to keep in mind—you make it round the compass with where you're from, your education, just a bit about each point. Quick, succinct examples on the later job experiences, emphasizing specifics that will help the employer see you in the job they're interviewing you for. Any questions so far?"

He shook his head, took up a pad, and scribbled a compass with points in bold, black strokes.

"Then you give a brief ending that overviews you and the job—leave 'em with three things you want them to remember about you. Got that?"

Jason nodded. Clare was glad to see he was taking notes. He'd not done that when she'd asked him before.

"Okay, Jason, tell me about yourself."

Jason looked up, alert. The watery eyes were gone, and he was leaning forward. She listened as he convincingly made his way around the compass and then ticked off his advantages.

Clare thought of her own three-point list of her skills. She had a terrific ability to spin the success genes in others. If she could help others, she could help herself.

When Clare reached in her computer bag to log the meeting with Jason, she pulled out the letter from Trenton—a handwritten letter was as hard to find as a teenager without a cell phone. She opened the envelope with a miniature letter opener she kept in her bag.

Glancing to the end, she saw it was from a man and apparently someone close to her mother, as it was signed, "Your affectionate kin, Tony."

> Dear Aunt Frankie,
> Your tenants are finally gone! You asked me to let you know when they left, and, now, thank God, they have departed, where I'm not sure.
> As soon as you get a chance to inspect, I'll be glad to rent to a more suitable family.
> Please let me know when you'll be coming up here.

Clare couldn't have been more surprised if she had learned her mother had a secret child. Rental property? In the mountains?

Clare tried to think of a time she'd heard her mother mention any property. And who was this unknown Tony? He apparently had been the local contact for this house—or was it an apartment? A farm?—and he was anticipating a visit from Frankie before leasing it again. How often had that idle Dodge in her mother's driveway taken her to the mountains and Clare never knew it? Clare wondered how many other areas of her mother's life were locked away from her, ready to spring out at her like a jack-in-the-box.

She bent over the conference room table where she'd been meeting with Jason. Relieved there were no more clients for the day and grateful for the curtains she'd drawn to make the session private, Clare put her fists over her eyes. She slowly drew in a breath. It had been a rollercoaster day, coming right after a day of news from banks and explosions from Willie that still gave off aftershocks in her body. And her mother was even stranger than she thought. She closed her eyes. With only blackness in her mind, she thought about an extended trip she'd taken to California in her old job. She'd stayed in a hotel in West LA, amazed at how brightly the sun shown in her hotel room every morning, streaming through the sheers like a message from heaven or at least the Resurrection. She'd finally had to close the heavy drapes over the sheers in order not to be awakened at 5 a.m. with a light that rivaled the aura around Christ at the tomb.

*It* is *sunny California*, she remembered thinking. But one night she woke in the middle of the night. The bed had shifted suddenly. It was so minute she'd almost thought it didn't happen. But it did.

A week later in a conference room where the marketing division was meeting to decide new strategies, she and the twenty others in the room were listening to the national manager's presentation when she felt that quick shift again. It was almost imperceptible—no one else around her acted as though they'd felt anything. Yet she knew what it was. Tremors. The earth was shifting underneath her.

Right now the earth was shifting under her again, and it was the Big One. She was in trouble. She pulled air in slowly. *Breathe in through the mouth.* Helene and Sherry said she knew how to fight. *Breathe out slowly.* Okay, make a list. Certified letter to the bank. Ditto for the mortgage company to report the fraud. Call Detective Scott to add the loan fraud to the case. Find a place to live.

# Chapter 4

## LATER THURSDAY

The conference room where she'd holed up seemed very small. Clare got up, walked around, shook the heavy load she carried from her shoulders. She'd written the letter, had it in her purse ready to take to the post office for certifying, called Detective Scott and left a message about the two-hundred-thousand-dollar home equity loan her husband and she seemed to owe although they didn't apply for one.

She started thinking about her contract with the company that was coming to an end. Jeff had told her that it probably wouldn't be renewed as the company was taking a break on the life coaching. So she needed to be thinking about new business.

Waiting for her next client, she picked up an Atlanta business newspaper to check for news of companies moving to town, a possible jobs source for some of her remaining clients. What about for herself? How was she going to keep supporting herself and look for an apartment? She recalled that last week, before her world shifted under her, she'd actually seen a notice in the paper about an unusual "career program on wheels."

She went through several of the past issues of the newspaper laying on a credenza there in the conference room and found it in a two-week old paper. Requests for proposals for career services were being publicized for locations in northeast Georgia, southeast Georgia, and northwest Georgia, near Rome.

"Consulting firms must be able to set up remote facilities using a custom RV and be able to move around the area," the article said.

Career programs she could do, Clare thought. *Would it be any harder to do them in an RV?*

On her laptop, she tapped in the name of the government training agency that wanted proposals for the career programs.

"Submit resume, outline of services to be provided, costs, overhead provision," she read to herself. "Must have been in business for two years."

That's me! she thought. Like it was made for me!

Her mood lightened, like a balloon released from a small child's hand.

Clare tore the notice out of the paper, noted a phone number to call, and placed it in her computer bag. When she slid the clipping in, her finger jammed on the envelope from the relative, Tony. She pulled it out and looked at the name on the return address.

*Sands*, Clare said to herself. *Find Tony Sands.*

Back at her computer, she clicked the Yellow Pages/White Pages website, and did a search in Trenton, Georgia for Tony Sands. After several screens, lots of hints of government records, and then a pay wall.

Then it hit her how her life was changing. She couldn't use her old credit card, as a new one hadn't been issued yet. A fraud alert had been issued by the credit reporting agencies. Alerting the Big Three to her fraud had been recommended, and she'd done it. But did that mean any unusual charges would set off alarms as well, catch her in a denial of credit, and just make this dilemma even crazier? She'd rarely used a paywall to go beyond the free information.

Clare took in a breath and entered her primary credit card information so she could access Tony Sands'—actually Antonio Sands'— information. Like magic, the computer spilled the details—address the same, with a phone number. What would happen if she called him? All she could say was that she had picked up her mother's mail, and here was this letter. She didn't know him but felt he should know that her mother was in a nursing home and wouldn't be able to come up to the town in northwest Georgia.

What was he going to think of her? He'd probably never heard of Clare from her secretive mother. How were he and her mother related? She tried to remember any aunts or uncles, but her memories of that era when she did visit in the mountains were wispy as clouds settled on mountains. Was he southern, older, friendly and loquacious like a lot of people she imagined in rural northwest Georgia?

She punched the number into her cell phone.

While the phone rang, she playfully tried out a response to the "who is this?" question.

She practiced in a bright voice what she would say when Tony answered: "I'm looking for Cousin Tony in Trenton!" The phone rang for a long time, and she thought about hanging up.

"H-Hello?" A man with a deep voice answered, breathing hard, as though picking up the phone was difficult.

"Hello, sir, my name is Clare Connor. Frankie Connor is my mother."

"Yes?" he asked. Nothing more. More heavy breaths. No "you must be long-lost Cousin Clare," no loose-tongued southern banter. Clare decided to keep it as businesslike as possible, as he was.

"Well, I'm calling because my mother is in a nursing home, and she's incapacitated. I picked your letter up when I checked her mail at the house."

"Oh, I'm sorry to hear that," he said with genuine feeling. Then a pause and a labored breath. "Happens to a lot of us."

"What can you tell me about the property?"

"Waal, I'm workin out in my garden right now, so I don't know that I can get ahold a the information, but these folks, the Pryors, done left outa your mama's propity there up on the mountain," he said, spilling details as though she'd been seated beside her mother with each of her financial transactions and knew the whole history.

"Mr. Sands—"

"Name's Tony, but that's okay. Your mamma told you about me?"

"N-No, not really. You see, my mom was pretty quiet about her business." *Try secretive and reclusive*, Clare told herself.

"Well, I'm not sure she told me much either," he said. "She didn't mention family much."

Clare took that to mean he didn't know about her. How strange was it that her own mother would have real estate in the mountains, but never tell her? That she would trust a relative with real estate but not mention she had a daughter?

"Well, tell me about the property. Is it habitable, ready for a new tenant do you think?"

"Hardly. Place has been busted up pretty well. I'm not sure I've got anyone who can go tend to it right now, and I'm not able, so I can't do it. Your momma liked to handle all the cleaning and the details."

Clare's silk blouse collar seemed tight and her skin felt warm. She couldn't imagine why her mother had withheld this part of her life from her. What kind of a mother would deliberately trick her own child, leave her to take care of business she knew nothing about?

"Well, thank you Mr.—Tony. Would you let me in if I came up there?"

"Got my son, Jerry, he can get you in. I'll have him open it up if you just give me the word."

"I don't know when it'll be. I'll let you know. By the way, are there any more properties you know of that my mother owns up there?"

"Nope, but this one's on a pretty fair piece of propity."

*More mystery*, Clare told herself. To the phone, she said, "It's nice to know I have a cousin up there."

"Waal, you'll see we ain't been family much, but we're here."

What did that mean, Clare wondered as she hung up. Was this a family trait to hide relatives away? She felt a pang of loss, loss of knowledge of her mother's life, her everyday dealings. Even if her mother held her at a distance, she still was—well, her mother.

Like unwelcome mosquitoes in summer, thoughts about her dilemma now buzzed about in her head. How was she going to take care of her mother's business up there, a place she barely knew, when she didn't even have a place to live here in Atlanta?

A young woman's face looked up at her, smiling and confident. What an attractive person, she thought. The plastic picture on her ID tag showed her corporate self caught in a moment of posing as she wanted to be seen— Ms. Can Do, specializing in helping the lost find their way through life's labyrinth of confusing choices. The eyes were so engaging, the hair cut in a swing style—it was her. She gazed at the reality of her, or at least what she wanted to portray as reality. Clare Connor, consultant. She fingered the now-soft edge of the plastic, worn through her three years of work here.

Then she got the idea—go up to North Georgia, clean up after the tenants, and stay there and do the contract work in the newspaper! Why not? She could wrap up her business here soon. There'd be lots of loose ends, but she could counsel employees still on her schedule by cell phone from up there! Then she could have a base of income from the contract, build her business, pay Sherry, and come back strong in any divorce action. Later, she could subcontract to run the business from Atlanta.

Good thinking, Clare. Go for it!

She grabbed her phone and extracted the ad for the career program out of her bag and dialed excitedly. A number of rings and then a receptionist answered. She was put through to Terry Harris, the program director for the Welfare to Work project. After giving her a few bona fides, Clare was pleased to hear her response. And excited to learn that the "near Rome" part of the work actually included Trenton, where she was headed.

"Well, we would welcome your application," Terry said. Bingo! It sounded like there was a perfect match between Clare's preparation and her project needs. "We haven't had any qualified applicants so far, and the deadline is next week."

Clare couldn't believe her luck in first getting through to the decision maker and then finding a deal fall into place so quickly.

"Great, I'll send you a resume and some information about my work," Clare said, already moving things in her briefcase to get to her marketing information, already thinking of a way to speed into the project slot even faster. The costs, the outline of services that they wanted—she could generate those after she'd talked with Terry. Putting career counseling resources into an RV and moving about the area would require some detail she didn't have right now.

Euphoria poured over her like light from a brilliant day, just like the day that was brewing outside her window, sun dappling waterfalls of green leaves on hardwoods, making them shine white-gold. She would be saved. She would prevail. For the first time since she'd been hit with the credit card fraud and the fake loan, Clare sensed she was on her way to a solution. Not just any solution, a brilliant solution. She'd come out of this with her head high, and Willie would not stand in her way!

The old Clare came back to her mind, the Clare that went to Chicago to college, who stayed in the big city for an exciting single life, who moved back to Atlanta with her successful job. And then trained and became a life coach, creating her own business. For once, she was using advice she gave to others to create her own magic. She was good. Damn good.

She looked in the mirror on the wall near the window. She looked attractive and smart. By God, she would tackle this thing, and she would win! The answer to that question about how she ended up with this strange person Willie was going to be resolved: The answer was, they didn't belong together so no need to stay together.

The brightness Clare felt dissolved as soon as she stepped into the home she'd known for five years. The light on the stairs seemed stale. Shards of light showed up dust sprinklings on the floor and on the stairs. Willie's jacket wasn't on the newel post where he hung it on arrival.

"He said he'd move out while I got my things together," she told herself. Something tugged in her chest as she thought about separation.

She felt frightened looking at the world she'd built—those were her carefully watered hydrangeas in a vase in the hall. The tomatoes ripening in a wire hanger in the kitchen were from her garden, her soiled hands, her sweating arms and fingers. Was it all going to go away, just like that?

She went upstairs to pack a bag before she turned coward. She'd beg a place to stay from Helene in her friend's tiny apartment, then leave for Trenton tomorrow. She'd make a small move now, a big one later. What was he going to do, throw her clothes on the sidewalk?

In the bath area outside her walk-in closet, Clare saw that her perfume was pulled slightly forward from the collection of bottles. What was Willie doing, wearing her scent? She looked at the pale bottle with the dashing gold script—*L'Air du Temps*—and smelled the light flowers, the feminine mist she'd applied with minimalist touch this morning. No, maybe Willie wanted the smell of her, just as she borrowed the perfume brand her mother favored. It was her mother's one indulgence that she knew of; she'd once requested it for a Christmas gift, and Clare had bought some for herself as well.

Clare struggled to pull clothes out of the bulging closet—blue jeans that the cleaners washed and ironed, tops, shorts. She did not own grunge wear, but she decided to take her older t-shirts and seriously faded jeans for chores. What would it take to clean up a house, get it ready for her and a later rental? For her possible job in northwest Georgia, she pulled out some older travel suits and dresses and the lowest of heels—just skimmers.

Don't want to look too Atlanta-like when approaching folks in Rome or Trenton.

A confusing image appeared in the bath mirror edge, like waking from a dream, at first Day-Glo clear, then murky, details erased, lost to memory. The unmade four-poster in the bedroom, linens humped in a mound. She turned from the mirror, and crossed the room, and saw that it was a long bolster pillow and a couple of sleeping pillows covered with her spread. Was Willie pretending she was there in bed with him? Clare felt cold chills, wondered if the air conditioning had been left on too high—why was Willie doing these things? He said he wanted her gone, yet he seemed to miss her already.

She scooted downstairs, glancing at the thermostat in the stairwell—nope, left at its usual temperature. What was he up to? Yesterday he was kicking her out and today he was touching her things, making as though she were with him. Had he changed his mind? She felt a twinge of tenderness.

She checked the refrigerator. He'd eaten her leftover pasta and tomatoes but didn't touch the salad. She saw crumbs dotting the space in front of the microwave. So he'd eaten the bread, microwaving it like she hated him to do. She pictured him gnawing at the glue-like fibers of the reheated bread—she frequently reminded him of how the toaster oven was better; it kept the white textures of the bread from fusing together like concrete!

A few minutes ago she had been feeling high and ready to take on the world, chuck Willie, go on and live her life, but now there was an awful lump in her stomach that felt like it was going to throw up, but it wouldn't come. It just stayed there making her ill, nauseous. How *brave* she was! Ready to take on the world!

But not. She felt coolness on her limbs, alternating with a hot head. She moved back to the downstairs hallway, idly picking at the empty message pad by the phone. She must keep going, not think about Willie. She had to get packed and go.

What was wrong with her body? What was wrong with her legs that they wouldn't take her back upstairs to that full closet? *Put your foot out, Clare, put it on the stair! Walk up there, go get the clothes you need. Keep it to a minimum. Get going, girl!*

She wanted to run out the door, down the street of other gabled European-style mansions. But the lump in her stomach wouldn't budge. She was going to have to move on with her plan no matter how she felt. She put her foot on the first hardwood step and ascended.

As she fled down the stairs later, all she could think about was that lump of pillows on the bed strung out like her body. How sad she felt! All the lovemaking, the tenderness, the intertwining of their lives—all that remained were lifeless bits of polyester stuffing and cotton coverings. And those elegant fabrics that caused her to feel luxuriant each time she changed them and eased into their soft envelope. Would she ever experience that pleasure again?

*Oooh*, she couldn't think about it! She wanted to cry. A tingling and aching hit the bridge and upper sinuses of her nose.

Clare shook herself, hoisted the bag, and let herself out of her quiet home.

His car was in the drive, and he was on the other side of it, away from her, his view of her blocked for the moment.

His shoulders jerked when he saw her. As he walked up the sidewalk, he pulled his sport jacket from where he'd held it over his shoulder with a finger and put the coat across his arm. His face looked ragged, like he hadn't slept much. Clare could feel her heart beating against her chest wall.

"What're you doing?" he asked as he drew closer.

She told herself to straighten her shoulders and keep walking down the front stairs. "I'm getting some things. I'm going."

"Where will you be?" He was less than four feet away.

"I'll let you know." *Why didn't he ask her to stay?* She wanted to stay. She thought she wanted to stay.

"Let me know who your lawyer is so mine can be in touch with him."

Lawyers talking to each other. Is that what we've come to? God! And of course he thinks it's a male.

Willie drew nearer to her. She could smell his cologne. She thought she saw something shiny in the corner of his left eye. But he walked sideways and away as he passed her, almost as if he wanted her to know that this meeting was over, and he was going into *his* house. She wanted to ask him if he missed her, if there was something different they could do. But his pudgy face, while worn-looking, also was firm, his eyes steady on her. Still, the shine was in them.

"I guess I'll see you later," she said weakly, and smelled his fragrance as he passed on up the stairs.

"Like I said, don't go after my family's businesses," he said behind her.

She felt bristling all over her body. She turned to face him; he was now on the landing in front of the door.

"That's all you think about, isn't it?" she shouted. "So much for loving and caring for each other till death do us part!"

She twisted around and went to her car. Her heart was beating fast, she could feel throbbing in her neck and ears. How reckless she was, not even worried about Joe and Mary Ann Shelton next door, or anybody else!

Before she pushed her stuff into the car, she looked back and saw him standing there with a mournful look on his face. She felt a tug in her embattled chest, then rage.

*Damn him,* she told herself. She shifted the heavy bag on the passenger seat, started the engine and left.

Her heart beating through the fabric of her thin blouse from the blow-out with Willie, Clare drove towards Helene's condo. She wasn't expecting the traffic jam going towards town; usually this time of day it was stopped the opposite way. *Could have been an accident,* she told herself. A man in a black SUV left of her texted on his phone and a woman in a Toyota sedan on her right anxiously looked at her dash and glanced on both sides of the interstate.

*So what kinds of relationships problems do you have,* she thought. *We've all got em.* A game came to mind that she'd watched at a neighborhood Halloween party. Two mothers, one of them in a long black witch's costume, and six or eight children in togs depicting characters from garbage can monsters to monkeys tossed large skeins of orange and black yarn back and forth, across and behind, first over, then under, until each was entangled, yawing left, right, up, and down as they fought to extricate themselves from the impossible web. But there was no escape. Like my relationship, she thought. Try to get away but can't. We all need each other, yet we want to separate at the same time—can't stand to see each other, yet still want to connect.

And it's never only a question of do I want to be with this person or why doesn't he want to be with me? There's always an even harder unknown: if I'm not here, where will I be? Where will I put my head tonight? How do I move my world and all I know to another planet? Because that's what it is—another planet. Thrown out of orbit on this one, how do I find a place on the barren reaches of another?

"God!"

The back of a shiny forest green SUV rose up in front of her. She hit the brakes, avoided a crunch of fenders. She felt a wave of heat over her face.

I'm thinking, not watching, she chided herself.

She punched in her quick link to Helene and waited for her to answer or her message to come on.

"Helene—I'm headed your way. Could I spend the night at your place tonight? Call me!"

Five minutes later when Helene called back, Clare was an exit away from her condo near Lenox.

"What's going on?"

"I'm moving on. I'm going to northwest Georgia tomorrow to see about work and a place to stay, and I just saw Willie and he's acting pissy." She was oozing stuff, stuff, stuff, the details of her life—the sordid falling apart of her life. She was getting crazy.

"—I'll explain when I get to your house. Okay if I stay with you tonight?"

"Girl. . . ." She heard frustration in Helene's response. Then, "Okay, you know my code?"

"Got it on my phone. See you soon!"

"Why on earth are you moving so fast?" Helene bit into a Cuban sandwich Clare had picked up for their dinner on the way up to the Lenox Road condo. Clare felt a sharp twinge in her chest as she sat on the patio looking over the condos clustered around landscaped grounds spilling over with impossibly large summer blooms. Her new home would not have this abundance, this variety.

"I don't have any choices right now. I need to find work, and I need to find a home."

"If I had more space, I'd offer it to you. But you *have* a home. Just move into a different bedroom." Helene was cranky, no doubt about it.

Lounging in mauve silk pajamas after her a heavy day of home mortgage refinancing, Helene looked serene and collected even in her critical mood, different from Clare who felt both sad and excited about her move. Clare was like a kid with a new puppy but going to a funeral at the same time.

"I can't stay there with him. He'll bully me every time I see him, but still send signals he misses me."

"What kind of signals?"

"Would you believe he's bunched up pillows next to him in bed, so he'll think it's me?"

Helene smiled a moment. Clare thought of an Egyptian cat—sleek and powerful, unperturbed. Clare had begun to think of herself like an alley cat, a stray, left on the beach after nearly being drowned on purpose by her uninterested owners.

"Both could be true—hates and loves at the same time. What do you think is going on with him?"

"I don't know. If I knew, I'd be telling you. Or listening to him tell me."

"Hey," Helene said, her brown eyes flashing more life. "You're a life coach—what do you think?"

Clare sighed deeply—why couldn't Helene just listen to her, empathize, not put to her the question she was constantly asking herself.

"Maybe we're just made from different molds."

"And his mold is—what?"

God, the questions! Clare thought.

"Well, I know that he and his dad don't get along, that his father holds him to this real high standard." Clare waited to see if Helene would be satisfied with that bit of news. She wasn't.

"And I know his mom grew up poor—poorer than you can imagine. Ask her where she grew up in Atlanta and she'll step around the question, change subjects. Her father was a horrible alcoholic who never worked a day in his life. Her mother begged space in the dirt basements of old Midtown houses for them and their family of five children in exchange for washing and sewing.

"They had to move a lot, as the arrangement was rarely satisfactory," Clare said.

"I can imagine."

"The bathroom was often a freestanding toilet used by the help. Picture that."

Helene's face darkened; Clare could only guess if Helene's parents or someone further back in her family working as domestics might have experienced something like that. And a lot worse.

"To this day, Grace's best friend is a bottle of Clorox, cause you can imagine the mildew and dirt smell of such places."

"Eew!" Helene grimaced, her mouth turned down at the ends.

"I'm sorry. TMI."

"So some of Willie's family comes from some desperate circumstances. And he grows up with a grasping mom. So—?"

Clare didn't know what to say. What could she say? Who knew what was on Willie's mind? She was without answers.

Helene stretched her neck, looked over the balcony to the manicured lawn below. Her prominent nose and slender high cheekbones gave her a regal look.

"You ever wonder about all these people crowded in these condos, or on the streets of Atlanta? They're all like Willie's mom or like Willie—trying to make a buck, trying to make it beyond their roots—roots that go back to rural Georgia or the poor side of Atlanta. We're all out here wearing Peachtree Road's finest, buying shoes to rival a rich dictator's wife and trying to be seen in the right places with the right people. But you scratch any one of us and you find all these unexpected stories—people with money, people without any money, and they're all here trying to make a buck and trying like hell to cover up that old life, those humble beginnings."

Clare took in her friend's outpouring of insight. She looked at Helene, her long legs on the opposite chair, her pinkish-lavender outfit beautifully complementing latte-colored skin set off by long black hair. She was the picture of what she'd lamented, Peachtree Road's finest. But she was right, as Helene often was. They were all pretenders, and they all knew it.

"But how the hell do I figure out Willie?" Clare cried. "He kicks me out of my home, and I'm supposed to guess why?"

Helene drummed her hand on the glass top of the table.

"Reckon you've made your mind up you aren't gonna try at this point."

"I'll be better off to go up to northwest Georgia. And it's just to get some income flowing in so I can deal with all this. I've got to get a fat retainer together, for starters."

"What about other lawyers?"

"Know any that don't want big retainers plus all the income information Sherry wants? I'm caught right now. Whoever I get, they'll subpoena financial records. There will be an explosion over that." Clare gazed inside the condo where Helen had hung a large exuberant folk-art painting over the fireplace: An ancient cabin with profusions of purple wisteria covered a wide porch, and a line of wash nearby showed honest yellows, reds, blues and greens against a cool azure sky. She longed for the painting's clarity and honesty in her own life.

Her life was like an engraving from an old newspaper she'd once seen of the New Madrid earthquake in the fault across the west end of Tennessee, near Memphis. In the early days of the country, a series of seven-point earthquakes lifted a portion of west Tennessee, eastern Missouri, and eastern Arkansas where they joined along the Mississippi River, throwing open huge lakes—the Mississippi actually ran backwards for a few minutes—and the impact created new bends in the Mississippi.

Sometimes when she heard about earthquakes in China or LA, she went to websites that carried pictures and first-person accounts of the crack in the earth. She'd escaped the quakes during her brief stay on the West Coast. Now she felt astride a closer fault, unable to move, unable to decide where was safe.

She decided she could not think about this possibility. Not now. She had to get down the road.

"There's not much I can do about that right now, is there?" Clare said, watching her friend closely.

Helene shrugged and stretched her feet on the wrought iron chair. But she didn't move, gave no clue about her thoughts.

There was silence.

"What about your mother?"

"'S not getting better. The nurses and the doctor say there's not much chance of it given her age and the severity of her stroke."

"You don't feel like you're abandoning her?" Helene's voice was sharp. Now she sounded accusing.

"She sleeps almost all the time, doing that praying thing. When she's awake, her words are all confused. The nurses and doctors say that could go on for a couple of months—or even longer, but she'll deteriorate and die. Don't know what I can do. I can't bring her to a home with me right now. I don't have a home."

"I don't mean bring her home. She needs that nursing home. But if you don't visit her, who's going to look after her?"

"The nursing home is going to have to do it right now. I call them every day as it is. There's never a change."

"Well, I'm not going to let you leave her alone. No mother should be left without relatives around. You give me the information where she is, and *I'll* go see her."

Now Helene was accusing her of abandoning her mother! But what could she do? "Okay. You're right. I need family or the closest thing to it with my mom."

It was hard going to sleep in the unknown expanse of Helene's fold-out sofa. Clare felt many things—but mostly fatigue and worry. She'd put umpteen miles on her car and had traveled untold distances of emotional life between the session with the divorce lawyer, the visit to her mother's home, her work with Jason, and finding the career program on wheels. And then the visit back home—*her home*—and the fireworks on seeing Willie. And the latest worry—how to take care of her mother long distance? Maybe sleep would take it all away.

Clare inhaled the lavender spray Helene used on the sheets and tried to get some positive thoughts going. She was grateful for a place to stay. Twice today she'd called Helene and asked for her help on short notice, once for lunch and then tonight for a bed. Now here she was, getting a place to sleep and help for her mother. Helene was as close to family as she could get.

Clare had a place, a harbor, a friend, and someone to check on her mom while she maneuvered to get on firm footing. It would not be easy, yet what she did have would help her steady herself—go away, get the income, get a grip, come back strong enough to fight. She could do that. Yes, she was like that stray cat cornered by the mad dog right now. Willie had all the family, especially his father's support, and he had her home. She had her wits and her plan and that was about it. But she was in the game. She would play.

A few more shifts on the thin mattress and sleep finally came.

# Chapter 5

Clare pushed down on the accelerator to give her small SUV a boost up the now sharp incline of the mountain. The yellow square back of her car bore a model name that suggested fleeing, which was what she was doing—leaving all behind. The road on either side of her showed an unbroken line of pine, oak, maple and hickory forest. This was her second mountain since leaving Cartersville. She thought if she came down the other side she'd be in a valley for a while, but that's what she'd thought about the last mountain.

The road made a hairpin turn to the left, taking Clare up the face of the mountain while revealing a quiet valley below. She was awed by the sense of looking forever down through that flattened area stretching out beneath her. The mountains—really very long ridges—ran northeast to southwest, and the valley in between ran toward a distant horizon. A gentle mist obscured the details of the valley to the southwest, making it seem like an Impressionist painting, light-to-dark green tinged with buff and brown.

*Hail Mary, full of grace.* A familiar prayer started in her mind.

She thought about her mother's lips moving, saying it over and over. She prayed it now. She needed spiritual help in this new life in the mountains.

The car's straining motor made her think: What if she got stuck or had car trouble? A pain that had begun as discomfort now flamed into a burn, traveling up her right leg, the limb that had pressed on the gas for many of the miles from Helene's condo. With every push on the gas, pain like a small lightning bolt flashed from foot to ankle, leg, knee and thigh and on up the back. She pulled off to the side of the road. They both needed a rest. She leaned on the car for a moment, breathing in the clean air.

Passing through Cartersville earlier, she had seen a mini-Atlanta going up—new developments of houses, all Lego-like pristine whiteness and neatness as they sprawled in open fields. She saw other new neighborhoods lopping off the sides of hills and mountains, heavy traffic that seemed a budding imitation of Atlanta. Horns hooted at her to speed up in the left lane. She shifted to the right, then got cut off as a small car tried to beat her to the red light at the crossing of the major highway. As she recovered from the rude driver, she recalled what her some of her clients had told her about the economy of this area. Big-box chain stores stood on both sides of the roads. A huge beer production plant had broken the sleepiness of the area and also had raised a little ruckus in the midst of the Bible-dipped populace. But it had brought a new busyness to the town. Now a growing city was drinking at the fountain of prosperity as other businesses trailed the suds maker.

Up here she was away from that. She looked down into a valley set between long cords of mountains. She wondered about the houses she saw dotting the green expanse that ran back into the shadows of the mountain. She slipped her body into the driver's seat that now felt like a glove on her hand, and continued driving, as she thought about the people in the valley. She'd seen a sign calling the area Varner, the same name as a prominent family in the state. Why did the sons and daughters of that settlement push beyond the mountains into the plains and river valleys to the east? Were they shunned when they tried to revisit home? Clare imagined little enclaves of relatives and suspicious farmers peering out at strangers, including the returning kin, who might appear on their front porches.

*Damn Willie*, she said to herself. Why on earth was she having to disrupt her life like this, run off to some godforsaken mountain community, try and make a go of it—even if for just a short time—in some deep, dark corner of the state? She could feel her eyebrows draw together as she thought about her lack of fortune.

"Damn his ass!" she yelled to the car's windows. Then she was ashamed. Here she'd just been saying a prayer, and now she was cursing the man she'd married. What was the rest of that prayer? She searched her memory.

*'The Lord is with thee.*

She repeated what she remembered, hoping for more peace. A kind of calm descended on her. She saw the humor in her going back and forth between cursing and prayer.

Her mother-in-law, Grace, popped into her mind. What did Grace think of life, so different from the smelly, dirt hovels she had been raised in? How did she and Dan Clem relate? How did they even meet—one from family that had grown wealthy from timbering southeast Georgia, the other a generation removed from not having the proverbial pot to piss in? Clare felt her blood run a little hot as she thought about her father-in-law. Did that whole family always marry below them? Did Willie get advice to look for a low-rung woman?

She didn't have anyone to puzzle this with right now. Maybe it was the loneliness, maybe it was just the sight of the trees so profoundly in charge of the land around her, but Clare found herself searching deeper for why the marriage went wrong.

"It takes two to tango," her mother had often said when there was conflict between her and her sister, or on that rare occasion when she'd told her mother of problems with a friend at school.

Willie always seemed oblivious to their differences. Take the Mary Ann and Joe Shelton dinner—he joked about her academic smarts and painted himself as a dufus next to her. Maybe their contrasts bothered him more than she knew. But how could she help the differences?

Yesterday, when he was coming up the walk toward her, she saw tears in his eyes, she was sure of it. As he approached her, she thought his arm might reach out to fold her into his chest. She could have sworn he wanted her to stay, but he went cold, and his words pushed her away. What were his words? *Keep away from my family's businesses.* What kind of love was it that folded in front of a balance sheet?

Clare felt coldness in the car. She could see trees bending as the wind blew through and a sprinkling of rain pelted the windshield, then grew heavier. She drove through the valley, and the shower turned into a deluge as she tried to find the road signs for her turn. Fog coated her windows as she slowed the car, trying to find the dogleg in the highway. She turned on that road and dropped her speed again to figure out how to clear her windows. That's the first thing Willie would have done, cleared the windows, she thought. He was always criticizing her for being slow to get things, slow on the car buttons.

Was she slow in getting Willie's ways? The night they had the Sheltons for dinner—Mary Ann couldn't keep her eyes off Willie. Had he flirted with her? Was he using his charm on someone in a Buckhead bar right now? She could picture any of a dozen places, and a silky-haired blonde sidling up to him in a dark interior while he stood grinning with a beer in his hand.

She made a mental note to call another lawyer as soon as she was settled. She might be on top of a mountain far away, but her Atlanta cell number would help her make the many contacts she needed to finagle a way back to her former existence. She missed the comforts, she missed the certainty of knowing where she would lay her head. She missed Willie and his lovemaking.

Through a heavy coating of mist on her windows, she made out gas pumps and a store—actually a small frame house converted to a store—on the right side of the road. She decided to pull in and adjust the heating and defrost buttons so she could clear the car windows. She nudged the car into the gravel parking lot, avoiding the two gas pumps, and pulled in as straight as she could to avoid the other cars parked like second and third thoughts near the station's door. Immediately she wished her car was not bright yellow.

"What the hell," she said to the fog-bound car. "Might as well go in and wait out the rain."

She pushed open a glass door almost solid with poster ads for ammo, a rodeo, and a church bake sale, among others. As the door opened, she heard a clear bell above the door jangling excitedly. Inside she felt warmth and hugged her chilled body.

"C'mon in dearie, it's mizable outside," a low hoarse voice hailed her as she stood wondering where to go next. Beyond displays of crackers, cookies, and paper diapers heaped at the front of the store, she saw a counter to the right. A rough-looking, tan blonde woman in a denim shirt leaned on a cash register behind the counter, smoking a cigarette. Sitting in front and just to Clare's right—a line of stools on which she saw the large, rounded backs of four men hunched over the slab.

"Great day for ducks and hogs," the woman yelled cheerily. "What can I get yuh? D'rections? A beer? We've got several brands, just name your p'ison."

Clare brushed the rain from her sweatered arms and walked over toward the woman, carefully avoiding the men's massive backs. None of them looked at her until she'd drawn up to the counter near the woman. She felt eyes cutting toward her.

"What'll it be?" the woman asked again.

"I—I just wanted to get out of the weather for a moment," Clare said. "Is this expected to go long?"

"That thar weather ain't gonna make it over Taylor's Ridge, so you might as well just set a spell," the man nearest the storekeeper growled. "Course, you just crossed Dick's Ridge, but yew didn't know that."

Taylor's, Dick's. Clare was confused. Then she realized they were messing with her.

"Yeah, ain't gonna be any real estate deals goin down in this kinda weather," said the man next to him, a face barely visible under his baseball cap. "Take a load off, honey."

"Don't let them boys bother y'honey," the woman said, leaning harder on the cash register and dragging on her cigarette. "They ain't very good company. I'd take muh old pigs next to them, only I ain't got none no more."

Clare heard mumbles and guffaws from that side. The four were all drinking longnecks and all wearing ball caps except for the first one, wearing a fishing hat. They wore t-shirts displaying different graffiti, the shirts so old Clare couldn't make out the words.

"They think I'm kidding," the woman said, "but I'm not."

Clare smelled what she thought was chicken feed mixed in with the scent of tobacco and beer. She wondered if she should buy rat poison or some such protection for the mountain house she was going to. She decided to wait on that.

"D—Do you by any chance have any coffee?" she asked tentatively. The first man let out a big laugh.

"Do you mean truck stop special cankered coffee? I know ol Shirl's got some of that, ain'tcha Shirl?"

"Never you mind," Shirl said, stubbing out her cigarette. She flung the man a dirty look as she went to the far end of the counter and brought back a stained decanter nearly empty of coffee.

"That's fine," Clare said. "I'll take a cup. Do you have cream?"

Shirl gave her the pot—Clare could see brown streaks in the glass—and nodded her head toward the end of the counter where cups, powdered creamer, and sugar holders stood next to the coffee maker.

"Help y'self."

Clare looked around at stacks of Moon Pies in front of the coffee counter. There were boxes and boxes of them, the vanilla and chocolate she knew as a child and the many varieties since: banana, orange, strawberry. Ugh, strawberry. She couldn't imagine. She poured herself some of the overheated coffee and turned up the creamer package to whiten the blackness and hopefully help it go down better. She sipped and choked.

"Gahh!"

"Told you it was cankered," the man in the fishing hat laughed.

"Here, dearie, I'll make some more." Shirl took the coffee pot and moved back to the coffee maker.

"You must be special—she don't do that for us," one of the other men laughed.

"Yeah, I done choked on Shirl's coffee every day for the last two years," the man at the right end said. "It ain't a rat day if I don't end up upchucking it." The others laughed and mumbled agreement.

Clare tried to ignore them and looked around the store. She'd never seen such a variety of food and farm supplies stacked in such a small space. On top of the baby diapers was a garden hose. Behind the counter was every kind of fishing and hunting gear, including stacks of ammunition boxes.

Over on the left side of the store, up above the merchandise, and hanging from the wall were antique wood halters and chains for horses and mules.

Clare's breath stopped for a moment as she came eye to eye with a vicious bobcat in mid-snarl. Her eye followed to the next fur-clad animal, a red fox creeping across a cabinet top lined with no less than three giant copperhead snakes, one curled as if to strike. Fine works of taxidermy. A third furry animal, a small mountain lion, crouched from a tree branch as if about to spring at her throat.

Clare stared at the animals in wonder. How long ago had they been captured? Did these animals still roam the woods up here?

On the left wall of the store she saw in the dim light a boar's head, a black bear head, and a rack of buck antlers. She yearned for a cup of decent coffee and she lusted after familiar surroundings of home: clean, white walls, gourmet coffee, fresh herbs and vegetables from her garden. What was this place? Was she going to rot in some place civilization left with no forwarding address? Would she be safe in a countryside village where being armed and dangerous was the norm?

She felt a movement on her right side and looked up into the small eyes and pink folds of wrinkled skin belonging to one of the stool sitters. Her chest felt tight, like it was bound by a rope, and a flush rose from her chest to forehead. The man's arms were raised over his head as he moved toward her, zombie-like, as if to pounce. Clare felt burning all over her body. She stepped back, knocking an ammo box to the floor. She grabbed the metal edge of the shelf for balance.

"Hoo, hoo! Hoo!" the man laughed with a hollow, bitter sound. "Scared you, didn't I?" He kept laughing, his body caving into itself, the shape of a comma. The laugh turned into a smoker's wheeze and then a hacking cough he couldn't stop. His body, still bent over, jerked with every spasm, saliva running from his open mouth.

Clare stood still, not sure what to do. Still that stinging in her skin. She was rattled. If she reached out, he might hurt her with a swat from his large, thick arm. The arm and attached rounded ham were at his throat right now. Crinkled white letters clung in tattered bits to his black shirt, trying to proclaim, "Live Free or Die." His chest rose and fell with each strangled cough.

Clare wanted to run, but her feet felt part of the floor.

Finally he stopped. Clare was aware of his foul breath as he moved farther into her space.

"Watch yerself, little lady," he said, his throat straining with the words and his face contorted. "You folks run up here from 'Lana or Birmingham and think you can do things jes like back home." Clare felt acid pushing up into her throat from below. The animals surrounding her, so fierce moments ago, now seemed as calm as Bambi next to this man. His face was flushed red.

"Folks just 'love the country'," his voice was singsong, heavy with sarcasm. "And then you just go about changing it all." His eyes were wide open, staring into hers. The sandy brown curly hair sticking out from his cap looked like steel wool. Her heart beat high in her chest, blood throbbed in her ears. She feared he would move closer, pinning her against the bullet boxes.

"I'm not here to change anybody," Clare said evenly. Truly, right now she did not want to be here but back home in Atlanta, far away from all of this.

A denim wall grew between Clare and the man.

"Hank, get yourself over to the counter," Shirl said as she squeezed in front of Clare.

Hank faded back toward his stool, Shirl's words seeming to beat him about the head.

"You belong with em in Alana, down in that cesspool of sin," Hank flung his words at Shirl. "Cain't make your mind up if you're Shirl or Earl." He turned and wobbled toward his buddies at the counter. "Damn transvestite or dike or whatever you call y'self!"

"Don't mind Hank," Shirl said. Her voice was deep, like a man's. Clare was confused, trying to match the sound and the woman's face. Be interesting to know her story, Clare thought.

She took the Styrofoam cup. Her hand shook, and the coffee shimmied. She saw that Shirl was younger than she thought, and that her eyes were a crystal blue, made more intense in a browned face that looked weathered and tough. Clare liked her.

"You live here long?" Clare asked. She heard the men on the stools continuing to swap lies about who'd drunk the oldest coffee Shirl had ever made. Hank exclaimed to the others, "I cain't' believe that woman—she's a man, she thinks!"

"I moved over here and took over the store from my uncle," Shirl said. "You see them housing developments over there near McCainsville? I'm outrunnin em, I hope. They done messed up my life big time. I had a great hog farm—a hundred of them boogers, and the giant Caterpillars and Kubotas and John Deeres started coming in and moving dirt like it was a sand pile, and builders started comin in and throwing up these teensy little houses with yards no bigger than a baby diaper."

Shirl's eyes narrowed as she looked at Clare. Clare had the idea she was delivering a message for her benefit, in case she planned to move here. She let her face relax, listening.

"And then the new homeowners that boogie on down to the barbecue joint on Satidy called the county on Monday to go do somethin about the smell of them hogs. Ole Hank here does have a point, I have to admit. Had to move away from that mess—hey, you up here looking for real estate?"

"No. I'm kinda running away from home," Clare said. Shirl smiled knowingly.

"Man trouble, huh?"

"You might say that. Been told to hit the road, basically."

"Woo, that's tough. Mean sumbitch, I bet." Clare felt sympathy from the blue eyes.

"Not till now. Thought everything was fine, then I got into credit card problems—someone saying they were me had a high old time at my expense in California—then my husband's ID was stolen, too, and he had a fit. But I really think he's trying to hide something he's doing."

Clare stopped. What was she doing telling this stranger all about her life, her suspicions about Willie?

Shirl put a hand on her shoulder. "Don't worry, Hon, you're tough, I can tell. Either that or you're gonna be!" Shirl laughed, showing teeth—discolored, snagged—that looked older than she was.

The bell over the door—it swung freely on a metal extension at the top of the door—rang loudly as a young, medium-sized Hispanic man dressed in working clothes entered. He stood hesitantly and looked in the direction of the counter, and Shirl quickly passed over to the right side of the store and scooted behind the counter.

"What can I help you with?" she asked loudly.

"Cigarette?" the young man asked, his accent thick.

Shirl turned to the rack behind her and put her hands on different boxes as she spoke. The men at the counter were perfectly still. No one drank. No one spoke.

"Marlboro? Camel? What kind?"

"Camule." He nodded when her hand lit on the packs.

"One or two?"

"Uno—one."

Shirl quickly plunked the cigarette pack down on the counter, took the man's money, and rang up change. With no other words exchanged except a mumbled "Thenk you," the youth took the cigarettes and change and exited the store.

Clare felt the tension in the store, as though strands of tightly wound wire were strung across the aisles, left side to right. If the men's bodies were made of glass, they would have shattered from the pressure of breaths held back.

"Damn wetback come in here, takin jobs, gettin money, goin back home and gettin more hombres to bring back to move in with im. No shame about how he looks or talks," the left back complained to the others.

"Do nothin but brawl and shoot each other up on Satidy nights," Hank joined in.

"Got that rat," the man on the end said.

Clare's heart sank as she heard the comments. Similar comments were regularly directed at another group—big time. Guns had been used in a mass murder in a church, a murder based on the race of the victims. So many police murders.

She pulled herself away from the dark thoughts. She needed to be on her way.

She drank the rest of her coffee, waved at Shirl, and stepped back out into the rain, determined to clear her windows and get on up the road to her new home on the side of a mountain.

She slid into her car seat and breathed deeply. She still felt like her skin was separated from her body after the scare Hank gave her back there. She turned on the engine and switched the fan and rear defroster on high, the heat on high. As the warmth cleared the windshield, she stared out at the debris-strewn parking lot and the little store with its dirty white clapboard sides. She rubbed her arms as though touching them might help her return to herself. She would never be able to live here, she thought. Clare leaned her head on the steering wheel and breathed deeply again.

"Breathe in, count of ten," she ticked off the count. "Breathe out, count of ten."

After a while, she calmed. She was entering a world unknown, but so were Shirl and the young man after the cigarettes. They were the minorities. Shirl was not finding it easy being in between her two lives. The Hispanic man was always under suspicion, and he knew it. Even the men lining the counter saw their lives changing because of people like her. And Clare was without her identity, her work, and Willie.

The light changed in the car. As she sat there, the clouds cleared, and the rain stopped.

Within a few minutes, there was a bright reflection of sun in a puddle in the parking lot.

A smile broke across her face as she thought about how mystified and, yes, a little superior she'd felt when she first entered the store. At least these people had a home. She had yet to find hers.

"We're all freaks!" she told the windshield.

She started the engine of her flee-mobile and backed out, turning on the highway that would take her up higher mountains.

Clare finally descended to a wide valley and drove into a large town, Lafayette. She remembered it had been the location for a change of venue in a famous wife murder trial, moved from Atlanta to a place defense lawyers thought pretrial publicity had not reached. The defendant, a lawyer laundering money for his drug crime clients, was convicted anyway.

The weather cleared as she began her ascent over her next-to-last mountain, Pigeon.

Fatigue grew, and while the pain in the back receded, her right leg felt like a thin string of fire was making its way from calf to hip. She stopped at a crossroads to catch her breath and just look. The road to the left was straight and its pastures green. The long, blue-gray wall of Lookout Mountain leaned against the horizon. Hundreds of acres below it looked flat and ideal for a long bike ride. But she couldn't travel that way now.

She grabbed a map and a package from the glove compartment of the yellow escape wagon and opened a piece of sugared gum she'd found there aging and hardening., Slowly, she opened the map and spread it across the hood. The map gave no hint of truly high cliffs and deep valleys she knew were on either side of the mountain as it descended at its north point into Chattanooga.

Clare thought of the porcine name of the road to the left—Hog Jowl, a long road known to bikers as a clean, long, scenic ride. Bicyclists traveling west entered the long mouth of the hog, surrounded by mountains on two sides, then looped back through the long cove. The pig head image came to mind again as she pictured the tip of the mountain thrusting into Tennessee, almost like a pig's snout, while its hairy cheeks lay squarely in Alabama and Georgia.

Already she was getting a sense of the remoteness and desolation of her destination, the perch on the west face of the mountain. She quickly formed a bubble with the gum, blew into it. It wobbled, sank, softened and then collapsed in her mouth, sweetness sinking there, too.

Dark fell by the time Clare pulled across the rolling expanse of the mountain top. She looked for the landmarks Tony gave her when she'd called him on her cell earlier. He told her to find a roadside cross marking a traffic fatality, a closed-up country store, then a road going off to the left. She found that road, and now she was off the main highway. After a mile or so, she spied an opening in the weeds to her right. That had to be the drive Tony had told her about. It was marked with an oddly new mailbox.

Fighting drowsiness and a body vibrating from several hours driving on hard pavement, she drove toward the opening and felt the crunch of gravel. Then dirt took over, and the SUV tossed back and forth as the trail headed into fields thick with high dog fennel on either side.

"What, did you think all this was gonna be easy?" she chided herself as she pointed the car farther into the dark.

"If I ever get up here, I'm never coming down!"

The four-wheel drive kicked in as she maneuvered down the lane. There was nothing but blackness beyond the short distance of her headlights. Could she fall off the mountain's edge? A headline popped into her mind: "Life Coach Found Dead."

The first sign of her new home was a child's red Big Wheel, then a small white plastic chair tossed bottom up. Clare braked as she approached the trailer, which she could almost see now. Tall grass stroked the sides of the car. Sticking up in the grass were angles of a blue-and-white striped swing set turned over. Pieces of clothes—why had they been left behind?—spilling from a broken cardboard box. A home—large, mobile, up on cement blocks, a small set of stairs and a landing leading to the front door. She ached for the drive to be over and to get out of the car. But she was afraid to see inside this house.

She told herself she would pretend there was no debris, nothing of the child's left behind. Even when she went in, she would not notice the leavings of a family's life. She pulled herself from the car and grabbed her overnight bag. She approached the door, sodden, soft ground thick with weeds beneath her shoes. But the minute she touched the metal door she knew she couldn't go inside tonight.

She returned to her car. A storm of pressure built, almost like her body was its own weather system, making her feel the closeness of the air on her chest, around her face, causing the air she breathed to catch in her throat. Ringing in her ears, shock in her chest as she felt some reminder of hurt, something she was responsible for. Clare couldn't think what she'd done but it was bad. There was shame and the car handle she touched to make herself feel real was cold. Her hands, arms, and shoulders were cold, too. Dark across the mountaintop, dark in the car, dark in her heart. She could not touch the fear. But it was as real as the car handle, broad as the dashboard, hard and unyielding as the metal cage surrounding her. What had she done? She'd felt it as soon as the car had inched its way up the path to the house. It would not let her go in the house. It would not leave her.

Her car was going to have to be her home for the night. She and the car had kept company now for four or five long mountains and a wide valley away from the rolling hills around Atlanta. The car was all she trusted right now.

She climbed in the back seat, relocated some file boxes, and loosened her slacks. She pulled her bra from underneath her shirt and settled down under a fleece blanket Willie had convinced her to carry in the car for emergencies. Now he was the emergency she had to cope with. She grabbed a towel from her overnight bag and stuffed it under her head as a pillow.

"Willie was a real Boy Scout when it came to the car," she said to the dark.

No way she was going to spend the night in that trailer. She moved around to get comfortable.

She kept picturing Hank, whose face kind of resembled a hog, and the scary animals now no longer alive perched around Shirl's store. Willie's face as he uttered his last angry words to her about his family's businesses.

Her life was a mess, and she didn't feel strong enough to face more disarray inside that trailer.

Come morning, she'd decide. Come morning.

# Chapter 6

Clare woke stiff, unable to move. It was as though her body was glue poured out of a bottle onto the back seat of her car—she covered the whole expanse, and she couldn't lift one arm or one leg up off her bed. When she oozed out of the cocoon of blanket she'd wrapped herself in, she looked through foggy windows onto the ground outside. Light showed long green grass, steps to the porch of the trailer, and the long gray expanse of the home.

She opened the door. She saw no toys, no broken cardboard box, no swing set. Had she imagined last night's child's things?

That weight, that fear she'd felt, returned. The child's toys had been like those of her family home on Melanie Street. But they were so real, the fire engine red of the Big Wheel, the blue diagonal striped paint of the swing set so familiar to her touch.

She grabbed for her purse on the floorboard and extracted a thin wafer of a receipt. She dug for her pen.

1. Get going.

2. Forget past.

Sometimes the reality of black ink on white paper gave more direction to her than her own rattled mind. Time to open the door to this house and get busy.

She fixed her underclothes, stepped out of the car. Moist, frigid air on her cheeks reminded her that she'd just spent the cool night either in or above the clouds. She smoothed her clothes and got back in again, using the rearview mirror to brush her hair with her hands.

"Ugh, what eyes!" Rounded puffs swelled below. "But keep on going."

She approached the trailer, went up the stairs, but she could not open the door. Something about the cold metal again pushed her back. She knew she needed to keep moving, but she didn't want it to be into the house yet. Pulled out the old receipt again, wrote over whatever transaction was recorded there: Clorox, Pine Sol, mop, broom.

*I'll find a store, keep moving that way.*

As she rode in search of a store, there was nothing on the highway. Slips of fog lay in front of her, then escaped to the side, revealing as straight a road as any in the coastal plain of Georgia, hardly like a mountaintop. Why had the swing and the Big Wheel disappeared? She had seen them as real as her hands in front of her last night. But they weren't here this morning. Was it the fog that she saw? But the stripe of the swing set leg—it was like her old set.

The road began to dip and rise, reminding Clare that she was indeed very high in the sky. Then morphed back to a straightaway. This was a very old mountain, worn down by eons of rain, snow, and wind so that the original upheaval of earth's crust had been mellowed and shaped and scraped. High, sharp upward thrusts had aged, leaving a giant loaf of bread loaf that was now somewhat flat on top with lumps of rocks pushing up, like fists of hard dough within the soft mixture. Yet beyond the smooth top were treacherous bluffs on either side of the mountain, precipices that were often hidden by dense trees. Now with the fog flitting in and out of her vision, she realized how tricky it was to drive here. Seemed she was going from one hazardous existence to another.

Still, few signs of life showed up on the road. Hadn't she seen a closed store the night before when she'd arrived? She peered at homes close to the road and a shuttered appliance repair store and noted expensive painted signs for high-end mountain homesites.

Her back hurt from the unusual sleeping quarters in the back seat of her SUV. She felt cranky and unprepared for the days of cleaning that probably awaited her. She was confused from her vision last night. When she finally saw a store on her right, she turned in, thinking back to Shirl and the men back at yesterday's store. What would she find here?

When she emerged from the car, she straightened her slacks and sweater, trying to see in the car's windows if she looked a fright. Her car tires wore arcs of flung mud, and a fine mist of dirt covered the windshields and side windows. She assured herself that the store, actually a house with weathered wood sides and windows filled with colorful Coca-Cola and tobacco ads, would be different from Shirl's.

"How're yuh? C'mon in," a youngish, slender man greeted her at a counter across the front of the store. His pale gold hair and beard were matted as though crushed during sleep. Clare did a double take as she saw his face repeated in a black and white picture on a flyer attached to the cash register.

There was his face, bushy whiskers and light eyes peering out from dense eyebrows. He was propping up a banjo and a guitar with each hand.

"Mountain Sublime—CDs here. Gordon Frick, Lookout Mountain Troubadour" the sign read.

The picture was much more flattering. Gordon looked bleary-eyed this morning. On the other hand, the store was well kept. No wild animals or other mountain creatures among the neatly stacked shelves of mayonnaise, peanut butter, and other goods.

"Musician, huh?" Clare asked.

"Yep," Gordon said. "Call myself doing music anyway."

"That's cool. Well, I need about every cleaning help you've got—Clorox, Pine Sol, mop, broom, rags—"

"Whoa, wait a minute," Gordon said. "You cleaning up after a crime?"

"I don't know. My renters were just a step ahead of the sheriff."

"I got the picture. Well, I think I know where you're talkin about. You're not far from my cabin."

"Yeah?"

"That singlewide down the pig trail to the right as you go down the highway toward Georgia?" Amazingly, Gordon had nailed the place.

"How'd you know?"

"I'm this side of it."

"I had no idea anyone was around."

Gordon laughed. "Welcome to the mountain. Nobody knows where anybody is, but everybody knows you're here. Or will fifteen minutes after you arrive."

"That so?" Clare felt her skin prickle. "What kind of people?"

"Most of 'em are okay. I can tell you the characters to look out for." Clare felt only moderately better.

"Really, the worst ones we have are the butt pains who've retired here from the big cities—" He blushed, and a flash of recognition shot through Clare's body. She was an outsider, too.

"At least you got one thing right," Gordon said, quickly recovering from his gaffe. "Everybody up here refers to Tennessee direction, Alabama direction, or Georgia direction. No east, west, north or south here. Had a famous art show up here called Plum Nelly, cause this part of the mountain's plum outa Tennessee, and nelly outa Georgia. Alabama's just down the other side of the mountain, opposite from where you came."

"Artists live up here?" This could be interesting, Clare thought.

"Got some artists—and musicians." His blue eyes lit up. The smile got bigger. "Some of us are pickin tonight. You need to drop by."

Clare pictured in her mind the mess she'd probably left behind. "I gotta work today. Maybe later."

"Do it this way. Work all you can and then walk down to my place later. My pig trail's just off your pig trail. I'll draw you a map."

"What's a pig trail?" Clare ventured.

Gordon laughed with a big, open-mouthed "Ha!"

"Back in the day, lots of people made their living raising pigs and cattle all over this area. They'd do it for their own homesteads, but they also raised them for market, driving them down south to big towns like Augusta and Savannah. Name kind of stuck, because those pigs tore up the trails, what trails were there. Trails were left over from the Indians."

Clare nodded quietly. "You a native?"

His head down, he drew a couple of lines on a scrap of notebook paper lying by the register.

"Yes and no. Grew up here, went to college, moved away, had another life, then came back—hey, this doesn't start till after nine." He gave her the paper. "Here's the directions. I don't have a phone, but most people just come by. We're harmless. This isn't 'Deliverance' or anything. Promise."

Clare went on to get her cleaning items, thinking how strange it was to be in a place where people didn't have a phone, not even a cell. How little money Gordon must live on, she reflected. *How nice for him*, she thought. *And truly weird.*

Back at the trailer, Clare was scared to enter, thinking of the trash that might await her.

She walked to the front door juggling her plastic bags of cleaning materials and the new mop and broom. Before she opened the door, she put down the bags and looked around again, hoping the child's toys she saw when she drove up in the dark would pop up again. But there were none.

She unlocked and cracked the door just a little. She could already smell the mildew.

"Whew!" she yelled and held her nose.

She opened the door, and a stronger sour smell assaulted her. She flicked on a light switch to her left and gasped at the sight: a couch with its back covering torn in a large triangle, clothes trailing across every floor in a kind of abandonment ritual. Dirty curtains pulled half off the large window on the other side. She grabbed a tissue from her pocket to cover her mouth and nose.

"Crap!" she shouted.

In the main room of the fourteen-foot wide trailer, she found the source of the mildew. A window looking out on a back deck had been left open, so all the rain of yesterday and days since the trailer sat empty had swept into the main room, drenching everything. She walked through the mess, put down her bags on the bar separating the kitchen and the main room, and took out her cleaners and wipers. Then she went to the car, dragged in her duffle bag, and changed into jeans and a t-shirt. She began her assault.

For the next several hours, she lost herself in the acute confusion of someone else's life, moving old toys, discarded clothing, and other glorious stuff to one place in the main room where she reused the grocery bags and several large trash bags to stuff the derelict goods. An old kitchen clock that didn't work, a headless hammer, a can opener with a ruined jagged edge, old medicine cabinets, and broken particle board bookshelves. Were there any goods left that were in one piece, she wondered. Old clothing of every type dotted each room and the narrow hallway to a back bedroom. In corners of the trailer she found old sets of mismatched tableware bound with rubber bands, and pottery vases. Perhaps a woman's hope she could improve her home?

Maybe the family shopped at yard sales there in the mountains. She tried to imagine what the family looked like. She wondered where they'd gone and hoped the new home was near a job or relatives who could help.

Clare picked a loose, slightly curled school picture off the floor of the child's room and met the girl for the first time—about eight, she guessed—shy smile of one who didn't stand out in her school.

*There was a little kid here. I wasn't imagining those toys.*

Clare moved over to the blinds in the darkened room to let more sun in so she could see the picture better. Bright horizontal-stripe knit top. Slightly turned to the camera, eyes lively, as though intelligent.

The brown hair was inexpertly cut, probably by her mother, Clare thought. But didn't her mother cut hers when she was little? How like her own life had this young girl's been?

A kind of painful, hard place seemed to grow in her chest. Clare sat on the floor and looked at the picture. She looked like a Lucy. Clare wondered if Lucy was cared for. How did she survive the chaos of her family? She felt heaviness in her back and shoulders dragging her forward over her lap. How had she, Clare, survived? She wiped a tear from her eye and then found more tears rimming the edges of her eyes. Her head filled with moisture, and she let the drops come. She swiped her tissue at the tears. She leaned back against a single bed whose mattress was sliding off the box spring.

"Sit still!" Her back had stung from her mother's slap, and she had begun crying. "I can't do your hair if you're so fidgety!" Her father was dead. She was eight, and he'd been dead two years. Her mother was trying to cut her hair. Horribly, she was getting ready for a Father-Daughter dance at school. She would not, of course, be dancing but would be helping serve punch and cookies to the fortunate ones. Her fourth-grade teacher thought that it would be a fine Christian gesture for Clare to do this.

"I'll never be able to cut your hair to look right," her mother obsessed. Frankie was always concerned about how things looked, and now she was doubly frustrated, pulling so much of the family weight. How much her mother must have missed Paul Connor at that moment! But at the time her mother struck her, Clare just knew it was all her fault. She remembered her tears and her mother's tears, a girl and a woman caught up in the ringing tragedies of loss.

Later, there was another incident.

"Mother, the teacher was talking today about needing parents to pay their tuition—the sisters are behind on their bills because families haven't paid!"

"What nerve!" her mother's dark eyes blazed. "Your father helped pay for your tuition by carrying boxes of food to the priests and the few sisters who were left at their convent! And I did the same—week after week. Our best from the store—only name brands—Kraft, Hormel. How ungrateful to be pushing for money!"

"So I'm kind of a charity case?"

"Call it what you want—you are not as well off as those who pay."

Clare absorbed the anger in her mother's voice and made a little pocket with it in her heart. Later in her days at Saint Anne's School, Clare understood that she was expected to be appreciative of everything she received at the school.

That pocket of red anger emptied sometimes, but mostly she just made plans to escape. Yet she knew she was terribly afraid of poverty—that was why Willie's abandonment and this little girl Lucy's plight affected her so.

Here in the trailer, the little reserve in her heart erupted now, letting the hurt spill into the rest of her body. It was hard to know what she was crying for—herself, the little girl, or her dying marriage. If Willie called her today, would she return? She was angry, sad, and missing his touch. She was tired of cleaning up this house. She missed her spotless home with all its conveniences and the maid once a month to help with the heavy stuff. Clare snuffled and wiped her sleeve on her jeans.

"She didn't even tell me I was on a 'scholarship,' and there were others like me that were being supported—is that what mothers do, hide the truth?" Clare asked a skewed mirror on the other side of the room.

Quietly, Clare wiped her face and stood up to put Lucy's picture in her jeans. She pulled the discarded clothes from the bottom of the small closet, picked up dirty doll clothes and an armless rag doll off the floor and continued to think about how she and Lucy could probably have some good talks about growing up. Gradually, the heaviness in her chest lightened.

On a whim, she decided to leave Lucy's room for later. She wanted to be reminded of the effects of living with a little girl.

She needed a boost to keep her going. She went outside, pulled the car closer to the trailer and opened the car door. She turned on the car radio and looked for a station strong enough to pull in on the mountaintop. She found some country music, turned the audio up full blast, went back inside the trailer, propping the door open with an old boot so guitar riffs and amplified country sounds could blast through her own thoughts as she attacked the rest of the trailer.

Later, after following Gordon's scratched directions, Clare stood in the living room of an old frame 1930s house that was back off the road like her place. She looked around at old, pale blue, painted bead board running all around the room, top to bottom. The bead board made her think of tiny ocean waves lapping the shore, only there was no shore for many, many miles around. The wind picked up, and the windows in the house clattered in their frames. Clare shivered to think what the home would be like up on this exposed mountain top in winter and caught a view of the wood stove in the kitchen area that seemed to offer the only heat.

The house had been transformed into a listening parlor, with a couple of wooden rockers, miscellaneous stuffed chairs and a sofa, as well as huge pillows in solid colors of yellow and green and tangerine big enough for sleeping that were strewn about the floor. There was very little light in the room—a couple of lamps with shades askew decorated the far wall.

The kitchen was Spartan, sporting a large freestanding porcelain sink, and white, grease-stained open shelves for dinnerware, cans, and boxes of food. A single exposed bulb in an overhead light socket lit everything with a glaring brightness and provided most of the light to the living room as well. A small table in the middle of the kitchen was filled with bottles of wine, beer, and bags of chips, salsa bowls and other snacks. Clare was sure that the people here could smell the residue of Pine Sol on her even though she'd showered and scrubbed herself in a freshly cleaned bathroom.

"Meet a newbie here on the mountain," Gordon said amiably as he introduced her to some other musicians who'd come in to play.

"Good to meet you." She asked them about their instruments and where they played.

"I'm up and down the East Coast in a backup band," one young man, a dark-haired mandolin player, said.

"Guitar here," said a blond about Gordon's size.

"We drive wherever the nearest airport is—Atlanta, Birmingham, Chattanooga—and fly wherever there's work," a tall banjo player said.

"Man, you're lyin'," said the guitar picker. The others laughed and agreed.

"Yeah, you know we stuff equipment in our Kias or vans if we're lucky and go to all the big cities around just to get a little work," the mandolin player said.

"Now Gordon here, he's got a custom van—previously owned, that is—and he rides in style. We like to get gigs with ol' Gordon!" Everyone laughed, and the banjo player just looked down at his glass, totally defeated in his effort to reflect the glamour that sometimes worked its way into their gigs.

After endless tuning and wisecracks back and forth, the playing finally started. Clare sat entranced as Gordon's group of four played Hank Williams and Bill Monroe favorites. Then his banjo pickers had the audience tapping feet—two women clogged off to the side—as they led fast-paced Earl Scruggs renditions of "Foggy Mountain Breakdown" and "Orange Blossom Special."

Another enthusiastic fiddle player with long, brown hair and thin, pendulous fingers made an elaborate introduction of a solo selection called "Gray Eagle." Clare gathered that the number was one that competitors in fiddle contests used to beat out others—it was a sure crowd pleaser, probably the bluegrass equivalent of Vivaldi's "Four Seasons," she guessed.

She felt her senses tingle and goose bumps pop out on her skin as the song took off, carrying the listeners along in a furious tune with difficult turns of scale and swooping movements, like the extinct bird that gave it its name. When the last notes streamed out, sudden thunder seemed to fall from all the walls of the low-ceilinged house.

While Gordon and his friends played, the house filled with young to middle-aged men and women, some in couples, some single, all favoring jeans and t-shirts with windbreakers and sweaters or woven wraps for dress. Respectful of the musicians, they quietly entered and slipped onto pillows or furniture, hailing each other with whispered greetings and hand waves. A couple snuggled in front of her on some pillows.

Clare felt her nose and eyes suddenly fill and throb, wondered if she'd cry again as she did over Lucy's things. She put her hands to her nose to stifle the tears and not look obvious. She longed to feel as close to someone as the couple was. She wanted to feel part of a whole group like this, glued with a love of music and the mountains that gave them the songs.

The guitar-toting blond took the stage, a kitchen stool in the middle of the sprawled audience. A reading lamp was brought up so he could read his lyrics or chords pasted to the instrument. With a mournful high mountain tenor, he sang songs of love and yearning that continued to tug at Clare, making her more emotional. She left the house and went outside.

From a nearby parked van, a young woman and man pulled things from the back—amplifier, electronic keyboard, microphone—most of which looked like they would not be needed in the small space in the house. They continued to extract guitar and mandolin cases, nodding toward Clare when they saw her.

"Hi," the young man said. Bearded and dark-haired, he was moving the heavy stuff.

"Hi back," Clare said, smiling. The young woman, slender with long, curling brown hair and pale skin, looked at her and gave a big smile.

"Glad to see you here," she said.

Clare walked on down the bumpy road past the couple, gathering her thoughts. The stars showed brightly in the darkness above her, like so many loose diamonds in a jewel box against a black velvet background. She found the Big Dipper and the North Star and oriented herself, walking a few steps north in the direction of Chattanooga. How much more brilliant the stars were away from the smog of the city! Willie would know all the constellations.

Clare decided she needed to get back to her house and plan her job attack for Monday morning. She'd go say her goodbyes now.

Back in Gordon's cabin, the couple she'd seen at the van were busy setting up the electronics, and Gordon had such an excited look on his face, she realized she was not going to get his attention to make her exit any time soon.

"Folks, welcome Jill and Gene Weldon. They're trying out their equipment here for a gig in Nashville—woohoo! Nashville! Hope you'll welcome them as they give you a sample of what they're going to play for some producers at a small label up there. Stick around, they'll be ready in a minute!"

Intrigued, Clare took her place back on the floor behind the couple, now drawn closer than ever. She'd have to endure the spectacle of love in front of her for a little while longer. Jill and Gene tested the microphone amid friendly boos from the acoustically oriented bluegrass fans. Jane tuned up on a twelve-string guitar, and Gene plugged in the keyboard, pressing buttons for various instruments and effects.

Jill began singing, and Clare sensed immediately she was vastly different from the others. While the instruments were borrowed from the mountains, Jill's voice was different, quicksilver movements up and down, hard to know where it would go next. It was melodious and rich, but also haunting.

Her voice lifted up the scale then raced down to depths of warmth and intimacy and ardor. As compelling melodies came from her twelve-string, Gene played in the background, and Jill sang with words that didn't rhyme and that refused a refrain but ran on and on. Snatches of words repeated only enough to give an idea of the song titles, like "Widening Sky," "Ohio," and "River." Clare thought of Joni Mitchell in the hard-to-guess way the singer played with notes. Clare sat transfixed as the woman's eyes closed and her mouth opened with those wild vocalizations, eerie and chilling, filling Clare with electricity she'd never felt from music.

Then applause cascaded from all around, from that gentle audience of believers, wrapped in the spell of the music. Unafraid to speak in front of groups, and often chatty with strangers, Clare could not speak.

Others gathered around Jill, but Clare sat and drew in the spirit of her music. She finally wandered over to where the couple had placed some copies of their CD and read from the cover. Roots of Celtic folk and East Tennessee relatives were acknowledged in the notes. Jill, the writer of most of the songs, had moved from northern Kentucky to Lookout Mountain and was discovering more relatives nearby, so she'd incorporated all these threads in her lyrics.

Even though she hadn't heard Gordon play his solo, Clare quietly left the party. She'd see Gordon at the store tomorrow and tell him how much she enjoyed the music. Right now she felt a need to let the waves of music continue to wash over her. She felt peaceful and looked forward to returning to a cleaner house.

Back in the trailer, Clare changed clothes from her makeshift closet, the open duffle bag on the floor. She put on a knit top and pajama pants and rolled into a bed she'd made from layers of sheets and quilts placed on the single bed, now put back together. This must be how construction workers feel after a long day, she told herself, as she fell motionless into a deep sleep.

"Darn—no signal!" Clare yelled at the weeds in the front yard of her new home. She moved farther from the trailer and closer to the highway and tried again to get a signal on her cell phone to call Helene. "No dice," she told herself, then moved out farther still. She gave up after five tries and jumped in her car to drive to Gordon's store. She'd dressed and pulled some milk out of her cooler to pour over a small plastic tub of cereal for breakfast. The niceties of life, especially human contact, were in short supply.

She'd hoped that she'd have a call from Willie, but she realized it was a silly dream that he'd try to call her. And almost impossible, since she didn't have a signal. But maybe her phone picked up a message anyway.

Gordon wasn't there, and the store wasn't open, as it was Sunday. A shut out—the only phone she'd seen anywhere along the highway was in the store. So she got back in her car and drove down the road to an intersection. "Cloudland Canyon State Park," the sign read. Campsite sign—surely there'd be a pay phone for them. She turned north and drove up to a neat unoccupied guard shack that marked the entrance, dug in her wallet for a three-dollar entry fee, put it in a box, and then followed all the signs to campsites and the canyon overlook. Cabins peeked out of trees on the left, but Clare followed the road as it curved quickly to the right. She went straight for a parking lot that seemed to be on the edge of a cliff, detouring to catch a view as she searched for a phone.

She parked and walked as close to the cliff end as the safety chain would allow and leaned over to see more. The drop-off was dramatic. She overlooked a chasm that descended quickly, but another sharp ridge rose in the distance overlooking a long, misty valley. Clare saw that by going down a trail and following the creek that ran between the two, she might have a full view of the lands below. But that had to wait for another day.

She drove back toward the campsites until she saw a main building. There was a pay phone hanging on a wall outside near a walkway. Clare saw that it would take a credit card, so she used her reliable one and put in Helene's phone number.

"Helene," she shouted into the receiver, as Helene sounded as far away as she really was. "How are things going? Have you visited Frankie? How is she?"

"Nothing's changed much. Except that praying you described? She's not doing that when I see her. She's just real quiet, real out of it."

"What do the nurses say about that?"

"She's in what they call nonresponsive wakefulness. That reminds me. I need you to sign a form for me to get information from the nurses. Give me your address and I'll send it. I'm guessing you don't have a printer set up yet."

"Printer? Are you kidding? I don't even have cell service, only a pay phone several miles away. I'll call Tony Sands and find out the address."

"What's happening there?" Helene asked.

"I found a holy mess. It'll keep me busy for a while." Clare told her about the trailer. "Got my hands full juggling getting it clean and making phone calls from the state park down the road to check on my career program."

Helene chuckled. "Other than that small detail, how's the place seem?"

"Haven't decided yet. Found some nice folks next property over, a musician who has lots of friends who play. Jaw dropping scenery here—you'd love it!"

"Yeah, right." She imagined Helene's shuddering. She was definitely a city girl.

Getting off the phone with her friend, Clare thought about her mother. She needed to get things under way here as soon as possible so she could return and take care of Frankie. Feeling the slight bulge in her pocket where Lucy's picture hid, she wondered if it was possible to reconstruct her own family from her ruins. Maybe she could redo part of her family life, make it better by being at her mother's side.

She dialed Tony's number, thinking he might be at church. She guessed folks in this part of the world were pretty much there on Sunday morning.

"Hallo?" he said. The heavy breathing again.

"Tony! Clare. I'm here. Thanks for your directions."

"Glad to help. Not a pretty sight I bet."

"Well, the house could be cleaner, but that's not your fault. The area around is lovely. Where do you live from where I am? Can I come see you sometime?"

"You'd be welcome to come, but I'm a little indis-posed right now, a little under the weather." She heard snuffling. "How about Tuesday?"

"That sounds good. I'm looking forward to meeting you!"

"I should be better by then. Give me a call."

"Oh, Tony, what's the address here? I have to have mail sent right away."

He gave her a box number. "Rising Fawn's the town."

"Rising Fawn? I thought this was Trenton."

"Trenton's down the valley toward Chattanooga. But not far away." Tony sounded tired.

"Look, I won't keep you—"

"It's all right. Rising Fawn's a town just below you. And Johnson's Crook and your area up there on top of the mountain is also in that post office area. So it's all Rising Fawn."

"Lovely name. Where does it come from?"

"Old Cherokee tradition. Baby's born, the papa looks out the door, and the first thing he sees is what he names his child. The Cherokee town that was originally here got its name from an Indian named Rising Fawn—name stuck after the Indians left."

"Interesting. Like I said, I'm not going to keep you. I'll call you Tuesday morning!"

"So long. I hope I'll feel better then," he said with a snuffle.

Clare drove on west and then down a steep incline where the west brow of the mountain dropped sharply, taking the highway with it. She managed a double hairpin curve about halfway down the mountain that was steeper than any she'd been on in recent memory, short of the northeast Georgia mountains. Clare gasped at the same time at the view it gave of the valley between Lookout and Sand Mountain on the other side. As she descended, she saw there was civilization up ahead, the town of Trenton, probably, and she tried to remember if she had an address handy where she could check out the Welfare to Work program. Of course, she didn't have it on her— she was feeling more disorganized and un-life coach-like every day. She hoped she would be able to carry the project off.

She drove up and down a couple of the main streets in Trenton to see if she could guess where she'd go the next day, but she was unsuccessful. The town was buttoned down on Sunday morning, with all the cars parked at the large, steepled Baptist church or the Methodist church or the Church of Christ. She looked for highway signs and decided she had two choices for going to Rising Fawn: travel south on the interstate or follow a highway closest to the railroad tracks. The highway was obviously the back road, so she chose that.

Rambling through the countryside, Lookout Mountain was a constant to her east. She neared the village of Rising Fawn, and a moment of panic seized her as she looked up at the bare rock outcrop so high over the valley—the bluff where her trailer was. Tony had called it Johnson's Crook. A concave ledge on the mountain above, it loomed over the settlement. She could have fallen off the mountain to her death with one false step walking to Gordon's house last night. Good thing she'd followed her pig trail back home. She'd have to walk down to the end of her mother's property overlooking the valley real soon to get an idea of where she was.

As she drove down the narrow valley with the railroad to her left, she saw barns, a few homes, and one closed restaurant. She guessed there was no quicker way to advertise one's godlessness than to open a business during church hours. She made a mental note to check back later and continued down the road. There didn't appear to be many signs of industry. She did notice that roads going up a hill to the right had some older homes, but here on the main road through town there were only a couple of Victorian homes that would have belonged to the more wealthy of the town "back in the day." Now she was rising over hills, as the valley suddenly narrowed.

At the next rise, she came to a large expanse of well-kept lawn on the left, the beginning of a cemetery that seemed to spill on and on.

She pulled off the road onto a drive that looked like it was for visitors and cut off her engine. The early morning mist had lifted, but a light, airy fog lingered over the soft breast of the hill as it fell to a creek down below. The huge grounds appeared to hold many more than the current population of Rising Fawn. Still, quiet, gravestones.

Clare climbed out of the car and wound her way back to the older part of the cemetery.

Old graves topped with long, thin tablets, pebbly-faced and dark gray where there had once been inscriptions. She saw mid- and late-1800s graves—quite a few of these—attesting to the once-large size of the village.

As she walked among the markers, Clare saw wide variation in the dates. Some were of children of two or six years old; small lambs topped some of these. A man, Marcus Jones, died at age thirty-five, while his wife lived to seventy.

Some died so young, and some had full lives. There were no guarantees, no ironclad contracts when it came to knowing when your time would come. She fantasized what it would be like in heaven, imagining lawyers debating the fine points of the contracts some people were sure they had, the bargains people made to assure they'd have a long and healthy life.

She imagined heavenly lawsuits being filed for the contracts God had broken. The man who thought if he lived an upright life, he'd be allowed to see his great-grandchildren. But he'd been taken at thirty-five. Would Willie be punished in purgatory, that temporary hell she knew was set up for those who hadn't sinned grievously, but who'd sinned nonetheless? Would she be punished along with him? She thought the gravestones would give up some answers.

As she drew away from the oldest markers, a single upright gravestone spanning three graves caught her attention. It wasn't new, but it wasn't the age of those hoary resting spots she'd just seen. What was curious was that the oblong stone was definitely for three spaces, and the names were dissimilar.

"James Thomas Connor," Clare read. "My grandfather's name—my father's father!" she told the air. She checked the dates: 1890–1943. Those were his dates, she was pretty sure. But why here? She looked at the other two graves.

"Julia Mullins Webster 1920–1989; John Michael Webster 1918–1990." Who were these people, she wondered, and why were they lying together? "Beloved father, daughter, husband," the gravestone read.

Clare wasn't familiar with anyone named Julia in the family. Nor was there a John Webster. What was this all about? She was mystified. Why would her grandfather be in this town, lying beside these two people she'd never heard of? Obviously, one claimed him. Why was that grave here? Other than the trailer home on the cliff above, there'd been no Rising Fawn—that she knew of— in her family's past. Anne, James's wife and Clare's grandmother, was buried in Trenton. Although she'd never seen the grave, she had just assumed her grandfather was buried next to her.

Clare wrote down the dates and names on a piece of paper in her wallet and then moved toward her car. She looked up to see a woman walking down the broad grassy slope of the cemetery toward her. Probably a neighbor wondering what's a woman doing casing graves on a Sunday morning in June, she thought.

"Hello," the woman said as she drew near. Her short blond hair lifted slightly in the breeze. "Is there something I can help you with?" She looked middle-aged and casually but well-dressed.

"Just checking out the graves," Clare said. "I'm from out of town. Finding relatives." That part was true.

"We just try to keep an eye on it," the woman said. "Funeral homes come and bury people here without checking, drive over graves, every sort of thing. And of course the devil worshippers would like to use this as their church."

"Devil worshippers, huh?"

"Yes, they occasionally like to dress up and come out here. Don't ask me who they are or where they come from. If I knew, I'd tell some mommas and there'd be some warm bottoms. Never can tell with these young people what they're gonna be into."

"I get the idea they learn to behave in this neighborhood."

"You've got that right. I see somebody misbehaving, it's on the church agenda for a meeting if the momma or daddy don't set them straight."

"Church about out now?"

"Yes, I just came back, and I saw you here."

Clare was walking toward her car as they talked and that seemed to please the woman. It was like the graveyard was her special charge, and she was going to see that no strangers came around unless attending an approved funeral.

"How did the town get started?"

"Railroads. Coal mines. Iron furnace. This was a big place in the 1800s—only place they mined coal much in Georgia—it was especially big in the Civil War and after. Lots of people came here and then left after things changed near the turn of the century."

"You mean the nineteen hundreds, that century turn?" She saw the woman smile at the mild correction. "Were there any Irish families that stayed in this area? I noticed a name, Connor, on one of those graves back there."

"No, there aren't many Irish any more, at least not the Cathlic kind." She said this with a frown. "They left with the end of the iron furnace. Helped build the railroad, mine the coal, work the iron, but they left this area." Her words were quick, like she had better things to do than talk about the Cathlics.

"That so?"

The woman's eyes narrowed further.

"Wouldn't exactly say they fit in, you know? But some of them became good Baptists over the years."

"Oh yeah? Are any of those families left?"

"Well, the O'Brians and the Daileys went on to live in Trenton. You might find Margaret O'Brian at the library there." She clearly didn't want to talk about these people.

"Well, thanks for telling me about the town. I'm going to go on up the road now."

The woman waved farewell, and Clare drove off land she figured was really private property and turned north.

As Clare retraced the road through Trenton and back up the mountain, the music she'd heard from Jill and Gene floated through her head. She opened her window to absorb the cool air and ascended the double switchback road. She was tempted to pull off on a narrow shoulder to see the view over the long, open valley between Sand and Lookout Mountain. But she drove on.

Jill's electric guitar and her eerie voice trailed in Clare's mind, filling her with the charge she remembered from the night before. The riddle of a grave and the music played back and forth in her head. What was James doing in that grave so far from his wife? The Irishman who lay in the grave was from her father's side, the side that hunted and provided food for their table from the woods around Trenton. And Rising Fawn. She wondered if the unusual grave had to do with some shame, some circumstance. Just like the wild sounds of the Celtic music, James's life, Clare thought, was a tumult— stormy and wild and unpredictable—maybe even dangerous. Something to be ashamed of? She wasn't sure. But the music was a connection. It pressed down on a small nerve in her body and wouldn't let up. A thin but persistent connection to all that went on up here, all that her family did not speak of.

The picture of Lucy tucked in her jeans, Clare walked out to the end of the trailer property. It was a high cliff made up of large boulders. She could see the long valley, which lay between the two mountains. Sand Mountain stretched from Birmingham through a good portion of East Tennessee, part of the Cumberland Plateau. Lookout Mountain started in Alabama, climbed through the northwest counties of Georgia, and ended at a point overlooking the Tennessee River near Chattanooga. The valley in between the two mountains was shaped like a jagged lightning bolt, and she was located on the elbow of the bolt. Her view spread southwest, down the lower leg of the bolt, probably a distance of a hundred miles or more. Where the bolt crooked, on the elbow where she sat, Lookout Mountain seemed to grow away from Sand Mountain, but they still continued their parallel paths.

"Must've been some humongous gully-washer that tore through these mountains," she told herself. It was hard to imagine the eons of constant water washing out the curve of the crook, leaving a ledge that dropped to the valley below, a distance of seven football fields.

She pulled the image of Lucy out of her pocket.

"Were you safe here? Did your momma warn you to stay off the rocks?"

Lucy said nothing.

When she'd looked up at Johnson's Crook from down in the valley in Rising Fawn, Clare hadn't been able to see the trailer because of the dense trees and rocks all across the mountain face. Now she sat on a huge boulder perched on the cliff over the valley, surrounded by the same trees. Someone had planted irises in the rich soil between the rocks. Lucy's mom? They looked like they'd been there for a long time and had just come out with their lavender and deep purple colors. Here, about a hundred feet from the trailer, the land sloped to the edge of the mountain, then suddenly pitched up with rocks protruding out over the mountainside. Then the rocks broke off, cascading down the side of the mountain. A minefield of spewed boulders spread across the slope underneath. There had to be some tremendous explosion in the earth's crust or other action to cause such a debris trail. Thermal currents of air lifted the hair around her face. In the distance, a hawk circled down a column of air, scarcely moving its wings.

She wondered about Willie. What was he doing right now? Was he with someone? She hadn't even told him where she was going. She had wanted to spite him in every way she could when she left. Somehow, her anger was softening now. She missed his love of music and his company doing nature things. His ability to figure out the Milky Way and the North Star in the night sky, things her schooling didn't emphasize.

And she had to admit she was tired of her own thoughts.

"I'm ready for somebody's thoughts besides mine!" she yelled into the valley.

"Lucy, you're not very talkative company!" she told the picture in her hand. She put the picture on a crack in the boulder she sat on, anchoring it from the light wind that blew gently over her. She pulled her sweater over her head to warm up.

How did her mother come into the trailer and property? She knew her grandparents on her mother's side had run a restaurant in Trenton, but she didn't know they had any land. She'd heard they worked hard to provide for the several children they had. There wasn't any mention of extra money. But if they'd run that restaurant together, why was her grandfather, James, buried separately? And who was the woman next to him and the man next to her?

She only vaguely remembered Angelina, her grandmother, and the family restaurant. She was independent, large-bodied, warm, and engaging. She watched in the kitchen as her grandma slapped a giant iron skillet on the stove, lopped in handfuls of lard, and threw rounds of sliced potatoes into hot smoking grease. She'd press those potatoes down, the grease popping from the damp disks, wait until they got good and brown, and then expertly flip them all, brown the other side, season them with pepper and salt, and turn them out on a big platter that went with the big steak that was the house special.

No Italian food? Now she understood a bit of what it was like being different in this valley. You weren't, if you wanted to fit in. Potatoes were a mainstay in the area, perhaps showing the influence from folks like James and other Irish people in the mountains. Steaks and roasts were frequent menu items, and those could be Irish or English or Scot. Clare finally decided that Angelina and her family cooked whatever the locals wanted. And even though they were Italian, that probably wasn't spaghetti and other pasta.

Still, pasta had been a mainstay in her home with Frankie. That and huge antipastos and tomato sauces on veal and eggplant from fresh grown tomatoes. Just like she did now. Or did, in her home on Reidinger Drive. So she did have a legacy from the food her mother cooked. That and the love of food. She remembered always there was fresh bakery or home-baked bread at Frankie's. And lots of talk about food—how to know the seasons for vegetable dishes, why this bakery bread was better than that, but never better than home-baked.

Again the strains of Jill's music, with penny whistle and guitar, played in her head. Fragments of "Widening Sky" ran through her mind as she looked down in the chasm between the mountains. Green hills gently rose up through the valley, partially screening the two highways, an interstate and a national road. Railroad tracks roughly paralleled the highways and, between the tracks and the highways lay a long, stringy creek almost hidden by groves of trees and small ridges. The Rising Fawn buildings were nearly obscured below. The interstate, the two-lane highway, the creek, and the railroad crowded in to accommodate the narrow valley created by the elbow of the lightning bolt. Then all four spread out again, hugging their own sides of the long, northeast-running valley.

When her grandparents' families had come here, perhaps James's father saw a bit of Ireland in the green mountains and valleys. She couldn't picture what would have been familiar to her Italian ancestors, but Paddy Connor would have smelled the air, seen the rivers and valleys, and thought he'd come home, only to a better home, one where he could hope to own land and never be hungry again, as the family was in the famine-ravaged Old Country.

How far the descendants of those immigrants had come, Clare reflected, looking down from her perch. But then her own dilemma raced through her mind. Was this progress, to be booted out of her home and sent to scramble for a living up in the rocky soil of her ancestors' homes? Surely, she'd come farther than this!

The peace of the mountain rock was broken as a door slapped in the distance. Within a few minutes, she heard tromping on long grasses and looked up to see Gordon coming up to her perch through the tangle of grasses and weeds, guitar held high.

"Hey, I thought I'd come join you," he yelled.

"Great. I could use company!"

"These bluffs are where I try out some of my songs." He sat down next to her, folding his legs in and drawing the guitar into his lap. He strummed a chord or two.

"Sorry I couldn't stay last night to hear you. Personal issues."

Gordon nodded.

"Who's the kid?"

"I call her Lucy. Found her picture in the house. Did you ever see her?"

"Yeah, once, out on the highway waiting for the school bus. Cute kid. Shy. Didn't hear much from the Pryors."

"I hope she's okay."

He shrugged. "Mind if I bore you with some John Denver?"

"Go ahead, bore me. Things could be worse," she laughed.

Gordon began playing "Rocky Mountain High," then went on to "Thank God, I'm a Country Boy."

"Now I'll get to Bill Monroe," he said, and launched into "Blue Moon of Kentucky." Clare enjoyed the music and stopped thinking about anything else. It was a treat to sit on this summer afternoon on the side of the mountain being serenaded. She couldn't think of a time she'd enjoyed music more.

"Tell me about Jill and Gene and their music," Clare said, once Gordon finished. "It's eerie music—is that what people coming to the mountains knew?"

"It's Celtic in its roots. Probably predates the pioneers by a few centuries. Like the Celtic stories, the musical verses were long and wandering, following many paths, not neat with rhymes and refrains like we have in ballads and tunes we play today. But it's an influence. Brooding melodies, sorrowful stories. But their stories probably have more heroines than our stories do. The Irish had strong women as well as strong men."

"I didn't know that."

"I don't know a lot about it, but Jill has told me a bit about the culture."

"Amazing. I'm part Irish Catholic and part Italian, and I know very little about either culture."

"I guess we're all like that. I know little about my own family. Didn't really *want* to know—there's a lot of alcohol. So I just grab onto other people's traditions, like Bill Monroe."

"Makes you feel you belong to something?"

"Something like that." Gordon wanted to get off the topic and back to his guitar. Clare said nothing and listened to his playing, singing along when she knew the words, humming when she didn't. It was a great afternoon!

"So what brings you all the way up here?" he asked, after a few more songs. Clare was lying back on the rock, enjoying the warm sun across her body. She rose up and looked at Gordon, whose eyes seemed like those of a wise old man. His face, framed by gold-blond shaggy hair and beard, reminded her of an oriental guru.

"Love lost," she said. "I don't really know what happened."

Gordon began playing Gordon Lightfoot's "If You Could Read My Mind," pausing to say, "My dad had a lot of music in him, enough to name me for Gordon. But he got disappointed early in life and turned to drinking and druggin." He strummed again.

"Tell me more about your love lost."

She told him about Willie and her financial problems and her missing him and wanting the separation to be over. As she talked, a rushing feeling passed over her heart, and a stone about half the size of the one they sat on seemed to press down on her chest. For sure, she told Gordon, he was making it with someone else now, because she'd been gone for three days. She saw Gordon wince at this, but he said nothing.

Willie was a jerk, there was no doubt about it, she told the practical stranger next to her there on the rock. While she looked over the landscape, tears clouded her view. She told Gordon how their marriage had deteriorated. From shared pleasures it had become a matter of wondering how and if he would embarrass her with others or come up with another way of being far different from her or surprise her with an affair. Gordon continued playing and singing about love lost and the pain of not knowing why, not knowing how to return to the before.

Gordon picked up Lucy's picture, then looked at Clare intently. "You need one of these."

Now there was a small shock of anger at her friend. How could she impose her crazy life on a child?

"Can't even go there." Tears ragged her voice. "We're not even in the same part of the state now, much less together on something like that!"

"Have you tried calling him from here?" He pulled his legs in, sat yoga-like looking at her, eyes showing concern.

"I can't make a stupid phone call without driving to the edge of a canyon around here!" she cried. "I go to town down below and all I get are middle-aged women suspicious of me and making sure I don't stay too long!"

She snuffled, wishing she had a tissue.

"Then I go to the graveyard and find my grandfather lying there next to a strange woman and another man!"

"Hey, that is bad," Gordon laughed, rubbing her shoulder. "Quick, tell me more, I feel a song coming on, and that would make a great story!"

Clare cried and laughed at the same time. "You're teasing!"

"Hey, I grew up with all those ironies, just like you did. I learned to ignore them, figured out that they had nothing to do with me," Gordon said.

"My old man knocked my mother around every payday. When he got some money, he got liquor. My mother was as bad or worse, always ragging him, always wanting more than the old man could give. I got away from them as soon as I could. And I learned I could still come back and see them, still live on the same mountain as they did, only as a different person. Of course, family don't leave me in peace—no-good cousins break into my house, rip off my stuff once in a while. You know, keeping me from getting cocky, evening up the score, mountain-style.

"What does it matter who's in a graveyard?" Gordon continued. "You're here. You have hopes and dreams and you contribute to the world. Who cares what happened in the last century? Who cares what happened before in your marriage? It can change. The important thing is to keep acting like you're the stable point in the universe. Every little disappointment, every little bend in the road can throw you off unless you become your own compass."

He smiled. She wiped her face with her sleeve again. She looked up at him.

"Do you want to hear something really crazy?" she asked.

"Sure. I'm ready for some good song material." He strummed an F minor chord.

"I'm a life coach. I'm supposed to have all the answers!"

Gordon laughed.

"A life coach—what a hoot!" He played a G chord.

"What you're telling me, although with much more interesting twists, is what I tell people in my workshops. I like that 'stable point in the universe' stuff. I'm going to use that."

"A life coach! That's great. I'm going to use *that*," he teased.

He waved his arm over the view below them.

"Invite Willie up here. If you can't get him to fall back in love with you on this rock, there is absolutely no hope. On the other hand, there might be some hope, and then you're really in trouble! Then you'll both move up here and be badass neighbors, cussing the local folks!"

They both laughed. Clare let tears flow, let the afternoon's light winds take cares up into the clouds.

# Chapter 7

## MONDAY

"Willie? Can you hear me?" Clare spoke into the state park's payphone.

"Yeah, I can hear you. Where are you?" Willie sounded surprised by her call.

"I'm a long way away. I'm up on Lookout Mountain." She felt the cool evening air curling around her arms and chest.

"Omigosh, what are you doing there?" Quick breathing. He sounded panicked.

"Don't worry, I'm safe. I'm just staying up here for a while." She made her voice sound deliberately flat: "If you get kicked out you have to find somewhere to live."

There was silence on the other end. "Willie?"

"Yeah?"

Butterflies flitted over her stomach. She needed to say it. Something about distance made it more important to speak the truth.

"I miss you. I don't understand why you're pushing me out."

"Miss you, too." His voice sounded soft, like he wasn't real mad. "But I'm still concerned about the mortgage and the credit card theft. What have you heard on that?"

Clare felt herself growing hot. And it wasn't from cleaning the trailer all day.

"I filed the police report," she said quickly. "I haven't heard anything. After all, it was the weekend."

"Well, it's Monday. I need you to take care of that. My dad's very mad—"

"Well, I guess that's the heart of the matter, isn't it? Your dad is *upset*." So much for reconciliation, she thought, feeling warmer.

"You don't know how much trouble you could get us in."

"Guess what? I don't care about your family. I care about you and me."

"Well, I guess that's the difference between us. I *do* care about my family. If you had a better one, you'd care too."

What? All this mystery about her family and he was blaming her for it? Her shoulders hunched over the phone. All the good she'd thought of Willie in the last few hours was crumbling in the face of the truth. He didn't love her. He never could.

There was silence on both ends. Then he sounded softer, but with a crack in his voice.

"Take care of yourself up there. But call me with some better news about the credit stuff." He hung up.

Clare stood looking at the plastic receiver in her hand. Oooh. No hope for anything different there.

"The hell with you!" she said to the phone. Then she looked around. Cars over by the canyon rim, people walking down toward the overlook, nobody nearby. "The hell with you," she muttered again, and walked back to her car.

When she arrived at the trailer, the sun was coloring the sky over the trees a hue of dark blue tinged with pink. Clare decided to take the rest of the daylight to clean up the front and began pulling weeds gathered under the stairs to the trailer door. She didn't want to run into snakes in the grass and Willie all in one day. All the frustration of the call was gathered into her muscles, and she let fly, pulling at the waist-high greenery with greater strength than she knew she had. In less than forty-five minutes she had a neat pile of pulled weeds. There was still a lot of overgrown weeds around the trailer, but at least the front was manageable. She went inside and dragged out garbage bags of debris and pieces of broken furniture.

"Now what?" she asked herself, looking at the heap. "No such thing as garbage service up here, I guess.

"Oh, yeah, I remember. The stuff tossed over the edge of the mountain there where the road starts down to Trenton." She would not throw it down the mountainside but find a public dump in Trenton or somewhere. She'd have to ask Gordon about a pickup truck for the furniture.

She figured talking to herself was going to become a way of life for her, alone with no telephone service. She stood by the mailbox and checked her phone just to make sure Willie hadn't called back. He hadn't. She touched her pocket holding Lucy's picture. What would Lucy do when she got her new life? Whenever that was.

Clare drove into Trenton the next morning, Tuesday. The new-looking county office building seemed inviting; the recent construction was reassuring. Maybe the city was open to new ideas. She parked close by, went in the courthouse, and walked up to an information desk where a young man was directing locals to various offices.

"The community development office?" she asked.

"Down the hall to the right," he motioned. From her first steps in the courthouse, Clare had a growing feeling of familiarity—offices, careers, business protocol—and she was back in her element finally.

Clare walked into the suite he'd pointed out, pushing a door that carried the department's name.

"I'm here to see Terry Harris," she told the receptionist at a desk.

"Did you have an appointment?" the young, tanned, dark-haired woman asked.

"I've spoken to her on the phone. I'm Clare Connor, from Atlanta." She thought that would mean something to the girl. It didn't.

"Just a moment."

The girl went to a door, pressed it open slightly, said a couple of words to the interior, then motioned to her to go in.

Terry Harris was maybe her age. Tall with light brown-hair cut stylishly, she wore a casual tan cotton suit, moderate jewelry, nice shoes. An open laptop beeped schedule prompts, notebook binders lay open on her desk. A woman of position, given her oversized window view of Sand Mountain. Clare felt immediately comfortable. She imagined them talking a common language of technology, business, and job training contracts. Whatever her new life was going to be, it would start here.

"About the training contract?" Terry said.

"We spoke by phone a couple of days ago," Clare said. "I had an opportunity to come on up here. Thought I could get an early start."

Terry ducked her head a little, gave her an odd look. At that moment her phone rang. She answered and began talking to someone.

Clare thought about some of the possible clients on this contract. Maybe the guys back at Shirl's or people like them. Visually, she tried to see herself in front of those guys, looking up to talk to them. She pictured the trailers like hers that she'd be trying to pull clients from to better themselves and the resistance they'd doubtless show. She might even encounter Lucy's parents.

Terry Harris was talking to either her boss or another superior, as she was quite deferential. "I'll be glad to," she kept saying. "Just let me know. I'll do everything I can."

Sucking up to someone, Clare thought. She was concerned Terry took the call. Had it been her, she wouldn't answer the phone during discussion with a consultant, as their time might be charged back. But then she wasn't Terry 's consultant, and she did just drop in. A lot of things were not the same anymore. Her leg, crossed on her other, bounced once but she pulled it in, so she'd hide impatience.

"I'll do it," Terry told the phone, then hung up. "Now, where were we?"

"The Welfare to Work contract."

"Oh, yeah. Got some bad news to tell you about the project." Clare felt her heart sink to the bottom of her stomach. "We actually had another consultant become available who has worked on the project before. So we gave her a renewal of a previous contract." Terry looked a little apologetic, but not much.

Clare's spirits collapsed as she listened to Terry's words. This was not good.

Terry spoke quickly. "She knows the area, and the employers like her, so we felt it would be best for the clients to stick with her." Clare felt like one of those boulders up on top of the mountain had just come crashing down, bowling her over in its path. Her worn checkbook register with its dwindling balance appeared in her head.

Here was that fear again. She'd be stranded up here in the mountains, just like she was running out of work in Atlanta. Silently, she chided herself about her hasty flight up here.

"So since Friday when I talked to you—" Clare began. Words almost strangled in her throat.

"Excuse me." The receptionist stood next to Clare talking to Terry, who looked up with an expression that told the woman to go on.

"I've got to cover Mr. Burdick's phones at his desk, remember?"

"Yes, yes, go ahead." Terry frowned. The woman left.

"I'm sorry, we've laid off county staff because of the economy so I have to catch our phones here while she gets the county manager's. I hope you won't mind. As I was saying," Terry's eyes wandered to the back wall, "we've had someone become available who's worked with us before."

"Well, I won't take your time," Clare could hardly manage to say.

"Perhaps there'll be something you can do in the future," Terry said, and stood.

Clare sensed an icy lightning bolt going through her body. She was alone again, adrift.

She left the office as abruptly as Terry had delivered her bad news. Thoughts of lawyers sprung into her head. "If this was Hollywood, I could sue," she said, drawing on a bit of legal trivia she knew about oral contracts.

But the sense of rejection trumped the legal options. It felt like someone had been beside her, supporting her, and now was gone. Only air remained.

*But this ain't Hollywood. And this isn't Atlanta.* She tugged at her suit jacket, hung her briefcase a little lower as she walked back to the building entrance. *And I need a job.*

Clare walked out into the parking lot and breathed through her mouth—hard. She would explode if she didn't have a release sometime soon. The quickness of Terry's dismissal left her not knowing what to do with herself. She turned from her car and began a slow walk around the block that framed the old brick courthouse in the middle of the square.

She saw the problem. She wasn't part of this area. But Terry was, and she probably had a lot of bosses telling her who to hire. And there was a long list of people who had firm ties to the county, and any contract would have to go to a local.

The structure she was circling, nicely renovated, reminded her of the many Georgia courthouses she'd seen over the years in the far suburbs of Atlanta, all dating from the late 1800s. It stood like a sentinel on the high ground of the town, people in cars circling the foundation. They looked like they had places to go.

She had thought the meeting would go like a tennis match, the way business meetings should be, a back and forth rhythm where clients and providers exchange needs and credentials, gradually settling into a slower, surer motion until there's a sale or conclusion. But the phone call and her assistant ruined all that.

As Clare walked, her feet hitting pavement in a pattern she could control, she wondered how she could have won the contract. Why had she just assumed that the phone conversation was a solid contract? Terry did say on Thursday that there were no applicants and the deadline was approaching. Still, Clare knew better! She was making mistakes like a first-time job hunter, not a skilled consultant. Where was her head?

Clare walked across the street to a coffee shop and contemplated her next step.

Darn this insular, ingrown world she'd escaped to. If she had time, she could blend in, network, and show Terry she could handle the clients here. She was tough. Give her a challenge and she'd meet it. But Clare didn't know if she wanted to live here long enough to beat the mountain bureaucracy.

She was going to have to get some kind of work right away, and this was her home for now, but what could she do? Even if she wanted to wait tables, as soon as locals knew she wanted the job, it was sure to vanish, just like this Welfare to Work project.

"Whatcha havin, Hon?"

Clare looked up into the clearest blue eyes she thought she'd ever seen, sitting in a round face with a tall pile of blond hair atop. "Coffee? How you take it?"

"Black, please," she responded. "And thank you for guessing!"

The woman's warm manner made Clare feel welcome for the first time this morning. She watched the woman's large form in its pastel uniform move quickly toward the kitchen. Should take back some of that bitter self-talk about losing even a waitress job because she wasn't local. What had she expected?

Better to focus on what was in front of her. Should she be calling the police or the mortgage company or somebody to check the status of her credit problems now that she wasn't going to work right away? Should she run back to Atlanta? Call client companies in Atlanta about new contracts?

She glanced at a paper someone had left on the table. She opened to the back to see what kinds of jobs there were here in the mountains. She swept through the offers for making $500 a week at home and scanned the more legitimate offers. Not much. She spied a brief ad for a horse farm hand. Caring for and exercising horses, mucking out stables, free apartment available. That sounded healthy, she thought. But she had a house of sorts here, so an apartment was unneeded. Probably she should rethink cleaning out stables, too.

As she skimmed through the thin newspaper drinking strong coffee, Clare remembered that the woman at the cemetery said a lady named O'Brian worked at the library and that she might have some information about Irish Catholics who'd lived in the area. James Connor's grave down the road still puzzled her. While she was killing time until her meeting with Tony Sands, she could explore those questions and figure out how—or if—she was going to live in this place.

Clare, feeling much stronger after the caffeine injection, carried her ticket, signed by Sonja, the waitress, to the cash register.

"Was everything okay?" an older, white haired lady with porcelain-thin skin asked her as she took her money. The woman seemed pleasant. After Sonja's friendliness and this lady's kindness, the weight of Clare's world lifted.

"Very good," Clare said, returning her smile. "It's a beautiful day, isn't it?"

"It really is, but there's rain coming tonight. You have a nice day now," the woman said.

Clare's step was lighter as she walked across the square to the library. She was glad to see that the library was at least half the size of the county administration building, a sure sign of literacy. She hoped the librarian would be helpful, not a baffle as Terry had been to her plans. She liked libraries and enjoyed spending time in them. Back in Atlanta, there were wonderful new buildings with book clubs and authors speaking and all kinds of exciting programs. She liked hanging out, borrowing DVDs and books. The local library was like the Red Cross for her laid off clients forced into a job search with free internet and a place to go to work looking for work.

Clare remembered the rich wood and the musty smell of the old library she'd hidden out in when she was a child, studying after school while waiting for her sister and mother to finish at the store. She'd dipped into every kind of children's books.

The library had been her anchor in the turbulent sea of her childhood. Seeing the rows of large bookcases at the Trenton library brought back her joy in being around books. The openness of the rooms, the touch of beautiful covers, the quickness with which she became immersed in the pages.

When Clare entered the checkout area in the front of the library, she saw a large older woman at the desk. Her hair was deep red and wavy. Her freckled arms extended from a dark, soft dress that draped her figure nicely. Clare figured that if this was not Ms. O'Brian, it was her twin sister.

"Hello," Clare said when the woman looked up and smiled. "I'm looking for a Ms. O'Brian."

"I am she," the woman said, freckled face crinkling in a bigger smile. "How can I help you?"

Clare noted the absence of country vernacular, the grammatically correct "she." Her heart warmed.

"Well, I'm on an ancestor hunt. The lady at the cemetery up the road told me that you would know about Irish Catholic families that might have been in this area."

"How far back are you talking about?" the woman asked, putting down a pencil she'd been holding over a piece of paper. "It's been a great while."

"Well, actually, there's a grave in the cemetery that lists a man, James Connor, who died in 1943. I think he's my grandfather." A veil of cold air draped across Clare's shoulders. What if she knows the whole story and it's bad? Shame crept over her. But she pressed on. "Do you know the name?"

"I know that there were lots of Irish miners and railroad workers who settled here in the mid and late-1800s, but I don't know all the names. I suggest you look in our special collections area over there in the corner." She waved to the right of the desk.

"We've got census data on microfilm. There are some family files— look in the cabinets. You'll find family histories and whatnot relating to families that were here. Some of the family genealogists and others in the community have donated those."

"But that name doesn't sound familiar to you?"

"The only thing that's familiar is that it's an Irish name," Margaret said, smiling again. Clare thought she'd be a kind grandmother. "So many changed the spelling of their names. Like that name might have been something like Caughron or some such before the family stayed here and became more Americanized."

"I guess some of these, if they were Catholic, became something else as well after changing their names?" Clare asked. Margaret flushed. She'd struck a sensitive nerve.

"There weren't any priests anywhere near here," she said defensively. "There was no one to bring the sacraments this far back in the mountains."

Clare reflected on the huge number of cars parked at the Baptist church yesterday morning. She'd seen fewer at the Methodist church in Rising Fawn, still fewer at the Church of Christ. No sign of any other churches. She wondered what kinds of pressures there were for those known to be "mackerel snappers," as the lady back at the cemetery all but called them.

"Thanks," she told Margaret O'Brian, "you've been a big help."

While the main library was full of computers and appeared very modern, the special collections area Clare entered was more old school, full of file cabinets. There was a table full of flyers advertising genealogy classes and programs at the national and state archives in Atlanta. She spied a stack of pamphlets on the natural history of Lookout and Sand mountains, and she took one.

She looked through folders and dog-eared index cards, searching for Irish names. She looked for O names, as it was possible the letter was original with the Connor name. But there were none. There was only one file with an O—and it was the O'Brian family, probably the librarian's. She decided to try the family files.

As opposed to the neat card files, the materials in the family files looked poured over and unkempt. She fingered the files, stuffed in a long file drawer in manila folders, looking under the Cs, looking for something that said Connor. She didn't exactly know what she was looking for, but she kept digging her hands into the leafy detritus of others' lives.

Urgency seemed to overtake her. She was unable to concentrate for wanting to know more. Her shaking fingers touched books, notebooks, files bound together with rubber bands and spilling, curling papers. Would she find something here, some clue to Frankie and Paul, her father, something more than the few pictures she'd seen growing up in her mother's house? She felt she had to know. Finding some shred, some link to that unknown past would be so helpful right now.

There was nothing.

She moved to the file section under S on a hunch that maybe there could be something under Tony's name. In a short time, she pulled out a file stuffed with clippings and a narrative of some kind typed in all upper case, ink fading to almost gray. "The Don and Lucy Sands Family," the sheet of paper began. Clare skimmed the account, which summarized a family's growing in size and prominence through a restaurant business over a number of generations. The clippings showed parties, banquets, and weddings with lots of large groupings of smiling elders, fashionably dressed young girls and spiffily clad men and young boys. There were family cabinet portraits showing dark-haired children and parents, all turned out in fine clothes, dark eyes steady with pride.

Clare passed her hand over the ephemera of someone else's family. Where were her relatives?

Tony's house looked like a tiny white monopoly piece set in front of a great overhanging stone. As Clare turned off the road coming up Lookout Valley, the mountain loomed overhead, and the house grew more life-sized. Tony's house lay on acreage, and a large garden sprang into view to the south-facing side of the house.

Lofty fantails of purple and white mountain phlox waived in a slight breeze sweeping through the valley and dwarfed smaller plants, mostly zinnias, in front of the house, which sat on a base of fieldstone. Clare was struck with the flowers and bushes and the sense that people lived here caring for the home, caring for the people inside.

When she went to the door, it was already open behind a glass outer door. When she rang the doorbell, nothing happened. Then Tony, seeming to blend in with the dark house interior behind him, emerged from the shadow in a wheelchair.

Clare quickly made the adjustment in her mind. In her daydreaming about this person she'd talked to on Sunday, she'd tried to imagine what Tony looked like and what kind of family he had. Now on Tuesday, she tried to think of clues she'd had about him. She remembered heavy breathing on the phone; now she knew it was from getting around in a wheelchair. A cold, which he'd had, would also do it.

She opened the door.

"How are you Tony—I hope you're feeling better!" She really was glad. She'd found herself thinking about him over the days, wondering about his connection to Frankie, and if he'd be a helpful link back to her mysterious family.

He took her hand warmly. He had thick salt-and-pepper hair and dark folds appeared under his brown eyes. The folds continued to his neck at his shirt collar. His skin was olive, and he looked to be in his late 50s or early 60s. He smiled and kept hold of her hand.

"Feeling a might better," he said. "It's good to meet family!" He tugged at her hand, let go, then quickly turned his wheelchair to the interior. "Come on in."

They entered a living room, a comfortable room where pictures of family occupied side tables and the TV top. They resembled the pictures in the Sands family files. Two vases of yard flowers perched on the side tables.

"My wife's at work. She's kept doing the same job for all these years. Started out to help support the family but now it's just cause she enjoys it!" He smiled and indicated a leather recliner chair for her. She sat, feeling comfortable sitting as Tony did.

"What can I get you to drink?" he asked.

"Water. Water's fine," she lied. She would have loved coffee, but she didn't want to trouble him.

"Come in the kitchen, and I'll fix it." Clare had just settled, adjusted herself to a slower pace for talking, and here he was wheeling away in a blaze of activity. She followed him into a pine-paneled, light-filled kitchen. Bright white figured curtains lifted in a breeze, colorful pottery pitchers and plates on shelves, sturdy breakfast table and chairs. A counter lower than the others held all the coffee-making gear. Tony was clearly self-sufficient and active.

Tony quickly grabbed a glass and filled it with ice and water from the door of a large stainless-steel refrigerator.

"Our biggest splurge of the last few years," he waved with an apologetic grin. His eyes were beautiful, his face welcoming.

"Nice. Do you freeze vegetables from your garden?" Clare wanted to know all about the garden. She was feeling at home. She wanted to sit at the kitchen table.

"Would you care to sit in here?" he asked.

What was it she'd heard once, that meeting family and cousins for the first time, you could sometimes pick up as though you'd spoken just yesterday? That was how she was feeling with Cousin Tony.

"I'd love to—I have so much to ask you. I don't know where to begin!"

"Your name is Clare?" he asked, making it sound like it was a foreign word. "I'm not sure I can place 'Clare,' and that's a puzzle. What's your middle name?"

"Mary is my first name. Clare is my middle name."

"Still doesn't register. I'm sorry." He looked embarrassed.

"I was too young to know relatives when my father died. There were quite a few there for the funeral, but I was just six, so I wouldn't know names. I'm not sure I met you."

"I wasn't traveling in those days, so I didn't go to the funeral." Clare wondered why he was in a wheelchair but refrained from asking. She didn't want to spoil her feeling of closeness to Tony.

"What did your mother tell you about family up here?" he asked.

"She talked about Trenton, but I couldn't connect many names, I'm afraid. I remember visiting Grandmother Angelina's restaurant once when I was very young. But otherwise, the names—it was as if someone sat down and started talking about their many grandchildren, but you didn't even know their children's names, so you couldn't associate. When I didn't catch on, my mother wasn't very patient with me. To me, it was a great fog of just names."

"Well, your mother and my mother were sisters. My mother was an older girl and Frankie was toward the end of the family, so my mother looked after yours."

Clare thought back to the thick files in the library. She had to know why there was nothing about hers. And she had to know why James Connor lay in his grave alone or next to people separated from the rest of the family.

"Tony, tell my why there is so much about your family in the library—probably a two-inch thick file. I feel like I know your family much better than mine, like mine didn't exist. Who *were* these people?" If she could just get someone to talk about her family, to make it real to her!

"I can't believe Frankie never told you about me!" she blurted.

Tony started. Glistening eyes looked at her.

"I-I'm sorry. I did know about you." He hesitated, cleared his throat. "I just knew you by a different name. You were Lucetta!"

"Lucetta?"

"We called you Cetta."

"Cetta?" It was as if a blinding flash came upon her. She didn't exist as Clare, but as a foreign-sounding Italian child.

"On the phone, when you called yourself Clare, I was confused. I've been disabled for quite a few years—crane fell on me at the foundry where I worked in Chattanooga—son Jerry was only a baby—but my memory's pretty good. I couldn't place you because your name was different from the little girl I met!"

No wonder she was a family outlier. They didn't know her name, even.

"When did you meet me? How old was I?"

"About three or four."

"So my parents changed my name?" Was that a shiver that went through her body?

"You okay?" Tony looked concerned.

"Yeah, I just wish I could get over not knowing my family. And why they would do something like that."

"How much time you got today?" Tony asked.

She felt giddy all of a sudden. She started laughing, unable to stop. Time. She had so much.

"I've got plenty—" Words caught in her throat. What could she say?

She didn't need to be anywhere, not on the mountain, not in Trenton, for sure not back in north Atlanta. No job, nobody needed her that she knew of. Her body started shaking and she tried to laugh but something hung heavy, as though the top of her body wanted to double over.

She tried to speak, but she couldn't. Now there was wetness in her eyes, seeping out like water from a spring.

Tony moved over toward her, his wheelchair touching her leg there at the table in his warm, light kitchen.

Her tears were welcome and sad at the same time.


Hot bread, preserves, butter, and coffee lay fan-like in front of Clare.

"Eat," Tony was urging. "You can talk later."

The food and fresh coffee had appeared almost without her knowing. Tony was in the background, a fuzzy presence as she had let the hurt and anger and questions flow out. A tissue appeared in her hand. Now she sat in front of a bright yellow plate and tropical blue cup with steaming coffee.

"We have time," he said in a soothing tone. "It will come easier with food." His hands lay on the arm rests of the wheelchair. His eyes were dark, seemed to bore deep.


After the delicious bread, Clare felt better. Tony looked at her as though he'd been waiting a while. She smiled and thanked him for letting her cry.

"I have time," she said, "because I've been kicked out of my home by my husband. No—I wasn't unfaithful or anything like that," she added quickly. "We got into some crazy financial problems and he's blaming me for it."

Tony said nothing. Then—

"You're a very bright girl—woman," he said. "But so sad."

Clare took a tissue from a box that had also suddenly appeared on the table and blew her nose, taking time to do it well, not holding back from politeness.

She only nodded.

"You've been hurt by him. And maybe hurt by this family here that you hardly know. I'm sorry."

Clare felt tears. Then she shook her head.

"I don't know enough to know if I've been hurt."

Tony moved one hand across his mouth, then spoke carefully. "A mother who called you Cetta then changed it to Clare without ever telling you, that's a start of keeping secrets from you. Sounds like secrets were common. . .." His voice seemed to run out of sound.

"You're hurt. And I'm sad, cause you're my cousin." Clare didn't know what to say. Here he was claiming her. Cousin. Someone kin. She tried to get her mind around the words. Her arms wanted to reach out to this gentle man, but she held back.

Tony had a quiet smile on his face, extended his arm, and patted her hand. So this was her family, her mother's family, up here in the mountains. He then sat back in his wheelchair and closed his eyes.

"Oh, I'm sorry." Clare immediately realized how tired he must be. "I've taken your time and you need your rest—especially after battling a cold."

His eyelids still not open, he held up his hand. "There's something you need to know. Changing names was sometimes necessary. So don't blame your parents for calling you one thing and then another."

She knelt down beside him and placed her hand on top of his.

"Did you have to change your name?"

"I didn't, but my grandparents did. Story another time." His seemed to start dozing. She squeezed his hand and held it before getting up to go.

As she crossed in front of a round table in the living room, she saw a large black Bible in a place of honor there. A fringed cloth with roses printed on it lay under the gilt-edged book. Clare saw that Tony still dozed in the kitchen. She walked back and turned the light out in that room and turned it on in the room holding the book.

She looked back again at Tony, then quietly opened to the first pages where births and deaths were often recorded. There were separate family trees showing the predecessors of Tony and his wife Silvia that had been carefully filled in on heavy parchment-like pages. She turned quickly to Tony's tree and located his mother's relatives—how Clare was connected to Tony. She saw Angelina and Sam Mathews, her maternal grandparents, and recognized her mother's name among their children, a few years behind Tony's mother, Lucia.

Stuck in the book was a half-sheet of copy paper. Opening it, she saw a rough, hand-drawn genealogy chart showing the lineage of James Connor, Clare's grandfather, probably the one in the Rising Fawn cemetery. Why would this be here? James was not related to the Mathews, Frankie's kin. The only connection was in her marriage to his son Paul. So here was Paul, his son, and the notation "m. Frankie Mathews." Then there was a space for Paul's brothers and sisters—four children in all and their spouses. But she noticed something else.

There was a trail of typewriter correction fluid under James's name, between Paul and the next sibling. After the little tears of fluid sprinkled down the page, there was a space, but a block had been placed over it. Whatever had been there, the writer thought the better of including it. Clare felt her heartbeat quicken. A missing person. A link erased. Could this connect to the graveyard? A birth once acknowledged then denied? The mysteries seemed to pile up, to evade her need to know the story of her mother's and father's people. Coolness spread over her shoulders. Another day, another time, she'd ask Tony if he made those notes—and why.

# Chapter 8

The next day, Clare was in another world in Tony's car. The large sedan, a re-stored older model Detroit lowrider, with a bench seat for a driver and two, maybe three, passengers in the front. She didn't help Tony get in. He was clearly self-sufficient in managing the door, the transit from the chair, the settling in behind the controls—although she did take charge of his wheel-chair after he was in. She struggled to collapse the chair's seat and back, fold them together, and hoist the chair behind Tony's seat.

"Great car," she told him when she slid onto the passenger seat and fastened the plastic gray seat belt. As she thought he would be, he was clearly pleased to show off his baby.

He put his arm across the headrest-free seat and turned to back the car up in the drive, smiling while keeping his eye on the edge of the house and the garden wall. He turned the boat-like car around. Gravel spun out briefly, and he gassed the engine to go forward.

"One of my few pleasures," he said, glancing at Clare as they moved down the drive to the main highway. "Hadn't been for my baby here and the garden, I probably would have lost my mind after the accident."

"Tell me about it." She was ready for a long retelling of his life as he knew it, the story of how everything changed as it must have after his injury.

He shrugged. "Just went from being breadwinner to being bread eater." He grimaced slightly, moving the gears on the steering column as they went down the road.

"But the car is one thing from the past that hasn't changed much."

Not telling, Clare thought to herself. When I get too close, he changes the subject back to the car, the weather, whatever. What is the story he won't tell?

They took the highway back to Trenton, the way she'd come this morning. She tried to remember when the last time was that she and Willie had been in a car for a long trip or weekend. When there was that space of time when talk was easy, the trivia of everyday life spilling out like some small gifts hidden away, stashed in the hall closet. As each small bit was exchanged, somehow Clare and Willie reconnected, reset their relationship. Since meeting Tony, Clare hadn't thought much about Willie. And that was a good thing, she concluded. Better to build new friendships, get used to a life without him.

The valley that had been so sunny when she drove down from her ledge on the mountain was now overcast. Signs were less brilliant white, storefronts not beckoning to her as before.

"Rain'll be here soon," Tony said. She followed his glance. The trees hiding the small ridges at the base of Lookout bent with a slight breeze.

"Time enough to see what we want?"

"Sure. Storms stall a little over the mountains before they finally make it."

"I'm glad you're so sure!" Clare laughed.

"They're a force to reckon with. Not your little hills like in Atlanta. Fact, these mountains here probably prevent some pretty bad weather, keep it trapped up in these valleys," Tony remarked.

Clare reflected on the "tornado alley" name that went with the northern Alabama area on the other side of Sand Mountain. Those two mountains, Sand and Lookout, probably protected the valleys to the east, including Atlanta. She breathed a little thanksgiving.

She was amazed at the drive between Sand on one side, Lookout on the other. She imagined the car they drove in as an ant in a large room, overwhelmed by large dark sofas on either side.

In Trenton, they turned left and began an ascent up the side of Sand Mountain. Businesses of all types, homes, and churches lined the highway on the incline just as they did in the valley. Large homes perched on hillsides with extravagances of land around them. Restaurants advertised all you can eat buffets and music on the weekend. The valley they'd just drove through peeked out between buildings; a miniature toy expanse of stores and churches and funeral homes. A flat expanse edged by wooded mini ridges, then the walls of mountain.

When they reached the top of the mountain, the land leveled out, and homes became sparser. Large wooded tracts seemed to fall away from either side.

"That was Shantytown back in the day," Tony said, gesturing to the left side of the car where now there were deserted woods. "Just one shack after another, thrown together by the coal company."

"Was it here when you grew up?"

"Long time ago, when I was just a kid. A few very poor people lived in them at the time, but the deep mines had shut by that time."

They took a left away from the edge of the mountain on a road called New Home Drive—somebody felt compelled to label this a home: were they immigrants? They followed it toward the center of the mountain.

He stopped the car after they'd gone a while, pulling off onto a road that was so deeply rutted she wondered if they'd ever be able to get back out onto pavement.

"This is where we stop. If you look to the right there, that road across the way's called Tram Road, cause that's where the tram ran out of the mine and down the hill to dump its load.

"Gonna let you look, I'm going to stay in the car," he said. "Yonder there's an air shaft from one of the mines that provided air to mines two hunnert feet below."

Clare looked up, saw a tall, sandstone tower in front of them, topping a heavy green undergrowth of weeds. She judged it to be about twenty feet high. It was like something out of a fairy tale, just appearing in the bramble. The mottled, caramel-colored sandstone rocks formed a tall rectangular column.

The air shaft was caged by ancient vines which now formed a kind of free-form crown atop the structure. Through gaps in the leafy vines at the top, Clare could see the edges of an iron grate to prevent exploring teens or others from trying to lower themselves inside. Tony had said it descended two hundred feet. Clare judged if the structure was twenty feet high, it descended ten times its height down below ground level.

Folds of her knit top pulled across her chest, and she straightened it. She was tired of these secrets, tired of people not talking. What happened? Why wouldn't Tony talk about the accident that maimed him? Why didn't her mother tell her about him and about her home here and the trailer? And scratched out information in the Bible's family record? Her skin tightened as a minor rage built up underneath. She looked outside for what to do. She needed to move.

She opened the wide car door and struggled over wet weeds to the air vent, rounded its far side, and found a huge hole looking into the dark interior of the castle-like shaft. Vandals had sledge-hammered their way in—a place to hide drugs? The stones on the ground were broken, jagged ends just peeking out of covers of weeds, so it had happened at least a season ago. The dark opening was like the vacuum she felt in her life. She'd thought she'd find something up here on the mountain, but she was as empty-handed as ever. Nothing.

She climbed over the pile of stones and felt them shift under her as she drew up to the hole. Her hands grabbed at the rough sides of the shaft and she pushed her chest in. Dank smells, musty as a mushroom farm, smothering air. The escape hole to the mine below was now covered with weeds. She kicked off the clogs and placed her knee up on the wall, pulled the other behind, feeling the sharp edges of the uneven rock on her knees through her crop pants. Then she tilted forward over the mound, holding herself up by gripping the shattered wall. Alice followed a rabbit down its hole; what was she following? She planted a bare foot on the interior mound of rocks, straddled the window, stood up on that foot and dragged the other over. Her body lightened and fairly sizzled as she moved. She felt like a little girl escaping all that the world demanded, daring to follow the fairy tale to its end. The ground beneath her was covered with rocks, earth, and weeds, but soft, loose. The wind whipped around the edges of the hole and rain dropped on her head still, but she was fully in the tale now. She was carried along with it, willing to just go, push, discover.

Then a jolt—a roaring sound filled her ears, wet ground jumped up to her mouth. Her body sank suddenly, shins and thighs falling into a dirt envelope. Her chest struck the pile, a rock punctured her cheek, and mud streaked her face. She was stuck. The pile of dirt had caved in under her weight, falling four feet at least. Her feet twisted, and mucky, cold soil spread around her toes. An earthen vise held her fast, twisted her body, trapped her.

The air shaft was still open, though weeds covered it. She could feel cool air escaping from the hole in the middle of the shaft, that lifeline of air to the coal miners below. The pile she was on shifted more towards the hole. If she moved much, she could be thrown a hundred feet below.

"Tony!"

Sound, too, was trapped in the tower. "Help! Tony!"

Tony was possibly asleep in the car. She was alone. She pictured her life's end with a TV news teaser, "Misadventure in the Mountains." She imagined a 30-second obit on the evening news—body at the bottom of an air shaft in a brambly, mountainside field, the very farthest corner of Georgia. Her best friend Helene, on camera, would hint at marital problems. *Oh, God. I detest Willie and what he's done, but I don't owe him a murder rap.*

I've got to get out of here!

The only good thing was that the rain was steady and light, not flooding.

She heard the car horn, sweet and full as horns on old cars were. Tony wanted her to hurry up.

"Help! Over here!"

Her life as a semi-orphan would end badly, mysteries unsolved. No more Frankie, no more Clare. A family blasted out of existence. Clare tried to shift in the wet soil. Pain shot up her back. But her limbs could move.

*Lord is with thee, Lord is with thee.* Parts of prayers she'd said for the first six years of school shot through her mind. Maybe she would be saved if she could pray. She made one up. *Lord be with me. Lord be with me.* She said it over and over again. How stupid that she'd climbed in. What a shock that the earth did not hold her.

Nothing was safe. Nothing.

She heard movement—a car's engine! Then there was silence for a long time. An image stuck in her mind of a statue of Our Lady from her childhood school, the one where the nun made her feel so small, so unworthy. Would that faith help her now? *Lord be with me,* she repeated. *Our Lady, pray for me.*

Then a faint, rattling sound. The wheelchair! So lucky she'd left the wheelchair in the back seat when she went to look at the mine. Tony, his instincts for survival perhaps sharper than hers, had insisted she put it there instead of in the trunk. But how could he help her get out?

*Lord be with me,* she repeated to herself. Air would not fill her chest, even though she was inhaling.

"Clare!" His head, a silhouette, peered over the wall. He was holding onto the wall with his fists, leaning in to keep himself stable.

"Help me get out!" She was short of breath. She needed oxygen—fast. The earth folded around her. Thoughts of construction workers suffocating under falling piles of dirt in work trenches filled her mind.

"Don't move, or you could fall further," he called.

She put her arms across the remaining dirt. Was it lack of air, or was it her fear, that kept her from exhaling, inhaling?

"Wait, stay still. I'll be back!"

The sound of the wheelchair rolling over grass. Then a car starting up and cutting off. After a while, a creaking, muffled clanging sound above. She couldn't breathe, the shaft was choking off her air, she was going to die.

"Here, grab this." Tony braced himself in the wall opening, the end of a giant chain in his right fist. She heard him grunt as he braced his back on the wall and pulled the dark snake up and over the wall. She heard *clink, clink* as he pulled sections of what must be a humongous set of links closer to him. She could hear her shallow breaths.

"Got the other end hooked to the axle." Tony's breathing sounded strangled. "Hold on to this—hard. I'm going to pull you out!"

She didn't dare speak.

A thick, cumbersome, welcome line of shiny metal ovals fell toward her face. She grabbed onto the metal links.

"Hold on tight," his disembodied head hollered down to her. "Try to get your feet up on what's left of the pile as soon as you can."

"Okay," she said, her voice shaking. "Go slow—don't jerk me!" She heard the echo of her voice against the rock column around her.

Tony left the window, and within a few moments, the car started, and she felt the other end gradually tighten. Breathing became a little easier.

*Indiana Jones, Indiana Jones,* Clare repeated to herself, trying to prepare for the climb. *What was his heroine's name? How quickly we forget the women!* She just knew she would not be able to hold onto the slippery steel.

*CRUUUNCH.* She heard stones falling from the wall above her head.

Tony's boat of a car pulled. Rocks hit the pile outside, and thuds sounded as some fell inside. *Maybe the structure will fall in on me!* Her arms stretched, hands ached, and she was pulled up slightly. Her midsection fell over the fragile pile of fill above her. She was making progress. The car strained, and she bent a leg and dug it into that pile, then the other leg. Her unfolding body burned at every bend, but one section of chain followed the other as she was pulled over the mound, then struggled to the window. She waved to Tony to stop, climbed over the window that she'd earlier so anxiously entered, and let her heavy, dirt-smeared body onto the ground below. She knelt, then stretched out sore knees and hugged herself in the rain. She was shivering, and her hands looked blue, but she was safe.

Tony's car door opened, but she motioned for him to stay.

"I'm coming!"

She unfolded her stiff body and moved toward the car, barefoot, wet. Bits of dirt fell off her as she walked. What a sight she must be!

Her clogs! She returned to the air shaft, found her shoes, and put them on, then continued to the car. She climbed into the passenger side breathing hard. Tony looked afraid.

"Get stopped, this'll be some story to explain, huh?" she said, her body exhaling, shaking.

"You okay? You've got a cut on your cheek. Let me clean it at least." He reached for a bottle of water in a caddy near the steering wheel, opened it, and wiped her left cheek with a wet tissue.

"It's not too bad. Brilliant bit of rescue, Tony. Who'd guess that the old Buick would be so handy? And that you'd have enough chain to pull me out!"

He relaxed a little.

She could hear her breaths, she still struggled for air.

"I shouldn't have gone in there, that was stupid. All this family stuff is confusing me, and I guess I lost my head."

"You could have lost more than that! You scared me to death."

"Tony, I'm still hunting for answers." She gulped for air, silently asking for courage. "What happened in the foundry? What are you hiding from me? Don't do to me what my mother did, avoiding talking about stuff that affects me. It makes me crazy!"

Now she had too much air, breaths wouldn't stop, become normal. What could she do to make him talk?

Tony's dark eyes looked at her steadily.

Clare grabbed for a patchwork quilt in the back seat, wrapped up in it. Her shivers were becoming full shakes of her body.

"I was set up by people on my job."

She didn't say anything. She didn't want to get in the way of whatever he had to say.

"It was a Monday morning, and I was called away from the drafting room to the floor where they said they had a piece of equipment I needed to see. A three-story crane was right over my head while I was talking with the two people who'd asked me to come over."

His eyes grew smaller as he talked.

"The crane made a strange noise. I looked up and saw it falling towards me. Last moment like a snapshot: the man behind the foreman, Barber, was gasping, mouth and chin contorted as if trying to speak. But Barber, he didn't yell out or change expression or anything. Just looked at me very deliberately. Next thing I knew I was on the ground, writhing under that huge piece of steel, back feeling cut in two—pain, shooting pain, through the right side of my body. Then everything went black for me. Later heard the crane driver barely escaped, jumped before the rig hit the ground."

"Horrible. What did Barber have against you?"

Would the pain of this family ever end? What could be good about all this?

"Nothing I know of. I never talked much, but every other conversation around me I'd hear the word Dago floating up or people would ask me what I was going to eat for lunch on Friday. Barber was the town gossip, always had an opinion about somebody that was tied to the tone of the person's skin or his religion. The usual stuff."

"But to do this? Was he capable of it?"

Tony looked at her as though he was trying to get a lesson through, but it wasn't taking.

"People are different back here in the mountains and where they go to work. You just got used to it. But this time it was not so subtle. Changed my life."

"It seems so strange that just odd comments could end up costing you your leg and lower body. How horrible!"

He turned around in the seat, put his hand to the steering column. "Let's get you back home and get you some warm clothes. No sense in talking about somethin that happened over thirty years ago."

"No, it's important! Y-You don't know critical it is!" For me, she realized. I'm the one who needs to know what happened cause I have to make some sense of this mess, my life.

Tony looked at her as he turned the key on the steering column. Cool winds replaced the light rain outside. He pulled onto the hard surface of New Home Road.

"Somethin I do, come up here, try to lose my self-pity by being close to where my people were. At the mines, might be able to tap into their spirits, get a taste of what kept them goin."

Tony's voice had longing in it. The strains in his speech were like the tautness in her own body every time she thought about her mother, how she'd rejected Clare, and what was left of herself now that Willie had exited her life. The rain returned, and fog atop the mountain kept her from seeing clearly. Tony started talking about his grandfather, Sal the Elder, who died young because of a "hell of a lot of coal dust" in the lungs and a smashed nose that restricted breathing.

"What happened to him?" she asked, already frightened to know the answer.

"Man hit him in the mine. Woke up in a pool of cold water, not knowing. He'd just come out of a hole he'd started—usually did that alone, as he was slight and could work into the seam before larger men worked it. Getting whacked in the back by some scoundrel happened regularly, but this was a full-on face smashing. Italians were less then human in some's mind. Sal didn't remember being hit or at least wouldn't let on he knew." Tony sighed.

"Went to an early grave not sayin."

Hearing about the waste of the man's life made Clare think of how murder victims' families felt—violated not only by loss, but by the fact that their loved one's life was so easily extinguished. To have a life become less valuable than a used-up rag? What did it leave her to hope for, to come from such people?

What was she searching for up and down these mountains, north and south in these valleys? Something substantial, maybe not a monument, but at least something that marked where her family had passed, some sign that their lives had more value than that rag.

Riding in the car, rain came down again in sheets, and the windshield wipers went back and forth. As it swept from left to right, a stretch of cleared glass would appear, and she could see the road. Within seconds, the rain filled it up again, so all was erased. Then the arm cleared right to left. Once more, rain filled the space, obscuring the road. She couldn't see anything for more than a few seconds, and Tony spun stories in a kind of monotone that was close to a plea. The blower exhaled to keep the chill off her, and she was almost in a trance as his words came, and she saw this ancestor Sal Marinelli—Sal the Elder—on his deathbed at the age of thirty, his nose pressed close to his face, breathing loudly and urgently. But the air was strangled, and Clare felt like she couldn't breathe either, and she was afraid. She shivered and there was weeping in the background. Sal's wife, Lucetta? No, it was her, crying for her lost family.

Sweep, sweep, the windshield cleared and drowned, again and again. *Clare. . .Frankie, Willie. . .Clare*, the wipers seemed to say. The blower hit her shins, but her bare, muddy feet were cold. Sleep crept over her, and she didn't stop it.

There in the Buick, Clare vaguely heard Tony describing Sal the Younger and how he met his wife through missionary priests. The priest travelled into the valley north of them and said Mass every couple months in the cabin of an Irish stonemason and his family, immigrants who'd built railroad bridges through the vast gaps in the mountains. They'd each had the sacraments there when the priest came through.

"So that's how Sal the Younger met Angelina and married. Sal the Elder had brought his wife, Lucetta, from the old country."

Clare struggled back from sleep. Her skin prickled at the name.

"Was I named for her?" Caught between sleep and wakefulness, she grasped for details that related to her as though those bits would put the puzzle together, make her life whole, free of the questions, the querulous way she went about her life.

"Possibly. My mother was known as Lucia, maybe to distinguish her from Lucetta, but she basically had the same name."

The wipers went back and forth, and Clare imagined the face of young Sal, who changed his name to Sam Mathews, moving from the mines at the top of the mountain and into the foundry in the valley at Rising Fawn.

"Prejudice a problem for Young Sam, too?"

"He dealt with it in a strange way. He pretended to be Cherokee. He was taller than Sam the Elder, so he could carry it off. As an Indian, he could be quiet, and everyone thought he might have a tomahawk under his work clothes, so nobody bothered him."

"No one knew?"

"One guy, actually the Klan grand wizard. But again, Sam sidestepped trouble by protecting that man's son."

"Klan was in here?"

"Everywhere in the South, actually it was a big movement all over the country, but where there weren't blacks, anyone who was different was prey for those scumbags. Sam actually was left alone, wasn't put on the spot to join them on night rides, because he was keeping the Klan man's son alive."

"How was that?" Clare found herself almost asleep now, her feet finally warm, the blower heating her whole body as she relaxed against the vinyl bed that was the Buick's front seat. The seat belt held her fast, saving her from sliding down or sideways. She wanted to pay attention, but her body would not let her.

"Son was a ne'er do well, the kind the Klan liked to beat up on, black, white, of any religion. If you weren't providing for your family, you were sorry and no count. Klan was likely to take you out to the woodshed or the roadside for a beating. So Sam kept the man and his family in food, mostly succotash."

"Succotash."

"Sure—lima beans, corn, peppers all mixed together. Protein, vegetables, and spice all in one big canning jar. Actually, Angelina gave him lots of vegetables."

"She canned succotash, and Sam would make sure he had a side of venison once in a while. And hot cornbread about once a week. Don't know what the son's problem was, could have had hookworm or something. Just didn't seem to be able to work like other people. Had six kids though. And Sam made sure they didn't starve."

Clare looked out the window at the valley traveling past, imagined Sam and his garden, plotting to stay alive there, and Angelina cooking their freedom.

The windshield wipers went back and forth. *Sam. . .Cherokee. Sam. . .Savior.* Phrases repeated with each swish-scrape across the glass. Clare's arms, legs, eyes seemed to press down on her. Then all was dark.

Clare heard a baby's cry. She stirred. She moved back and forth for a moment, straddling sleep and consciousness. A toddler, she heard a toddler. Now she was awake, trying to make sense of the dream. She judged the loud child was trying to form words, but they were mostly screeching, attention-getting sounds, a rough echo of older children's sounds, but meant to pull attention to the young one. She was seduced by the sounds. The vocals sounded familiar. She remembered cuddling a child in her arms, moist fragrance of baby skin teasing her nostrils.

Where was this? The smell of birthday cake—Helene's niece had three small children, and she'd attended serial birthday parties for each. Walking around the home filled with outsized upholstered couches and chairs interspersed with plastic riding toys, she'd been the one grabbing up the kids in her arms, especially the small babies. The squirmers and screamers always got her attention first, and they quieted almost miraculously in her arms. She did seem to have a special ability in calming them. Maybe it was her pale skin that frightened them into submission.

Back in the Buick, the blower was about to burn her skin. She reached to shut down the fan.

Silence and tiredness saved her from trying to organize her thoughts. She let the sadness seep deeper in her skin, let go of needing to be in charge of the moment. Softness gathered around her, the image of her mother, herself, Willie, the faceless baby, they all swam around her. A shirring, vibrating bit of air surrounded her.

She could have died in the air shaft back there, but the dirt didn't give way under her feet. By some miracle she hadn't tumbled through the long deep hole to the earth's interior. It was a miracle, a wake-up call of some sort. She was due to return a favor of some kind. She thought of Frankie lying in her bed. If her mother couldn't survive the stroke, she owed Frankie the debt of living, and living a whole life, a life without fear.

There was a kernel of something hard in her, like the large quartz river rocks of these mountains and valleys—rounded, almost pillow-like on the outside, but beautiful, shining, sharp, and enduring like a jeweled cave inside.

# Chapter 9

**THURSDAY**

Morning light filled the room and woke Clare up. She felt for the soft gold coverlet she knew; it was not there. The space next to her was vacant. The bed was hard, not soft. It took Clare a minute to realize she was not on Re-idinger Drive in Atlanta. She was in a sleeping bag in a single-wide trailer on top of Lookout Mountain. It was Thursday, though so much had happened the day before, she couldn't be sure. She was in Rising Fawn. Her sleep had been so deep, she'd moved to another world during the night.

How she'd gotten home after the scare in the air shaft, she was not sure. Moment by moment, she recalled the rescue, being safe in the car with Tony, and descending Sand Mountain in his big Buick. Now she pushed sleep out of her eyes and rose with difficulty, stiff muscles and back not giving way to smooth motion as they usually did. Pain on her left cheek and her shins hurt from scratches from the rocks.

The mystery of Frankie's family was becoming a little clearer, if as-saults on relatives in at least two generations including Tony's could be called clearer. How vulnerable her Italian relatives had been! And maybe still were? No wonder her mother was so close-mouthed about her family. Shame and learning to be someone different than you were had caused her mother's tendency not to talk, not to reveal much.

The Irish side still puzzled her. Her mind went to that slip of paper with the hand-drawn Connor family tree she'd seen at Tony's. She pictured the large cemetery with the gravestone of James Connor and whoever was next to him. Again the mystery. Anne, his wife, was buried in Trenton. But here was James farther down the valley in Rising Fawn. If Tony had drawn the family tree, he had some knowledge of that family, even if he and the

Connors were not blood relatives. Was he a genealogy nerd and just drew it out of information from registers and census listings? Surely he had more interesting things to do with his time. That garden for sure kept him busy.

She didn't dare go to Tony's house unannounced. But she wanted to talk to him—soon. She thought of all the things she needed if she was going to stay a couple of weeks here. Cups and saucers, bowls, a coffee maker, coffee, food. Yes, food. She'd been living off a few things she'd bought from Gordon on Saturday, but here it was Thursday, and she had nothing other than cereal to eat. Be nice to have a banana.

Searching in her purse for a piece of paper to write on, she located the pamphlet on the natural history of the mountains and read for a few moments before flipping to a blank side and writing down what she needed at the store.

"My wife says we've got to stop meeting like this," Tony said from the other end when she called him from the Dollar Store in Trenton.

"But she's okay," he laughed. "Really, I told her about our outing yesterday, and she's mostly concerned how you are doing. Thought I'd done a poor job of trying to disappear a relative!"

It took Clare a moment to realize he was joking. It really was okay. It was just his first line that still had her thinking. She'd have to get used to his sense of humor.

"If it's a problem, I'll try to not be too much of an intrusion," she said. "Maybe we can invite her on our next date!"

"No, it's fine. She's actually glad I've got something other than the garden to do."

"Good. Because I have a question about a piece of genealogy."

"What's that?"

"What do you know about James Connor?"

"Not sure I know what you mean."

Should she tell Tony she'd seen something in his house on the sly? That certainly would not build trust. And trust was what she had now in this bit of family she'd discovered.

"Not only am I an intruder in your family, but I'm a sneak." She took a breath. Should she continue down this road? She was already on it. She had to go on, find out what the big mystery about James Connor was.

Tony was silent on the other end. He waited.

"I-I took a look at your family Bible when I was at your house Tuesday. I saw your family lines, but I also saw a piece of paper that had James Connor's line. I looked at it out of curiosity. Then I saw something that raised more questions. I apologize for invading your privacy. I-I. . .. You know how much I want to understand this mystery of my family!" A loud buzz came through the line just as she said her last words.

She let silence fall between them.

"We got a bad connection here," he finally said, speaking slowly. "It's kind a hard to talk about this on the phone, and I'm not sure I'm catching everything you're saying. What if I pick you up at your place in a bit? I want to show you some of the mountain anyway."

Was he going to avoid her question about why he was researching someone not related to him? Connor was on her father's side of the family, and Tony was her mother's relative. Nothing to do with the Connors. Or did he have a connection?

"Okay. Give me time to get back home and put groceries away."

They rode for a long time—across the top of the mountain, traveling from the west brow where her trailer was back towards Cloudland Canyon and then over toward the east side of the mountain. The scenery passed in a kind of blur. Clare was thinking about her question for Tony.

"So about the family tree. . .," she began.

A frown crossed Tony's face.

"It's not that I don't want to tell you about what you found. It's just that I'd rather wait. Let me show you some of the area round here first. You don't have to leave for Atlanta yet, do you?"

She didn't know if he was kidding her or avoiding her question. He knew she had nowhere to go now that Terry Harris had taken care of her one career option.

"I can wait. . .for a while. Why don't you show me what you want, and then we can talk."

"Suits me," he said with a shrug. Clare didn't know if that was the truth from Tony or a delay tactic. They continued driving down the east brow of the mountain, where houses grew sparser the farther south they travelled. June here had the trees turning chartreuse as they budded later than the trees in Atlanta. The lighter trees budding showed themselves among darker green pines and other evergreens on both sides of the road.

With no warning, Tony pulled off the road to the left. Only trees and overgrown roadside vines greeted them. Across the road to the right was an open field undulating up to the mountain's crown. Not so much kudzu here as in the northeast Georgia mountains she knew from hikes, Clare noted. She knew the story—1930s soil erosion was so bad that the government encouraged planting of the green, leafy vine imported from Japan, only to find out that it grew so fast it covered telephone poles overnight, it seemed.

Maybe, she thought, these areas had not been farmed as had northeast Georgia's rolling valleys and mountains.

She saw a dark green and white sign on her right: "Lula Lake Land Trust" with a web address.

"Here's where you can help," Tony said. "Get that key out of the glove box that has a long, leather fringe holder, and open the padlock on that gate." She saw they were parked near a two-sectioned dark green gate, and she emerged to unlock the heavy fastener, which hung from the back of the gate.

"Tony, this all yours?" she joked, as the car rolled in and she closed and relocked the gate. She got back in the car and they continued deep into woods. There were swells of ground over on the right, and the wooded hillside closed in on them from the left.

Tony smiled. "Wish it was. This all belonged to the railroad when the deep mines were going. We're driving on the railroad bed. Coal was hauled out of the mountain and down this gorge to the valley below."

He motioned to the right.

"Last fall, I saw a bobcat right there on that rise," he said.

"Wow. Were you scared?"

"Naah. What's to be afraid of? I wasn't going to go pet im, that's for shore."

The land then fell away from the right, and the sound that had followed them from the main road became louder, and the air smelled of pine and cedar. A rushing creek came into view. Not just a little creek, but a waterway that became wider and full of bigger boulders and rocks as they drove down the road. The atmosphere around them turned cooler and wetter.

"What's that structure?" Clare motioned to the right.

"That was a railroad trestle that spanned the creek above us here. There was some kind of rig where they would actually wash the coal in the creek. That's why the rocks are black, not gray. There's still residue from the coal mining that took place in the late 1800s."

When Clare thought the water would maybe dwindle and disappear, it continued to fall on a gradual down-mountain grade, the boulders getting larger and more plentiful.

"Should see this after a rain," Tony said. "It's awesome."

"So how do you get to open the gate?"

"I know the manager of the land trust that owns it now, and he gives me a key as a backup in case something happens to his key or to him."

"Is there a danger of something happening to him?"

"Not that we know of, but it's just a precaution."

Silence fell as Clare took in the woods, the rushing water, the deep tree canopy, the wildness of the scene. Huge boulders appeared along the road.

"Actually, Lula Lake had a history of thievery and desecration," Tony said in his usual monotone voice. "Even murder in the 60s."

Clare began looking more closely at either side of their rough road. There were few signs of anything unusual, other than the utter beauty of the place.

"Fortunately, a wealthy businessman bought it and cleaned up a lot of it. Then an environmental nonprofit got a permanent conservation easement and continued to haul out the debris—everything from old tires in the stream to baby diapers strewn all over—acres of trash. The land trust manages it now. The man who bought it spent years buying up the land so he could enjoy where he played as a kid and make sure it was never spoiled. You'll see why in a few minutes."

Clare took it all in. A place so special someone bought it all up to protect it, wanting to never let go of it. Land that had been so spoiled at one time that trucks had to haul out the trash left behind.

"Murder, huh?" Clare felt a chill cross her body. But she wanted to know more.

"No fences or barriers here for a long time. We used to have family reunion picnics here in the 50s. No bother. We'd spread on these rocks and sun ourselves, jump in the creek to swim, and set up all kinds of food on the shore. Had a great time." Tony looked wistful.

"Young people came up here to swim and hang out a lot, but often some locals would steal wallets and stuff out of the cars. The varmints would spring the lock on a trunk like it was child's play. Nothing worse, but then when the 60s and the hippie era came along, folks liked to hang out here and do drugs. People trashed the area. During this time, a couple was up here, and they were found dead farther on out to the edge of the mountain, chained to a tree and shot."

"Wow."

"So there's always been the creep factor here."

"I'd say more than a creep factor. Did they ever find out who did it?"

"Nope. Wasn't meant to be found out. Folks that live around here are very secretive. Maybe got some weed-growing and other stuff going on. They don't want to be found out."

Clare looked around trying to make sure no one else was sharing the woods with them. The rushing water continued to push down the mountain beside them on the right. Boulders larger and more numerous than any she'd ever seen heaped up in the creek, forcing the water flow around them. Spray from the impacts rose in the air, making it look like it was raining over the creek.

They pulled into a graded parking lot. There was an arched, green steel bridge crossing over the creek to a bluff on their right. It was clear that a railroad crossed here at some point in the past and went out through what was now trees and rocks. The creek below seemed to disappear over a ledge. Through closed car windows, the water sounded louder. A large gap opened in the mountainside where the creek was headed.

"Gonna park here and go over that bridge."

When Tony said that, Clare suddenly thought of the irony of her situation. Here she was on a lonely, out of the way road deep in the mountains of northwest Georgia, accompanied by a man she'd met only three days ago and with whose help she'd narrowly escaped falling into a deep, deep hole in the mountain. And they were treading on land that held secrets of murder and mayhem and who knows what. If Helene knew where she was, she'd be freaked and would be telling her in no uncertain terms to get her ass out of here. If Willie knew where she was. . .she thought about the hikes and water trips they'd taken in the mountains. *Actually,* she thought, *Willie might find this as beautiful and intriguing as I do.*

She looked at Tony across the seat from her, the only family connection she had. With her mother in her last days back in Atlanta, he was all she had. But he, like her mother, was secretive, urging her to hold her questions until he showed her something up here at the lake. Should she trust him? She did not feel threatened physically, as his body left him few ways to flee if he did something awful. But she did feel she was on emotional shaky ground because he had the power to play with her need to find out about her family secrets. Was he toying with that power now?

Clare opened her door and came around the large car to Tony's side. The loud "whisssh" of tons of water falling grew in Clare's ears, and she turned to see just beyond where the creek fell over a ledge under the walking bridge.

"I hope what you're going to show me is better than this little piddling stream," she joked with him.

"I think you'll like it," he smiled as she opened the door behind him and pulled out his chair. "They call it Rock Creek, a little obvious," he joked.

He was agile in lifting himself to the chair and wheeling to the footbridge over the water. Clare pushed the chair up the incline of the bridge and over to the other side of the creek, watching the water coursing down a shelf of rock into a cavernous opening in the mountain.

When she walked them past where the creek fell, she saw a large crater lake in the side of the mountain. The creek now fell in a diagonal staircase about thirty feet into the lake, forming a deep green pool with a dramatic rock wall that rose a hundred or more feet above the lake on the left side.

On the right where they stood, the railroad bed continued to edge the right slope of mountain. On the left and below them was a descent to the lake; a steep foot trail snaked down the ridge between boulders, bushes, and trees overhanging the lake.

"This is as far as I can take you," Tony said.

"It's gorgeous. It would be great to have some canoes and paddle around in this."

"People did swim in it when we were young, but at great risk," Tony said, motioning to some large "No Swimming" signs. "One of my uncle's friends dove off of one of those ledges," he pointed to the wall rising up across from them. Clare thought the layers of rock resembled thousands and thousands of yards-long thin pancakes compressed into a solid mass. On some of the edges, it looked like air bubbles were caught in stone forever. Trees grew on some of the ledges near where the creek fell, but there were ledges in the layers of rock jutting out where someone with good climbing skills could access a diving spot.

"Hit a rock in the water and broke his neck. Died of course."

"Places like this seem to have their legends," Clare said. "It's almost like they're these mythical people with stories growing up about them through the ages."

"Only these are true," Tony said.

"But the legends have their lessons. Like the man who provided for the preservation of this area. To think you can live your life, and then preserving a spot like this goes on giving to generations you never will know. It's a kind of redemption for all the bad things that happened here. People can now come here and be renewed and hopefully not have anything bad happen, only good things that can come from being near this amazing water."

"Didn' know you were such a poet, Clare."

"Well, I'm not a poet, but this place moves me."

"Before too much of the day goes, you need to go on down that trail to see what happens after Rock Creek runs off over there." He motioned with his arm to the trail on the right. "I'll be fine sitting here watching the birds and the waterfall."

"Okay."

"When you get back, there'll be a quiz. See if you can find Insurance Bluff. That's where car stripping gangs took advantage of all the new shopping centers in the 60s, stole cars, stripped them, sold their parts, and pushed the cars over the cliff."

Shivers again. Why was there always mayhem mixed in with beauty? Clare looked at the trail. She couldn't see much for the tree cover, but it was apparent that the creek continued its slight descent there on her left. The steep side of the mountain on the right held a trail that she could manage with care. She walked along it and eventually saw that the sky was opening up in front of her. The sound of water followed her, even though it disappeared behind trees that began to separate her from the creek below to her left.

After a few minutes of walking the trail, she emerged to see a huge gorge that opened up toward the valley below. It was as if the mountain wore a deep gash in its side with the creek at the base, only it was covered in trees, green on green, with little ground visible through it all. A wall of green grew up across the gorge from her. When she looked to the left, she saw a dramatic waterfall, water lopping over a ledge so high she could not see the end of it, and misting lifted from below where it was hitting rock. The sound was louder, more than the sound of the creek tumbling over rocks. It was just a wide sheet of water falling over the edge, a waterfall of at least a hundred feet.

*Hawaii must be like this.*

Moisture from the mist formed droplets on her face. It was like nothing she'd seen before. So exotic, so removed from normal existence.

She figured the green wall across from her was probably Insurance Bluff, where car strippers had dumped vehicles once they were done with them. It was hard to believe, as the trees and growth were so thick there was no sign of a road. So much beauty mixed with the crime.

Like life, she decided.

She longed for a camera, but frustrated with trying to get a signal, she'd left her phone in the trailer. At the top of the falls, a refrigerator-sized boulder rested just before the veil of water tumbled over. What a wonder it perched there, never moving. The ledge underneath the falls appeared to be thirty or so feet deep, then quickly receded, as though there might be a cave underneath.

She descended toward the floor of the falls, picking her way on a rough trail through huge sections of rock. On her right, one cliff was so high she imagined a castle rampart above her with medieval soldiers launching flaming spears. She understood now why Gnome Lane and Giant's Highway graced street names in small subdivisions situated on the side of the mountain not far away. The rock formations scattered down the mountainside, spurred imaginations, and created scenarios, fantasy villages. In fact, she'd heard that during the Depression, an enterprising Lookout resident had made one of the world's most famous attractions out of the rock caverns on top of this mountain. Clare passed a threesome of giant boulders laid on top of each other, ending in a deep cave where chilled air escaped, inviting entry.

Coolness, all was coolness here in the vertical forest. She tripped down the path to get as close to the waterfall as possible. Her thoughts ran to the natural history of the mountain she'd read on the pamphlet she'd found. She recalled bits of data: hundreds of millions of years ago the ocean had covered this area, dropping tons of sea animals that formed the basis of limestone beds. Then as the seas pulled back, lush tropical vegetation grew, died, and became peat and formed coal layers. Next, more eruptions and the shifting of tectonic plates created the Appalachian chain, including this southernmost mountain. Then millions of years of rain and wind, then another upheaval, creating the Cumberland Plateau and Sand Mountain. Ice glaciers advanced and melted repeatedly along Lookout. Giant frost heaves in the rock cliffs split them apart, spewing trails of boulders and rocks down the mountain. Eons of time, incalculable geologic shifts.

She got closer to the waterfall's end point, but layers of fallen trees blocked her way. As she neared the falls, cooler air swirled around her. She turned back toward the mountainside she'd descended. She saw a few steps ahead of her on the right the overturned frame of an old car, hardly visible in the dead leaves. A chrome front grill was still attached that recalled the rounded curves of early 1950s cars she'd seen in Willie's collector magazines. Clare's mind went to the car strippers and that other crime, the double murder that had taken place many decades before.

*Better get back to Tony*, she thought. She turned and worked her way back, not stopping this time, not taking in the views.

"How was it?" Tony was in the same place she'd left him, near the staircase falls.

"Took my breath away. You ought to bottle this stuff. The beauty would change the world's bad guys into babies. It's gorgeous!" she exclaimed. "What happened to the coal mining that was here?"

"Found better coal in Alabama. The coal here needed high heat to start up, so it wasn't suitable for household and many industries. The coal from here went by railroad to Port Royal in South Carolina to fuel the Navy fleet and the shipping business there."

"So that explains why we think of coal, we think of Alabama and the steel mills there, not this area. Let's get back—I'm sure you need a bladder break pretty soon, and so do I."

"Waal, I'm going to need one fore long. Let's get on the road." He turned his wheelchair toward the bridge arching over Rock Creek, and Clare took up position behind him to push him to the car.

At Tony's insistence, they'd postponed the discussion of the mystery in Tony's Bible. For some reason, he wanted her to see the beauty of the mountains before he talked about the missing information. On the way back, she'd get the story.

"Thank you for taking me to such a lovely place," Clare said. They were driving back towards her area of the mountain. "It's a wonder no one grabbed it long ago and made a resort out of it. I'm glad they didn't, but still—so many people would crowd to that if they could."

"They have public access a couple of times a month, so people are able to visit, but otherwise, it's just like that—no one around, just the animals. But, yes, long ago, there was a hotel for a short time, but it went away. With the coal mining and then the shutdown, the land was vacant for a while with only locals knowing about it. Back when I was growing up, it was pretty far away from anything, so I guess that saved it. Or maybe mysterious thefts and such kept the curious out."

"Is it still dangerous?"

"Now there are so many volunteers building trails and taking care of the place that I doubt the kind of activity that went on could get ahold. Seems like the 60s, when they started building shopping centers—there was a time, you know, when folks shopped downtown, not in the suburbs—and they threw up these huge parking lots, it was just ripe for car theft gangs to go into stealing, stripping, and selling parts. So they got rid of the evidence by pushing them off that bluff. And insurance companies paid out tons in losses. Those gangs have long died out by now or gone into another line of business."

"I feel a *little* better." She noted the car front grill she's seen was very old.

Tony grinned at her, then moved his eyes back to the road. For a fleeting moment, she thought of how Willie would love what she had just seen. Back in another era, they had spent many weekends hiking in places like this, but nowhere so dramatic as the Lula Lake Falls. She didn't say anything for a while.

"So, I went to the cemetery in Rising Fawn when I'd just arrived here, and I found a gravestone with James Connor," Clare said finally. "Next thing, I'm meeting you, and I do something inappropriate. I admit it, and I'm ashamed, but I have been unraveling secrets up here, and that's one of them—who I came from, and why my mother didn't talk about these people."

Tony winced as he drove but said nothing.

"So I take a look at *your* family Bible and find this piece of paper that you or someone has written on that has a family tree with James Connor, my father's father. He's not related to you, but you've got this family tree for him. Only there's correcting fluid near his children's names."

Tony sighed, a deep sound like the water falling back there in the creek. He didn't say anything for a few moments. Clare waited, her throat getting tighter.

"James Connor had a child out of wedlock."

"Oh." The skin around her face felt taut.

"I found out about it many years ago when his daughter showed up on my family's doorstep. We'd never met her, and my mother didn't believe it at first. She was pretty pissed we were so suspicious of her. But she was a nice lady, even if she was mad. I was only about 20, the young one in the room, so I was just on the sidelines there in our living room when she visited."

"What was her name?"

"Julia Mullins."

"Where was she from? I mean I guess she was from my grandfather, but did she live nearby?"

"Long story."

"Gonna tell me, or do I have to wait again?" she asked impatiently. Her grandfather was an adulterer with an unclaimed child? What was with this family? She puffed out air from her mouth like she did as a kid. Her bangs would lift with the exhaled breath. She had no bangs now, but the blowing out was a great stress reliever, and she continued it.

"What?"

"If you go to the library, you may find some stuff."

"Like in the family files or what?"

"She said she'd bullied the priest at the mission parish we attended to give her back some letters she'd written to another priest who'd been at the mission years earlier. Why he still had those letters, I don't know. But she somehow got ahold of them. Said she wanted to leave it somewhere so it would be clear what happened to her father. Try looking in the files on families of the area."

"Well, it must have been a pretty bad experience if you erased her from the record," Clare said. She felt confused. And even more impatient.

"I know. I guess I have mixed feelings about putting this situation out there." Tony said. "You'll have to read the letters." He looked at her and gave a small smile, almost an apology.

"You know, you are not the sum of your parents' or grandparents' actions. You're Clare, you're unique. You are not them. If that were true, we'd all be in a heap of trouble!" He smiled more broadly. Clare tried to feel better.

"I never got off on ancestor worship," he said, his heavy brows knitting together. "What happened in my family was just too painful. Why dredge up the past?"

Clare thought a moment about the large file about the Sands family in the library. The pain of the past covered up by celebrations in the present. Or the permanent sign of hatred, Tony's crippled body, redeemed by his caring for her and helping her find her family.

"Well, I'm getting the idea there may be some ghosts waiting for me in those letters. Better to let them out, I guess."

Clare pawed through the oddly shaped files in the library, the soft holders under M for Mullins giving way, and fanning, and then falling back into each other as she moved her hand over them. She found nothing. Then she tried the Ws on the hunch she might be listed under the last name on her gravestone. There were several files in that drawer section, a collection featuring odd papers and plastic ring-bound booklets that showed some signs of care. Then a single folder with a name neatly printed in upper case in the tab with a large felt marker: Webster.

Of course Julia would file under her married name, Clare thought as she reached for the manila folder. A woman whose birth name might have eluded her would want to be found under her husband's name.

Two pieces of paper slipped out of the file onto the floor. She stooped to pick them up and began reading in a woman's hand a long epistle dated January 5, 1943. Above the address, a return address gave a street in Trenton. A round, faded red seal stamped in the corner of the first page of the letter noted, "Received, July 10, 1974" and "Dade County Public Library." Clare lowered herself into a nearby chair at a long table and began reading.

> Dear Father Patrick,
>     I'm writing to you to pray especially for the soul of my father, James Connor. He was killed last week in a terrible accident on the railroad here. He lay across the tracks in an inebriated state, and no one saw him; the morning train dragged his body and injured him terribly. Of course, there was no way a priest could be brought this way.

Clare began coughing, gagging on the musty smell of the paper, shocked by the revelation about James. No wonder she didn't know much about him. Her mother was probably glad to keep this quiet.

On a visit to her mother in the nursing home about two weeks ago, her mother had seemed agitated, kept motioning to Clare. Clare had moved closer.

"Must," Frankie kept saying. It was one of the few times she could hear her say a clear word. But it was mixed in with words that had no meaning at all.

"What do you need, mother?" Clare said. "What are you trying to tell me?"

She was trying to signal something of great importance, but Clare could not interpret what she meant. She'd pulled back from her mother, taking in her familiar smell.

At the library table in Trenton, Clare continued reading, compelled to know all the papers held for her. She peered at the neat, expansive handwriting that spanned both sides of the thin paper. The ink bleeding from the other side only made the story more poignant.

> This is probably a surprise to find that I am requesting these prayers. You probably do not know that James was my father. You see, James actually had two families, that I know of. My mother, Jenny Mullins, lived in Rising Fawn, as her mother did also. Both ladies did not know their fathers, as my grandmother's mother had not known hers. So you see, Father, my mother and her mother and her mother were indeed like the sinning woman Jesus forgave, not exactly ladies with the cleanest sheets.

Clare's throat caught. A secret family! With a prostitute! Did her mother, now lying in a nursing home in Atlanta, know about this? Were those mysterious urgings of "Must!" meant to lead her to this family story?

> I pray, Father, that you will intercede with Our Father in heaven so that my families' sins will be forgiven. I believe my father was a good man, although he had many failings, and I guess the main fault was his changeable spirit. He was reluctant to stay in one place and he could not be faithful to one kind of work or one woman. My mother met him when he frequented our home where there were several young women living and making a living of sin. Rather than continue to entertain the men of the neighborhood, my mother, Jenny, wanted a better life. James set her up in a house. A shack, really, but a shack with nice things like a porch and a stove and a well on the back porch. She could not hope to have a marriage, as James was already married and living in another part of the world, around the mountain, on the Tennessee River near South Pittsburg.

Her grandfather had two families, Clare thought. The wandering must have come from a restlessness a family couldn't help—maybe it frightened him. How did he end up in Rising Fawn?

My father first came here when he was a young man but already
married. From South Pittsburg, he took the train to Chattanooga, and then switched lines and came south into the valley between Sand Mountain and Lookout. He came to Rising
Fawn, he told Jenny, because his father, a stonemason and an
immigrant from Ireland, told him he could always find work
here if he looked for it. My father always told me that he was a
new immigrant in search of work. Of course, he couldn't have
been new to this country, because his father was that. He did
work some, but the coal mines had shut down and the foundry
had gone away, and the town was like a ghost town except when
the trains of tourists and railroad workers and highway builders
came through.

James got work as a railroad laborer and then he met my
mother at Grandmother Eileen's place. The ladies had to move,
though, to where there was more business along the highway
being constructed over the mountain. That's when James bought
Jenny a shack here and set up housekeeping. He didn't want to
see her move as Jenny's family had over the years, following the
newest work camp.

Clare found herself imagining this big bloke of an Irishman lurching
through the valley, spending time with one family, then another, always secretive, always hiding. He had to be full of guilt about what he was doing
and frightened of this wildness that had him wandering around the mountain, struggling to support one family, and then starting another.

I will say this about my father. He didn't have a passel of children
as so many of the women in my family did. Jenny didn't let him
close when she knew she was most likely to get with child. I
won't say any more, Father, I have said too much already for
your holy ears. But I do think if there is any reason God should
show mercy to my father, it is because he did right by my mother
and didn't leave a large family to starve.

So James was a sinner and my mother was a sinner and I
have prayed for the repose of her soul, too, but I think you knew
my father because you priests baptized him and confirmed him
and gave him Communion and you knew his family at South
Pittsburg. Perhaps your prayers for his soul will work better
than mine.

Where did the priests come in? Clare wondered. Mrs. O'Brian had said
they weren't in this area.

I didn't think you knew he had passed away and I wanted to tell you. Not many knew about us, his other family that lived in Rising Fawn, but now you do, so maybe you can pray for his soul. We are why he died in Rising Fawn rather than Trenton. Anne, my father's real wife, was very devoted to him. I guess she had to be. She had four children by him. There were Thomas and Paul and Lacy and ? Anne had to provide for them, and she couldn't do it by herself. So, lo, about 1930, she moved the whole family to Georgia, just up the track in Trenton so he could help support them. I was not allowed to go to Trenton, ever, the whole time I was growing up. My father thought that Anne, his other wife, might see me, and that would make things difficult for everyone. So my father spent several weeks with his family in Trenton and then another couple of weeks with us here in Rising Fawn. He'd just hop the train and come down the track. Everyone here knew, but we think no one in Trenton was aware not just to pick up work but to see another family. Except Anne. Anne had to know.

But that was how my father solved his problem of wandering. I remember he walked a lot around our neighborhood, especially when he was out of money for whiskey. I guess he did the same in Trenton, walked the soles off pairs of shoes to keep his mind off spirits. Anyone who frequented both places was probably acquainted with that walking Mr. Connor.

I know the Church probably would have run my father out if they'd known about his two families. I hope you do not think badly of him for his deeds. In truth, I think the Good Lord actually took care of him and his families better this way. Some people are just cut out differently than others, I suppose.

Clare smiled at the understatement, wondered what other secrets her father's family carried through the generations. Did her father, Paul, know about this? Were there other secrets?

I hope that I can meet you one day. James always spoke very highly of the Church, and he was pleased to be baptized and confirmed. He told me that when he died, he hoped that a priest would be coming through the area so he could receive the last rites. I guess he didn't get that wish.

But I remembered his regard for the Faith, and I myself have begun instruction in a little church up on the side of the mountain that overlooks Alabama. Now that I have a car I can get myself there. From this letter, you can probably tell that I was able to get more book knowledge than my father or anyone else in this valley, in fact. I became a teacher and now help children in these neighborhoods.

Clare wondered about the writer, her distant relative, lying in the grave next to her father. Had she tried to care for him, get him to stop drinking, become respectable?

So you see, Father, my father James had two families. I was the first in mine to go to school all the way through. I still do not bear my father's name, but that will change, too, when I meet a beau and get married.

Some of the ladies I see in the town still shake their heads and *tsk* at me as I walk by because they know the family history of the Mullen women who kept their names and passed them to their children because the fathers would not claim them. I knew my father. He just happens to be a shared father.

So, Father, please pray for James's soul. I hope a good and gracious God will welcome him inside the gates of heaven. And I pray God my mother, Jenny, has made it there as well.

Sincerely,

Julia Ann Mullins

Still holding onto the delicate sheet—if she let it go, would the revelations, the mysterious, disturbing caches of details about her grandfather slip away?—Clare sat in the library chair feeling numb and tight-skinned at the same time. She felt close to Julia Mullins Webster and wondered what her life had been like. She had spent her young life in shame, but became educated and married, two accomplishments that erased some of the past. But she might have had no children.

And she would have been her Aunt Julia.

Clare looked out the window at Lookout Mountain guarding the valley where she sat. Were there relatives in these hills that could give her more clues? Maybe Terry Harris was kin. The atmosphere felt spooky, as though the hills knew more than she, and hid more secrets of her origins.

She thought of pictures of Andean women swinging their children onto their backs in colorful, secure mantas, of the Madonna with child, of pictures of fathers and their children, all symbols of the lavish caring of parents. But in every crop, there were duds of peaches or tomatoes. In a clutch of eggs, some birds made it, some didn't. Was she the dud in the family group?

How much have I inherited of James? she asked herself.

How much of what I am is nature and how much nurture? Is all the fine education I've had for nothing because of faulty genes? Are there goblins in my background? Do I have a major flaw like James? Am I unable to be happy in a single marriage because of a quirk of nature like one of my ancestor's? What about the other relatives?

Clare closed the folder on the table. She looked at her empty lap and thought about what she'd just read. She felt like her journey to find herself had just started. There was more in these library files. Where had Father Patrick come from? She thought the Irish staple religion had shattered and split into pieces in these parts. As Mrs. O'Brian had said, there were no priests. Where had her grandfather been baptized? Where were his brothers and sisters? Now she was obsessed. The compulsion to know more from books and papers took a hold of her. Just as she'd felt the Rising Fawn grave-yard's insistent pull, she felt tentacles drawing her to more knowledge in the folders and books in that room.

A sound sliced through the silence and startled her out of the previous century. It was a shrill sound, but musical, and familiar. It was her cell phone ringing.

Clare dove for her purse to shut off the sound, then ran from the li-brary to the sidewalk outside to answer.

"Clare, your mom's taken a turn for the worse," Helene, breathless, said from the other end. "The doctors say she doesn't have long."

"I'm on my way," Clare said. "I'll leave right away." She clicked off and felt a hardness in her chest, then a sob trying to make its way out. She made her way to the car, climbed in, and lay her arms on the wheel, letting the feelings of loss and confusion come. Tears emerged, fell onto her cheeks. This was final. All the time of her mother's stroke and coma aftermath, Clare had held on as her mother held on. Now it was certain. Her mother was leaving. And she would take all these secrets with her.

# Chapter 10

## LATER THURSDAY

Clare plugged in her phone to charge in the trailer while she prepared to leave. The thought that she would be connected to the world now filled her with dread. After all the fuming about not getting a signal, she was now fearful of joining back into the world she'd known before. She didn't know her place in it right now. Her heart for being the hard-charging professional was gone.

It would not be easy to ignore that old world. A practical matter arose: She had just a couple of choices of clothes without returning to Reidinger Drive. Would she go there?

She thought about her mother lying in bed. She could picture her mother not speaking, her negligee slightly off the shoulder, her lips moving in silent prayer. But now?

The car was waiting. Dew covered its safety-yellow expanse, luminous against the bright-green weeds rising up to the chassis. Clare looked at it and wondered at her next move. She couldn't keep her mind straight enough to be sure what to do next. Her thoughts seemed to flit from herself to her mother, back to herself and her situation. She was in her new home here, but she was leaving to go back to the old. Where would she stay? She pictured Helene's sleep sofa. It would be temporary, just enough for her brief stay in Atlanta. She did not see herself as belonging there now. She saw herself as here in the mountains. Should she be thinking of how to break apart her life on Reidinger Drive?

"Enough," she told herself. "Enough to do just going down there and handling my mother's life. Not mine."

She gathered her clothing and toiletries and placed them in her duffle bag. She carried these and her couple of outfits on hangers to the car. She thought about calling Tony and decided to wait until she was actually on the way. It was best to tell him her departure time and then have a person on the other end—Helene—know when she was expected in case of an accident or a delay. *How different it is when you're no longer a couple, sharing that kind information with no more thought than reading a clock,* she thought. *Things are different now. Simpler, but requiring a few more steps. But why am I thinking about things like this right now? My mother needs me!*

After unloading in the car, she went back in to check windows to make sure they were closed and locked. Funny, she was now attached to the old sofa and the early Salvation Army furnishings. They weren't great, but they were serviceable. And they certainly were easily replaceable if anyone broke in. It's almost laughable to think about locking, she told herself, looking at the dining table where Jerry, Tony's son, had left her keys some days ago. She had different ideas now about furniture and the furnishings of her life—a far cry from her previous life when the choice of a sofa took days to decide.

Clare pulled the phone charger from the wall and carried it outside to finish recharging in the car. Moving everything outside, she felt the June air becoming moist and the light around her darker. She'd need to check the forecast when she could get a station on the radio. Did Tony tell her earlier it was supposed to rain?

The fact that Clare was here on the mountain and not by her mother caused a veil of shame to fall over her. Why did she feel she had to leave her mother and flee Atlanta in the first place? Maybe she should have found another lawyer or someone who could have devised a way for her to stay in her own home. *I didn't know any better,* she told herself. *Miss Know-It-All about everyone else's life doesn't know how to take care of herself. Not a clue.*

"Mom, I'm sorry I didn't learn self-care," Clare told the window as she closed the car door and put on her seat belt. "I had an education in how to do everything for everyone else but not for Clare. I became frightened when Willie told me to leave, and I didn't know what to do. I left you, and I shouldn't have."

The light on the road and around her was strange. Most of her trips across the mountaintop had been in sun or at least morning light. It was past three o'clock now and the roads and the grass and tree-filled roadsides were dimmer than she'd seen before, save for the night she'd arrived when only blackness clothed the mountain. Clare figured it would be at least seven or eight before she got to the nursing home, so it would be dark, and who knew what kind of traffic would be on I-75 nearer Atlanta.

A tall man loping long the roadsides of Rising Fawn, a worried look on his face, appeared in Clare's mind. What were the demons that drove James Connor up and down those byways, and onto the train shuttling between the two towns of his "wives"? She imagined him in the dungarees of a railroad worker, maybe wearing a short visored-cap popular at the time. He walked for hours, moving from church fronts past the porches of fine Victorian homes along the railroad.

Would he go to the cemetery? Where was the house he had with Jenny? Was it on a hill behind the Victorians, away from view but still near the railroad? If she, Clare, had a changeable mind and was so easily wounded and swayed from her path, could it be that she inherited this need for movement, for variety, for inconstancy from her grandfather?

Helene had asked her long ago if bipolar disease might be an issue with her. She'd never thought about it applying to her, as she was so competent in some ways. But maybe. . ..

Pasted in her vision next was Julia as a child. Clare could picture a photograph, one of those old-fashioned portraits mounted in a stiff cardboard folder so it could be displayed on a sideboard or a chest of drawers. She pictured a young girl in curls and a fine white lawn dress with ruffles, made to appear as attractive as a girl from the best of families. The picture was old, the edges worn, the colors shades of gray and white. She would have a large ribbon in her hair, and her hair would be dark and long, with curls. If Julia was eight or nine years of age, it would be just before the Depression, and Julia would be too early for Shirley Temple, so maybe the curls weren't as extravagant as the film star's, but she would have hair not unlike the color and texture of her own, Clare imagined.

Clare thought about Tony. She needed to call him. But she wasn't sure she'd have cell service yet. She'd wait.

By the time she let herself down into the valley below Lookout Mountain, slashes of water began to hit the windshield. She retraced the path she'd taken up to the mountain from the lowlands. Still in front of her were the ridges—Taylor's, Dick's, and all the rest. Focus came without effort as the rain made it harder to see. Her questions from before quickly dissolved, faded away as the weather and the increasing darkness challenged her alertness and control of the wheel. The rigid boundaries of the small SUV became a guard against elements, against possible injury. She was on this. The weather, the terrain, the darkness would not defeat her.

Clare picked up the phone and saw that she had bars, so she finally had cell service. She had her digital assistant call Tony's number.

"Hello?" a deep-voiced woman answered. It was Tony's wife, Silvia. "Silvia, this is Clare Connor, Tony's cousin."

"Bambina! I've been wanting to meet you!" Silvia exclaimed. Clare relaxed, no longer afraid of Silvia's reaction.

"I've been hoping to meet you, too. Tony has been so kind to take me to places around the mountain." Clare's forehead felt less warm. She pictured the kitchen Silvia spoke from. Full of light coming through the white curtains and sparks of sunny yellow, blue, and red painted pitchers and jugs on shelves around the room. She felt welcomed, as she did right from the start with Tony.

"I've been working, so I haven't been at home to meet you. You must come over on a weekend. Probably Saturday, not Sunday, unless you'd like to go to church with us. But you know you are welcome!"

"Thanks. I look forward to being at your house again." The warm temperature of the welcome surprised and freshened her spirit. "Is Tony there? I just wanted him to know I'd left the mountain."

"He's at the store right now getting some groceries."

"T-tell him that my mother has regained consciousness, and I'm headed to Atlanta. I should be there by seven. Tell him I will call him later."

"Be safe. And don't forget to call when you get there. This weather is going to be bad. What Tony calls a frog strangler." Clare could hear a smile in her voice.

"That's a great way to describe what I think I'm headed into. I'll be careful. Give Tony my thanks!"

She ended the call, picking up once more the resolve she'd finally gained to face the wind and rain. She felt people were on this trip with her, urging her toward her mother. How generous of Silvia not to be upset about her taking her husband's time. This must be what families do, she thought. And Helene, volunteering to stand in her place with her mother. What a great friend. She wondered how she would repay her. Take her out for a few nice dinners for starters, she thought. If she kept at this pace, she would be able to get to Atlanta and the nursing home by seven. It would still be light. She clicked on her cell phone a couple of times and called Helene.

"I just want you to know I'm on my way. How is Mom doing?"

"She's actually improved from when I called you. She's asking for you, though she can't say your name. She just says 'her.' It's what the nurse calls aphasia. The words come, but they don't mean anything. Like she'll say 'what-what-chair-day' and stuff like that."

"Is she comfortable?"

"She seems okay. Just very tired."

Clare didn't think Helene had met her mother more than twice. She wouldn't know that her mother was normally slow and subdued in her recent years. Unless she was there, it was impossible to know what was going on with Frankie.

"I'll be there about seven, I hope, if there's not a huge jam around the north Perimeter," Clare said.

"Haven't heard of anything unusual; most of the traffic is coming toward you."

"Thanks for all you are doing," Clare said. "I owe you, big time!" Clare ended the call.

The rain had stopped in the valley she was moving through. Light reflected off the dark green pines and lighter green oaks, sweet gums, maples and elms. She noticed the graceful arms of the hemlocks were missing along the road. She'd seen these at Lula Lake beside Rock Creek and along gracious lawns and in stubby fields while she was on the mountain, but they were no more, as she'd come off the mountain slope. Pin oaks and water oaks and bushes of who-knew-what else stood beside and between the pines, escorting her as in a parade, raising their limbs in salute. By the time she started up what she guessed to be Taylor's Ridge, she anticipated seeing Shirl's store on the left this time. She would not have time to stop, but one day she would. Shirl seemed to have some special knowledge of this area, and she'd like to know more about her and her life. What a challenge to be seeking sexual identity in the middle of the buckle on the Bible Belt. She probably had many stories to tell.

Was she planning to move here permanently? She thought for a moment about the realities of her life—no income, no source of support. Savings would run out eventually. What would she do?

She wouldn't think about it right now, she decided. No way to have all the answers. But she felt pulled to this area, and she knew there was a big city at the foot of the mountain, the one named for the "rock coming to a point" above it. She'd heard through her network of contacts in the job placement business that there were new industries moving in because of a large auto plant and all the suppliers that came with it. A new fulfillment center for an American distribution giant. Young people and young families moving in. Terry Harris notwithstanding, she thought, she could make some contacts in the surrounding area, just get closer to the big city, Chattanooga.

Clare passed by Shirl's—she looked for signs that would give a name to the store so she could look up a phone number. The only signs said "Gas" and "Food and Beverages" and there was a blinking neon beer sign in the window. "I guess if you need more information, you're not from here, so you don't need to go in anyway," she laughed to herself.

She began making turns that would take her up the ridge. An intersection marker pointed the way to Old Villanow Road taking off to the right, marking the original road over the ridge, Clare guessed. The road she was on was far better—broad and well-paved with gradual shoulders and moving up the grade with measured patience. When she was eventually lifted high over the valley below, Clare decided to pull off to the side of the road. On her way up—how many days ago was that?— she'd noticed through the heavy rain that there was a break in the trees where she likely could see what lay below. As she emerged from the car, a truck loudly pressed by her, straining its motor to reach the top. She could see a long patchwork of fields and roads and occasional homes spread out below, running south to north. The panorama looked like a pastel painting, as it was far away and there appeared to be a haze over the low-lying land. How far she could see, and how small it all seemed. She loved standing on the ridge overlooking the land below—the sweep of it, the lofty feeling of being above and seeing so much more than her little space. Now she saw why she loved hiking so much—you could escape your small world and be melded into another, larger scheme.

But it was time to move on. Her mother awaited. Frankie couldn't know how far away she was nor any of what she had discovered up in this home she'd tried to hide from her. Maybe she didn't intend for it all to be a secret, but it was. How strange it was now to give her mother these qualities of thought and planning, with her life coming to an end.

Clare got in the car, imprinting the vision of the valley in her mind. She wanted to remember this when she got into Atlanta traffic and hubbub and all the many distractions of the huge metropolis. Her life there would erase the memory like water washing away a stain if she did not guard it in her mind.

But what else would stay in her memory—the shoots and tendrils of the tawdry family history she'd uncovered? Still, she told herself, that should not affect me. I'm my own person, even though a person without much family. Tony was the closest to family she had. Tony and maybe Silvia, too. *Silvia*, the Hispanic and Italian spelling. *Sylvia* is the Anglo version. Tony had never suggested that his wife was one thing or the other. But Clare thought, now connecting the Sands collection of pottery, that a bit of the Central Mediterranean wafted through Silvia's bloodline.

The road down the ridge was followed by a gentle climb over a smaller ridge and then a winding through a pleasant valley lit up from the recent rain. It *was* important—her family there in the mountains. She was bound up in what had gone before. I need to know it all, she told herself. The good, the bad, the not important. Just as I know Tony by his steadfastness and his courage and Silvia by her generous spirit and her love of color and light, I need to know my traits, my beginnings, the starting stuff.

Her hand shook as she picked up her phone and checked the signal. Two dots. That was enough. She punched in Tony's number, hoping he would be home by now. The Bluetooth did its odd business and she heard an amplified phone ringing.

"Huhlo," he answered.

"Tony, it's Clare. I left word about Frankie with Silvia—did you get it?"

"Yes. I'm glad to know she's revived." The caring in his voice came through, crossing mountains and valleys, but clear as a good day without rain. "Let me know if I can hep at all."

"Silvia seems very nice, and I look forward to getting to know her—is that by any chance the Italian Silvia?"

There was a soft guffaw from the other end.

"She does claim a bit of the sunny land. But you didn't call me just to ask how I spell my wife's name, did you?" She could hear a hint of humor in his voice.

"I've been thinking of what you told me about James and what I found out about him from Julia's letters. They're so sad. I wish I'd known her."

"So you did read them."

She felt like she was avoiding the real reason for calling him, and Tony knew. Her hand lay a bit unsteadily on the phone, and she pulled it up to see. She now had three dots, a stronger signal.

"Tony, is that the worst about my family? Is there any more you need to tell me?"

No sound from the other end. She thought she heard a shuffle of an object or maybe it was Tony moving in his wheelchair.

"I'm speeding to my mother's bedside, and I have more of an idea about her family—my family—up here in the mountains. But I want to know if that's everything. I need to know all the stuff about my family." Her voice, enhanced by the Bluetooth speakers, was very loud.

"Why is it so important?"

"It's important to you, isn't it? I've seen how you or someone carefully gathered family events in the library's family files. Your family Bible shows close attention to your ancestors and your offspring. And their offspring. And my family. I've never figured out my family, and as I have these final days with my mother, I'd like to know who she is and who I am and have more than these tatters of history."

"You are not your family history," Tony said emphatically. Tony was sparing with directness, so this was new to Clare.

"Well, let me decide that, okay?" She was irritated with Tony. He was being stubborn about this family business.

"*Madre Dio,*" he finally breathed out. "I guess I'm the only one who can tell you."

"Tell me what?" She heard muffled sounds of pans clanging in the background. Silvia would be in the next room preparing dinner.

"You have a different mother than your sister Angela."

The skies over her, now filled with dark clouds, could have opened up and rained *Walking Dead* characters and Clare would have been less surprised.

"What do you mean?" She thought there was a squeal in her voice.

"Your father Paul had a problem with drink," he said gently. "He and my mother had a brief affair very late in life. But before you moved to Atlanta."

Clare felt fire around her. Then she realized it was her skin. Her body vibrated as though her limbs, her torso, her head were the strings of an instrument receiving a strum, again and again, from an insistent hand.

"You've got to be kidding me. My father—and your mother?"

"Right."

"So that makes us half-brother and sister! No wonder I felt so connected to you!"

"'At's one way to look at it. It's bad news, but it's not all bad news as far as I'm concerned."

"How long have you known this?"

"Since I was a young man. It was long after the visit from Julia, so I was probably in my early 20s."

"So how old was your mother?"

"Close to menopause—so maybe they thought they could risk sleeping with each other. I'm sure it was a brief fling, as my mother was real emotional, and I'm pretty sure Paul gained her sympathies, especially since Frankie appeared pretty distant in the marriage. Mom ended up pregnant, but I was one of the few to know.

"She took a long visit to see relatives in another state, to take care of an 'ailing aunt.' Gone for months. My father was distraught, and he almost became violent. We were all upset. We had to decide what to do. My father was horribly shamed, and there was no way he was going to accept this child. So the best thing we could do was to move Paul out of Trenton and have him and Frankie raise his child. You." This all sounded like a radio drama, as the Bluetooth made everything loud enough to carry through the car.

The heat around Clare grew closer. She opened the car windows to cool off. The air was still warm around her. Her skin felt like the surface of her car baking up there in the field near her trailer on the mountain, closer to the sun than it had been before. She could imagine wavy vapors radiating from her body like the surface of a highway through the desert. She looked in the mirror expecting to see rays about her head, but all she saw was herself as she was, brunette and needing lipstick, eyes strained, bags beginning to show underneath.

"Why can't anyone in this family do anything RIGHT?" Clare yelled, mostly to the car.

"I know," Tony said. "It hurts."

"It hurts and it makes me feel useless, like a discarded kid in a crackhouse. But poor you. Your betrayed father. And Frankie.

"So I became Lucetta, little Lucy."

"She was about your size. She also had your smile. That little left dimple, for instance. That's what would have given you away in our town."

"You seem adjusted to this thing—it's maddening me. I'm steamed. I'm crying for all the people who were wronged—you, your mother, your father, MY mother, Frankie."

A sob broke through, labored and straining her throat.

"Frankie's not my mother. No wonder she was so distant from me. She was probably frigid toward my father, though I never knew it. That would explain the fifteen years between my older sister and me. Only it was a forever distance between us after my aunt carried me, my father's baby." *How crazy was all of this?* "Can you even imagine the pain of all that?"

Tony said nothing. She could hear the water running in the kitchen as Silvia continued to work there. Would she be running water for pasta? Clare found her mind wandering to other matters, hoping what was in front of her was maybe not real, maybe a family rumor that sprang up when families were separated by many miles and not in touch over a generation. But the hard truth of betrayals up and down her family line stared her in the face. From the time she was fatherless and attending the Catholic grade school in Atlanta, she'd tried to erect an edifice of normalcy to make up for the pain of his loss and the wound of her family's neediness.

"The legacy I carry! Two adulterers for parents, one the son of a wandering Irishman with two families, both creating me on the sly. You'd think that I would be running off with the newspaper delivery man or at least an attractive client in Atlanta. But I've no desire for that. I'm a one-man woman. Got enough on my plate with Willie."

Tony didn't say anything to interrupt her rant, and he remained silent after she stopped.

Clare's insides felt crushed, as though one of those huge outcroppings of stone along the old railroad bed at Lula Lake had just broken apart on a clear day and bowled her over with its force and weight. She was flattened as sure as anything would be that lay in the path of such an enormous stone.

"Do you have Frankie's power of attorney?" Tony approached the practicalities of what she was about to encounter.

"Yes."

"Then you need to be thinking about what she has stated about her final days. I realize that she has revived, but my mother Lucia also seemed to recover some strength in her final days and then suddenly died. I want you to be ready for this."

"I'm sorry you lost your mom. I'm sorry I didn't get to know her—at all. I was denied that."

"She would have been proud of you. She knew that I knew, and she told me how it hurt not to be able to acknowledge you. But everything we heard about you was shared and gone over as news of a very close relative. My mom cried a lot about your loss. But she also knew she'd done wrong. I felt like her early death was because of all the guilt she carried about her one act of unfaithfulness. As far as I know, she never spoke to your father again."

"I never saw my father drink. There was none in the house. I wonder if all this affected him so deeply he just gave it up? It must have been a shock to have to leave the mountains," she said. "The home where his grandfather had settled from Ireland and his father had been such a known part of the community, even if he was a pariah."

Clare was tired, and she knew that she had a long way to go on the trip. Rain was spotting her windshield. It was as if nature cried with her, weeping over the slicing cut that has just been sawed across her skin, going deep through the whole structure of what had so far protected her.

She wanted to get away from Tony and his story. "I'm going to ring off now, Tony. I'm tired."

"I'm sorry I had to bring you such sad news," Tony said. "I'm sorry we let you go on thinking this was your mother and that everyone conspired to keep you in the dark for so long. I know you care deeply for your mother. But everyone owes you the truth."

"Well, she is my aunt, technically," Clare managed a half-laugh. Then she stopped. Her heart felt heavy as that mammoth stone she'd seen. "But she was the only mother I knew. Do me a favor, Tony, will you?"

"Sure."

"Don't pretend with me anymore. I have to have the truth, even if it is difficult for you to say it."

When she closed her phone, Clare was about to leave the curving roads through wooded hillsides, valleys and plains, and enter the heavily traveled interstate highway that ran from upper Indiana and Illinois all the way to Florida by way of Atlanta. She dreaded the change. If land could be nurturing, the ridges, valleys and mountains she'd just spent a week in were the closest to a mother she'd had. Their rainy leaves and boughs waved at her as to a friend. The ups and downs of the terrain required patience and understanding and thoughtfulness, just as a close family relationship demanded the same. She did not take these hills for granted. They were part of her.

After news of her true mother, she felt like her guts were splayed over those green hills. She had to work to keep her hands on the wheel. The news cut into her like sharp fingernails, red like fresh blood, pouring over her. If she was unsure about herself before, she was doubly so now.

She merged onto the highway, and the rain increased. She pressed on the accelerator to jump onto the mad ride, designed to test her abilities to hold a steady course while rain, wind, and other drivers sought to throw her off. She drove like the Atlanta native she was—fast, deliberate, and ever-conscious of the cars around her, watching for the outlier, the guy or woman who wasn't following the pattern. The ones that switched lanes like crazy were the deadliest, but more murderous than them were the ones trying to text from the side of the steering wheel or the lap. Then there was the nervous driver she tried to pass, but who would then speed up, making it impossible for her to get by them.

On this evening, people were being good. They spaced themselves well and didn't crowd her. In fact, after a number of miles on the straightaway, she saw that there were a couple of cars that appeared more than once at her side. First she noticed the rag-top Mustang. It was orange-red, the top beige—and it looked like a pretty old one, although in great condition. It was in front of her, and later, despite her efforts to keep aware of all the cars around her, suddenly it appeared behind her. Other cars moved in front of the Mustang, and she thought she'd left it behind in the mist of rain—but then it was alongside her.

"Strange," she told herself. She couldn't see who was driving. The car was keeping pace with her. Then it moved ahead of her but remained not too far ahead, still in the left lane.

In front of her now was a newer white hatchback, a small car with a woman driving. Her dark hair was short but full. Clare noticed a white monogram on the left lower edge of her rear window. She decided not to attempt to read the initials, trying to keep alert in the rain. She'd seen this car earlier in the stretch since she'd joined the interstate, but she wasn't sure if it was behind her or beside her earlier.

A mysterious white pickup truck followed her. She wasn't sure of the truck brand, but it wasn't one of those huge monster trucks. She could bare-ly make out that the driver was an older guy, white haired. She kept driving with a vague awareness of the other drivers, wanting to keep her focus on her journey and what lay ahead at the hospital.

Not too long after she'd noted these travelers, they switched positions. The Mustang was ahead of her, the Versa behind, and the truck alongside. She saw now that it held a white toolbox across the back and under the rear window. The man's head was in profile, and he was watching the road.

"They're not trying to stay around me, for real," Clare told the windshield. "That would be crazy!"

But it was almost as if she had an escort. She couldn't lose the group, even if one or two moved off from her for a bit. As she traveled south through formerly rural counties, now becoming good-sized cities circling north Atlanta, she had a vibe of being cared for, watched over, even though no one made an overt move toward her.

A song came to mind, a 70s folk rock number with a mind-sticking guitar and strings melody, one that her mother and father-in-law had in a rotation that piped through the ceiling of their large home. Harry Chapin's hoarse voice spun out the long story, "Cat's in the Cradle." The song title evoked a children's game played with cotton strings that played back and forth——if one hand pulled, the other hand lost string, and it became harder to recover. At school she would play, starting the string between her two hands and passing it off to friends in an attempt to see who could keep the connections of string and thumbs and fingers going and not drop a related string and collapse the cradle. The father in the song seeks a relationship with a son he neglected while chasing work and outside interests, always making excuses, leaving the boy with a shell of a dad. The boy returns the favor to his father when his dad, many years later, wants to spend time with this son. The son turns him down. The father's previous actions collapsed the cradle.

But Clare was suspended by this thin network of escorts, the cars and truck on her front, side, and rear. For twenty or more miles, the cars stayed with her. One would range out in front and she would almost lose it, and then there it was.

Until Clare and the others reached the outskirts of Marietta, the signal for approaching Atlanta, the cars accompanied her. Vehicles coming in the opposite direction, reverse commuting from town, slowed to almost standstill as Cobb County residents and others patiently waited their turn to move a few feet in the heavy traffic. Finally, the Mustang took off on a Marietta exit, and the white hatchback departed soon after. Only the truck continued, following her until she peeled off to join I-285 eastbound. As she made the lane change to go right near the new Braves stadium, she thought she saw a wave from the truck driver in her rearview mirror.

Did it happen? She thought so, but that would be so bizarre.

She was alone again with thoughts of her mother, the mother that was not a mother. But who was.

# Chapter 11

## THURSDAY NIGHT AND AFTER

Clare lifted out of the car and walked across the small parking lot into the Angel's Wings nursing facility, anxious to see Frankie. She had not been responsive for weeks, but she hadn't gone much beyond her after-stroke condition, so if she was declining, that was new. Clare's layers of thoughts about her philandering grandfather as well as her father carried on in the back of her mind like quarreling teenagers, but she ignored them. She would do this work for her mother, even if her technical status as a daughter now hung like a half-opened envelope, ready for revelation.

Rain puddles grouped around the pavement, the active downfall now stilled. She looked at her cell phone. She was earlier than she thought she'd be, six p.m.

"Good evening," a nurse in deep blue garb greeted her as she went inside.

"Hi," Clare said. "My mother is Frankie Connor. She's in the same room, isn't she?"

"Check with the nurse's station where she was last," the pleasant, short-haired blond said.

"Thank you—I will."

It was one floor up. She caught the elevator up in a corner of the windowed, plant-filled foyer.

Clare passed near the room where her mother had been. She pressed the door forward to see if she was still there.

"Hold it! Give me a minute!" A male voice hailed her.

A tall African American stuck his slender head around the door, with a gloved hand holding to the door.

"We'll be done soon." Dark eyes, a little challenging.

"I'm looking for my mother, Frankie Connor." For a moment, she imagined the aide not believing her, asking her to prove her blood relationship, unsure now.

"I'm taking her vitals."

"Oh."

Clare caught herself starting to get irate. Then it was as if she was behind a video camera and she saw herself in the viewfinder, pushing ahead, oblivious, unaware of how she was affecting the fine clutch of routines that were set about her mother's care. Like clock hands pointing to the hours of the day, there were specific jobs for each part of each shift: bathing, vital signs, diaper change, bed position shift, medications. Who cared that she just blew in like a squall over the ocean, propelled by fears, alarm and anger about her own life? She wasn't the show here. Frankie was.

She watched that abrupt shift in her own attention from checking at the nurses' station, as the nurse on the first floor suggested, to just bulldogging it through to her mother's room. Echoes of her father's and grandfather's inconstancy, a tendency to go off what was normally expected on a whim. She owned that now.

"I apologize," she said, with a smile. "I'll check at the nurses' station."

She arrived at that hub of blue scrubs moving around, grabbing charts, pulling up the medication cart, handling phones while drinking from bottles of water. Each person seemed very sure of his or her direction. An African American woman lifted her braids-ringed head a few moments after Clare stood at the desk.

"I'd like to know if my mother, Frankie Connor, is in her same room."

"She hasn't been moved," the full-faced woman smiled. "She's in 207."

"Can you tell me about her condition?"

The nurse pulled a file from a group at the top of the desk. She opened and scanned the file and smiled more broadly.

"She seemed to go down real fast. We called Helene Johnson."

"Yes, she called me."

"Then she sort of roused herself. She's able to verbalize a little." This was terrific—like a miracle, Clare thought.

"Great. Does this mean she could fully recover?"

The woman's face lost its smile, though her eyes remained friendly.

"It's really hard to say. Sometimes it happens. But she's been able to eat a little today!" The last part she said brightly.

"Thank you. I'll go wait outside for the assistant to finish."

"I'm sure you can go right in. Just explain you are her daughter."

The slender young man was just wheeling his rolling pole with blood pressure cuffs, computers, and equipment from the room. He smiled and held the door open for her.

"Come right in. Know she'll be glad to have company." To her mother, he said, "You've got a visitor!"

Her mother was sitting up in bed, dressed in a fresh nightgown, white with blue flowers sprinkled across it, one of several Clare had provided months ago when she'd brought clothing in with sewn-in name labels, as if for a child going off to camp. There were oxygen tubes in her mouth, but her feeding and hydration tubes were gone. Her yellow DNR bracelet was still on her wrist. She'd been clear in her living will she did not want to be resuscitated if she was near the end of her life.

"Mom! It's so good to see you! How are you feeling?" She moved to her mother's side and gave her a hug. Frankie's thick hair rubbed against her chin. She smelled of baby powder.

"D-Day," Frankie said. It was hard to tell if she was happy or not about being able to say something. "Not day it is."

It sounded like she wanted to know what day it was.

"It's Thursday. I'm here with you. I was away, but now I'm with you. I see you've had dinner!"

She motioned with her hand over the tray. "Not good."

"Well, I'm glad you ate some. You know what they say about hospital food."

"Home!"

She put out her hand to touch Clare's top, an orange baggy knit she'd worn for comfort, one that would not show wrinkles that were in most of her clothes now.

"Where? Where?" said Frankie. Clare was pretty sure Helene had told Frankie everything, but she was having trouble making sense of things.

"You had a stroke. Remember when Willie and I brought you here? You'd fallen at the store. We called an ambulance, and you ended up in the hospital. You probably don't remember that."

"W-Wuh!" She was trying to say Willie's name. Funny how she could go right to the quick, to her vulnerable flesh.

Her mother looked around the room, her dark eyes getting larger.

"W-Wuh?" She looked at Clare directly.

"He'll be in to see you soon," she lied. If her mother had any idea of what had transpired in her life in the last week, she'd be angry. She'd be the first to condemn her for leaving her man. Didn't she stick by her own man through the unfathomable injury he did her? Clare thought about all she'd learned about Frankie and Paul and Lucia. Should she say anything about her secrets she'd found out to the woman who kept them? Where would she start? Gee, I found out I'm not yours. How did you do that, raise me up without a complaint, never telling on Paul's unfaithfulness that brought a "love child" into your home for you to pretend was yours.

*Just love your people.*

That came out of the blue. She knew it was what Tony would say right now. And it was true. All she could do for her mother for the rest of her life was love her. No trying to ask her questions.

She needed to call Tony to let him know she'd arrived. She also needed to reach Helene to let her know she was here. It would be so easy to pick up her cell phone here in front of her mother, but she was afraid her mother would relapse if she gave her the shock of connecting to the cousin she'd taken such pains to hide from her.

"I'm going to step out in the hallway and make a couple of calls. I'll be right back. Now don't go anywhere!" She joked.

"Helene," she said when her friend answered. "It's me, Clare."

"Silly, I know it's you. I'm glad you got in okay—early, from what you told me. How does your mom seem?"

"Kinda hard to understand, but she's at least awake after all these weeks. Fragile, but with us. I really owe you for taking care of her."

"It's only been a week."

"Seems like a month. I promise you some special treats to make up for this."

"You don't owe me anything. You'd do the same if I needed it. You know the code to get in my condo development." Clare clicked off the call feeling a little guilty about Helene's last statement. The way her world was moving, she might not be around to help with Helene's family. Unless they wanted to come visit her on the mountain. More and more, she felt like it was her home now.

She tried to reach Tony, but his voicemail answered, so she let him know she'd arrived okay and spoken with her mother and seen her awake for the first time.

She returned to her mother's room in time to see an older gentleman emerge.

"I'm from Our Lady of Grace church," the man said when she arrived at the door as he was walking through it. "I just brought her Communion. We heard that she'd revived. I know you are happy she is back with us!"

Clare again reckoned with the church life of her mother. She had been a stalwart of the volunteers, so no mystery here. And it was a kind of resurrection for Frankie. Clare thanked him, and he left.

Frankie was lying back in her bed now as if ready to sleep. Angela, her long-gone sister, came to mind. Where in the world was she, and why hadn't they heard from her in all these years? Was she still alive? She decided that Angela, even if she were found, may not want to know about her family. But she should know. Clare made a note to look up Angela Connor in the search engines on the web.

Clare cradled her mom's head in her arms and put a kiss on her cheek.

"I hope you sleep well, Mom. I'll see you in the morning. I'm so glad you're back." Frankie's eyes fluttered.

"I love you, Mom."

"Yu yu."

The words sounded strange to Clare. She didn't hear them that much from Frankie. But then she hadn't told Frankie often of her love for her. Clare touched the blue flower-flocked gown on the shoulder. There was the baby powder smell again.

Clare left to drive to Helene's, not so far from the nursing home. As she felt in her bag for her keys, she brushed the change purse that held a small white envelope, so small it was able to nest there almost unnoticed. It was the key to her mother's safe deposit box at the bank near her house on Melanie Street. All her mother's documents were there.

"Maybe I won't need those anytime soon." she told herself.

"Clare! Wake up!" Just before this, Clare was in the middle of a dream about Angela and her in her mother's house arguing over a little wreath her mother had made for the May crowning at her church. Every early May, special services and processions were held involving the children at the parochial school associated with the church. The girls wore white dresses and carried flowers, and the boys wore dark pants and white shirts. The highlight was the youngest girl accompanied by the youngest boy laying the crown on the statue of Our Lady in the courtyard. Always, Frankie made a crown using muscadine vines soaked in the tub and then dried and wound into a tight crown filled with flowers from her yard. In Clare's dream, Angela and she each had one end of a small crown, and they were yelling and pulling at it.

"It's mine! "

"No, it's mine!" Then Helene's nudge to wake her. Dawn light behind the curtains

"Angel's Arms called. Your mother has fallen into a coma again. They've moved her to the hospital up the street."

Clare rose, threw on some clothes, and Helene greeted her with a cup of coffee.

"Be careful. You're not quite awake!"

Clare nodded her head.

"I'll just take a few minutes to drink this." She looked at Helene, who stood with a very worried look on her face. "I didn't expect this."

"I know." Helene put her arm around her. "My guess is she's not going to come back from this. I've seen some people who are gravely ill make a big improvement. They rally and then, poof, they're gone. I don't know if it's to give us our last moments with them or what."

Clare gave her a hug. "Thanks, Helene."

"I'm going to drive over there to be with you."

"You're such a friend, and I'm grateful."

Driving to her mother's home two days later, Clare felt relief and tension. She'd rushed to the hospital, found her mother in a hospital bed with tubes reattached all over, where she seemed to slumber solidly. The nurses explained that Frankie had slipped into a full coma and was not likely to revive. Clare asked about the prognosis, and they described a vegetative state that would not be relieved. They asked if Clare wanted to continue the hydration and feeding. Sadly, Clare said no, because her wishes were to not be resuscitated if she was near death.

They helped Clare fill out papers and moved her to a hospice unit of the hospital on the next floor. Helene was with her through the decisions, then left to go to work. After that, Clare and Helene took turns being with her, except overnight, when Clare spent the night in a lounge chair in her room. A nurse would come in and check filtration bags and advise that there would be a progression over a few days, that gradually kidneys failed, and that usually brought the end.

There were no big events, except that a young Filipino priest came to deliver the Last Rites. Clare and Helene searched on their laptops for Angela Connor, first in Florida, and then in all states, but they found no public records.

On the morning of the second day, the nurses told her that her vitals showed the end was near. They left Clare alone as she lay next to her mother in the hospice bed. She held Frankie in her arms as she labored with her last breaths. Clare pulled her to her, then heard what sounded like a straw pulling air from the bottom of a nearly empty milkshake cup. Then Frankie was still. As she lay with Frankie against her, stiff and all signs of life going, Clare felt a warmth invade her own chest and arms. She stayed like this for a while, then pulled herself away from her mother's body and called the nurse.

Now entering her mother's house, she looked for an outfit to clothe her in for the funeral. She had visited the funeral home to select a casket and funeral package. All the while, that heat, a kind of buzz, filled her body. At the meeting with the undertaker, she wrote out pieces of an obituary for the newspaper announcement, to be carried in the paper the day of the funeral, she understood, though she doubted she'd see the paper. She no longer had a home, least of all home delivery. She paused when she listed her name and Willie's with hers. She included Angela's name, wondering where in the world she was, or if she was still alive.

She walked into the dining room of the old house and was struck by the smells of old things piled undisturbed for a while. The light through the windows, covered in sheers, made the room luminous. Light reflected off little statues and porcelain flowers perched on the dining room buffet, the bookshelves, and windowsills. Clare sat down at that dining table still littered with business forms, junk mail, and various bits of her mother's life. Her eye rested on a clear plastic-topped box about the size of a candy gift box, resting half-covered under an old newspaper section.

She pulled the box out and saw to her amazement that it was one of the wreaths she dreamed about, fighting with Angela, just when Helene woke her two days ago. It was lying half-covered in sand inside the box. Clare removed the plastic cover so that the white cardboard box was exposed. She looked at dried roses, lilies, and other smaller flowers perfectly preserved in the crown. Clare could picture her mother winding and winding the vines into the small, thick wreath no bigger than five inches across on the inside, and then inserting the live flowers—reds, yellows, pinks, blues—to create the full, flowering headpiece. She could picture it on the chalk white statue in the courtyard between the church and the school where the May procession took place. She'd been part of it when she was younger, year after year, walking in line with the other girls, singing in celebration.

> Bring flowers of the fairest
> Bring flowers of the rarest
> From garden and woodland
> And hillside and vale.

Clare fingered the delicate flowers, saw her mother again cut them, trim them, and place their stems between the spirals of muscadine vine she so carefully wrapped. She thought of her own hydrangeas and roses back on Reidinger Drive. How she missed them! Now the buzz that had been in her body grew stronger, as though there was a presence in her body. There was an eerie slant to the sun through the curtains, like there were waves in the sunlight. Her own love of plants and flowers melded with her mother's. Even though Frankie was not her mother, the Italian sense of beauty and care for growing things leapt across generations, across family lines, and

Frankie and Clare and Tony and all were one. Clare felt the electric charge in her body recede for the first time since she held Frankie as she passed. Tears rimmed her eyes, then fell on the table in front of her. She put the wreath down, stretched out her arms, put her head down, and let go, crying.

"Mom, I'm so lonely," she cried. "There's only me now."

She didn't have to be anywhere, take care of anyone now. The tears flowed.

When she finally felt finished, Clare went to her mother's closet to se-lect an outfit for her burial. As she pushed hangers holding plastic-covered clothes, she thought about her own need for clothes for the funeral. That meant she'd need to go to Reidinger Drive. Today was Sunday, and Willie would be at home. She wasn't ready to see him. There was something hol-low in her when she thought of the man who had kicked her out. She was compelled to leave the city, and she missed being with her mother in her last days. She'd had few options, and he'd had a great many, yet she she'd had to go to the mountains.

She breathed deep and hard several times to clear her head, reclaim some calm. It was just her now. No more of the Connor family. She slowly pulled her phone from her bag.

"Helene, would you do me a favor? Would you call Willie and ask him to let me have the house alone for a few minutes this afternoon?"

"Sure. Anything else?"

Almost without thinking, Clare said, "Tell him to clear out the dancing girls!"

Helene laughed, and said she'd call her back to make sure the coast was clear. "That business of the late hours and strange calls still bothering you, isn't it?"

"I guess it is, since it just jumped out of my mouth."

"Why don't you track the house phone calls in case he's slipping up and using it. A repeated phone number at times he's home—it'll show up."

"We let the caller ID go last year when we wanted to save on all our tech expenses."

"Well, then, that might not work," Helene said. She clicked off.

Clare looked at her cell phone and did a search for the phone company. She called up to see if she could restore the old phone plan with caller ID. She could, and so she did.

"Why didn't I think of that before?" she asked the sheer curtains in her mother's dining room.

Clare sipped on a latte at a coffee bar near her old home, waiting for Helene to call her back. She looked out at skies that had cleared as though the storms she drove through the night before didn't happen.

"You're good to go," Helene said when she called. "He asked about your mother's arrangements."

"Feel free to give them to him."

"I'll see you tomorrow, but don't forget to call me if you need anything."

Clare drove to Reidinger Drive and pulled in with the car's front next to the garage. As she got out of the car, she saw across the street a shade quickly drawing closed in one of the front windows. She grasped in her memory for the neighbors' name. Travis and Lela Tremont. And their teenagers.

She was just entering the front hall when the phone rang.

"Hello?" The empty hall echoed with her voice. A giggle, then a snort. Then a hang-up.

This time, instead of dread and fear, Clare felt energized.

Now she could see the phone number. The 770 prefix was typical for the outer Perimeter area. The next three numbers matched the exchanges in the north Atlanta suburbs around her. So it was probably a landline and not too far away. She'd learned that with a landline, at least with older ones, there's a series of telephone exchanges that were originally serviced by a telephone company switching station in a given area. Just some of the trivia her job-coaching strategies had turned up. When looking for ways to contact people who don't necessarily want to be found, telephone exchanges provided a clue.

Clare went upstairs to her office. There was dust on her desk and across her computer keys. It had been a while. It all looked so foreign to her now, and the self that used to bang out resumes and whiz through data files and job postings seemed a stranger to her. She turned on the computer, let it warm quickly, entered her password, and did a reverse phone number search. Just as she'd begun to suspect, the number belonged to the Tremont family.

Clare flew across the street and rang the doorbell. At first, no one answered. She repeated the rings, then knocked, hard and loud.

"Hello, anyone home?" She yelled loud so the other houses might hear her. She was going to get this tended to and in earshot of the other neighbors if need be.

The door opened a little, and Clare saw an orange head belonging to a teenaged girl peering through.

"Tell me why you are calling me and hanging up!" Clare said. The door started to close.

"Who is it? Is it one of Mom's friends?" a voice yelled from behind the door.

The door opened wider.

"C-come in," a young girl in a black t-shirt advertising Twenty One Pilots said, her hands clinging to the edge of the door.

Clare stepped inside and glared at the girl.

"I didn't mean any harm," the carrot head said. Clare looked at the heavy black eyeliner and other overdone makeup and decided the hair color, actually it was two shades of orange, was too freaky to be natural.

"Why are you calling my house?" Clare asked in a voice she knew was shrill.

"We were just trying to prank you," the flame-headed girl said. Another teen, younger, emerged from behind her. Her hair was royal blue. She approached cautiously, kind of sideways with her head bent.

"Do you have any idea what worry you caused?"

"Were you scared he was stepping out on you?" the older one challenged, tossing her bangs. "That's what we thought would be fun, create mayhem."

"Why on earth would you want to do that?" Clare stood in a foyer, with an elegantly furnished living room just beyond.

"It's fun to disrupt. Our parents' marriage is breaking up. So why not watch others come undone, too?" Flamehead smirked, her kohl-lined eyes wide. "Happened to us. Maybe we could watch it happen to someone else."

"Do you know how totally screwed up that sounds?" Clare protested.

"Where have you been? Did you move out? Guess it's working, huh?"

Clare wanted to hit someone. She would have loved to grab the orange or blue hair or both, pull on it to make them yell.

A heaviness draped across her body. The girls' cruelty stirred her old feelings of worthlessness.

"Why are you doing this?" Her voice sounded shrill as the words came out. "Is it fun to see more misery when you're miserable?" Unable to stand, she sat on the stairs going up to their second floor.

She saw the blue-haired girl's face distort, and then tears rolled down her perfect-skinned cheeks. The orange head hung her head and averted her eyes.

"Our dad's got an apartment, and he and Mom are getting a divorce," moaned the older girl. "We might not get to stay here when the house sells. We'll lose our school and all our friends. We're in clubs and everything. It really sucks!" She put her head on the stair rail near Clare.

"I agree," Clare said. "Change like that really sucks. Tell me about it!"

Clare stood and put her hand out to the orange head. "How about you help me keep things together and don't make those phone calls? You help me, and I'll try to help you with your problem. I can't promise anything, but you can come over and hang out with me when I'm here."

Now the orange top was crying. The girls' tears became noisy snivels. Clare reached to a nearby tissue box from a table in the foyer to hand them.

"You know there's a rule: Only one divorce or separation going on at a time on Reidinger Drive." She smiled at the blue-haired girl, trying to buck up her spirits.

"No more calls. Then you come over in a couple of days to just chill out. Deal?" She put her hand out again.

The flame head shook it, then the blue head shook it.

"Okay, on top of all of this, my mother died, and I need to get clothes to wear to the funeral. Promise me you're not going to call when I'm in there getting clothes?"

"Promise."

"I promise."

"Good. I'm going to come over and talk with your mom and you as soon as I get the funeral over with. Just don't make any of these prank calls. Think of something you can do to make life easier for your mom. It really sucks that your lives are turned upside down now. But she really needs you."

A part of Clare's riddle was solved. So they were trying to create mayhem in her life—and they did it. She thought about warming their bottoms but decided that was unrealistic. She'd call Lela Tremont after the funeral. In the meantime, maybe the girls would give all their intended targets a breather.

The room was hushed, the sounds of voices of about twenty adults muffled by thick carpeting throughout the rooms, rooms that seemed to flow continuously, one after the other, with no end. Monday night, Clare walked into the parlor and straight to her mother's bier, set at the right end of the second room. The shine of the metal in the casket caught her eye. There were large funeral sprays of lovely red roses set in thick greenery on either side of the casket.

Clare was shocked at seeing her mother, so alive just yesterday, so still in the coffin. Frankie looked wooden, but light shone around her. The casket lining of soft white satin was echoed in the chalky streaks in her mother's hair. She was dressed in the two-piece royal blue outfit she had chosen. Clare couldn't deal with the hands. They were so absolutely stiff, and she always remembered her mother as busy, making lists, working at the store, ironing and carefully folding linens. The stilled hands meant she was gone.

Frankie's makeup, although she rarely wore makeup, had been applied well, and her cheeks had just enough rouge to highlight her nice cheekbones without being laughable.

"I'd like to work with the dead."

A slow-talking woman's statement sounded in Clare's mind like it was yesterday. She'd been leading a workshop in the south metro area, a phone company facility where the employees were being offered career assessment workshops, counseling, and generous tuition grants to help them move from jobs that would soon be no more due to technology changes. So she asked the class to reflect on their values, their personal goals, and some possible career choices. A young woman had come up with the working with the dead.

"My grandpa has a mortuary, and I sometimes help him," she said. "I like doin their hair and makeup and making them look soooo pretty." Clare had reflected on that as one of the most unusual career goals she'd ever heard, but she saw the young woman had a strong spiritual connection. It was like making a lady or man beautiful for meeting God was the holiest thing a person could do. Clare proceeded to help her draw up a plan focusing on cosmetology and mortician training.

A young priest approached Frankie's coffin, prayed at a kneeler there, then rose and greeted Clare, holding out his hand.

"I'm Father Doran," he said. "You must be Clare." She'd called the church office about the funeral and spoke on the phone to an office person who helped her with funeral Mass details. It was clear Frankie was well-known at church, and the church wanted to show its respect at her passing by assuring a nice farewell.

"I am, Father. Thank you for all your visits to my mother. It meant a great deal to her."

"If you have time after rosary tonight, let's sit together and talk so I'll have your thoughts on what I say tomorrow."

"Sure, Father. Uh, Father?"

"Yes?"

"I don't have rosary beads. Do you have a spare by any chance?"

"Here, use mine. I'm able to keep up without them."

He put in Clare's hands a set made of olive wood.

"I'll be sure to return them. They look very special."

"They are. But so are you and your need for prayer in the loss of your mother."

He turned to another parishioner, a thin lady with white, carefully curled hair. "You may know Mrs. Lindsay. The two of them took care of all our altar linens."

Clare took Mrs. Lindsay's hand, and the smaller lady pulled her to her shoulder with a strong arm for a hug.

"I'm so sorry about your mother," she said. "We had so many talks while we laid out the altar cloths and lavabo towels and the other items. About what God had waiting for us after He called us home. I know she is happy to be in heaven with your father."

Clare's stomach felt tight at the thought. That assumed Paul made it to heaven. That really would be an interesting scene, and she wasn't sure she wanted to be there. That the two ladies talked about this spoke to the longing her mother had for her Final Reward, and how her life on earth was only a matter of marking time. In all her years serving the church, she'd apparently not shared her husband's betrayal with anyone, and that made Clare sadder than before. How long had she been waiting for her transition to heaven—all her life? Clare would never know.

She first noticed the posture, the dark suit top and pants, unfamiliar garb on a familiar body. He was standing in a corner where there were a number of flower arrangements not far from a couch. He was a little slumped, but she recognized the hair and face. He pulled up straighter when she saw him.

"I'm sorry, Clare." Willie looked at her with hurt in his eyes. She could tell he'd been drinking. And not sleeping a lot.

"I'm sorry, too, that you didn't get to see her awake there at the end. It didn't last long. But she did ask about you."

He looked at her woefully. "At least you got to see her."

"The only few hours she was most like herself for the last two months. Then gone—so fast, like lightning. Tonight, the casket, I can't believe that's her."

She was surprised at how loquacious she was with Willie. He probably wasn't comprehending much.

"Gimme a hug," he said, his eyes dark with tears, and reached an arm toward her.

The bile in her throat rose, not from anger, but from nervousness. What should she do? For the first time, Willie was chastened by his loss of her. He was sad, he wanted contact with her. She still wasn't sure how she felt. She was not ready to open any doors right now. He had thrown her out.

"I appreciate you wanting to hug me, but I need some time. It's a strange time for me." He didn't react too much, just lightly touched her on the arm and walked away.

She still thought he was handsome, even if he didn't look his best, even if he tried to get too close to her.

Clare went to her purse, pulled out the rosary beads, and moved toward the main parlor where people were gathering around Father Doran.

# Chapter 12

TUESDAY

A light rain fell the Tuesday morning of Frankie's burial. Clare greeted a few people outside the church and started to go in, when she decided to linger in the church's vestibule to wait for Helene and her family. She had called Tony the night her mother died and expected him and Silvia to arrive also. She wasn't sure she would be able to go through more of the goodbye to her mother. Again she thought of Tony's revelation on her way down from the mountain that evening in the rain—so long ago, it seemed, even though it had only been Thursday.

The brick, 1920s-era church reflected the centuries-old tradition of a small, low vestibule to enhance churchgoers' sense of wonder and awe from the openness and spaciousness of lofty ceilings and high stained-glass windows once they entered the sanctuary. Clare pulled open the heavy door to the holy space and breathed in the familiar smell of stone and wood and slight mold. All those years of kneeling in the pews, gazing at the jeweled colors in the stained glass depicting the incidents in Christ's life. Always she wondered about the family names inscribed in white scrolls at the bottom of the stained-glass windows. Who were the people, and how did they have the funds to purchase such luxuries as windows imported from Italy? Those had to be families of substance, not like her own.

She saw the same statues, including the darling Infant of Prague with its tiny cloak with colored stones that changed with the seasons. Mary was still there on the left. St. Joseph on the right. And a wall of beautiful flowers of every description filled in between. If flowers were a sign of love, then Frankie Connor was much loved by this parish of believers.

Clare returned outside to the vestibule. Posters for upcoming services, the weekly church bulletin, and advertisements for an upcoming choral concert benefiting a mission in Jamaica filled a bulletin board. Another board with similar announcements in Spanish hung adjacent to the first one.

"Clare!" She heard a familiar voice.

"Tony," she exclaimed, as she saw Tony wheeling himself toward her from the side handicapped entrance. His hair was slicked back, and he wore a dark blazer over summer weight pants. Coming behind him through the narrow passageway was a shapely blond woman of about 55 or 60, and she wore an immaculate gray linen suit.

"Clare," the woman said, "I'm Silvia. I'm so sorry about the loss of your mother."

She embraced Clare, then pulled back. "But I'm glad to finally meet you—Tony's sister."

"Half-sister," Clare automatically corrected. But she looked at both of them gratefully.

"It's so good to have family here with me!"

A few others gathered around, but Clare decided she needed to talk to Tony and Silvia first.

"I've spotted a small alcove over here. Let's go talk before the service begins."

"How is Willie—have you seen him?" Tony asked, once they were off the hall. Clare felt a cloud cover her chest, a slowing in the excitement she'd felt on seeing the two.

"He actually came by the funeral home last night—pretty obviously he'd been drinking.

He wanted to hug me. But I'm not ready yet. I don't know how I feel."

Her glum feeling shifted.

"But I did find out where all those mysterious phone calls were coming from!"

"Let me guess—you finally figured out it's telemarketers hanging up!"

"No, my neighbor's teenaged kids were deliberately pranking me, calling just when I got home, and before Willie arrived every other night. Seems were in pain and wanted to inflict some more. I saw signs of life next door just as I arrived at my house Sunday night after Mom died. Let's just say I took care of that issue. So, no woman on the side, though that still leaves unexplained late arrivals."

"Come here," Tony said, and reached out his hand. Clare moved to him. Silvia stood on Tony's other side with her hand on his shoulder.

"You're my little sister. You and I have gone through a lot these last few days to know who we are to each other." He smiled warmly. "You were born in a sad situation that became better when you entered the world, odd though your family turned out to be. I know how quickly things can change at any moment in life." He shifted a little in his wheelchair.

"Look at me." She looked in his dark eyes, the eyes that had seen so much of her lately. "A crane came crashing down and my life was changed forever. Something just as devastating could happen in your life. If you knew that, how would you be living now? You don't have forever. If you really understood that, how would you be treating Willie now?" Clare sensed the deep caring her cousin was showing.

"Here's another thing—a guy reaches a point when he is ready to have children and devote himself to his family. If it's not you, Willie will find someone else. How will you feel about that?"

Tony looked at her deeply and went silent. Silvia moved over and put an arm around her while touching Tony's hand on the wheelchair.

Clare felt her eyes swell and tears rimming them, then slowly making their way down her cheeks. She started to mentally beat herself for not thinking to bring tissue. Tony whipped out a large cotton handkerchief and handed it to her.

"I'm just so confused right now. I miss my mom. I wish she was here so I could talk to her." She pulled the white square to her face.

Silvia brought her closer and placed Clare's head on her shoulder, her low voice murmuring to her.

"We're your family, Clare. We're here for you."

Tony squeezed her hand. The sound of steps and low conversation, mourners filling the vestibule, rose outside the alcove.

Silvia turned Clare's face to her and used the handkerchief to dry off the tears.

"Here's my compact. Fix your face a little, then let's go be with the others. Keep the hanky."

A dozen people came up to Clare as she walked through the hallway. All spoke of how much they admired her mother and missed her. They were a blur to Clare. Light filled the area when the funeral director opened the large front doors to the church, and her mother's casket was brought in, still wearing a huge spray of red roses Clare had ordered. The spray was moved to a stand to go in the church, and a white cloth, representing the purity of spirit gained at her mother's baptism, was laid across the casket. When all were seated in the church, Clare, Silvia, and Tony followed the wheeled bier to the altar, then moved to a pew on the left just below the pulpit.

On the aisle side, the pew was a little shorter than the rest behind it, allowing for Tony's mobile chair to be placed near Clare and Silvia.

Willie's mother, Grace, her dark blond hair cut short and sporting fresh highlights, appeared with Dan, and the two sat behind her. She wore a black dress with pearls, and Dan, silver-haired and one and a half times the size of Grace, wore a dark suit. What should she do about Willie? She looked around for him.

Almost as soon as she thought about him, he appeared in the church aisle at her left, genuflecting deeply, then joining her in the pew. She smiled, grateful to not have their separation be so obvious right now. He reached his hand to her, and she took it.

"Thank you for coming," she said.

Grace inched up to Clare from behind and whispered in her ear.

"I realize the church will have a reception here, but I'd like us all to go out afterwards for a drink if you're up to it," she said.

"We'll just wait and see how you're doing," Grace added helpfully.

During the service, Clare heard Grace whispering to Dan to stand or sit when the rest of the congregation did so at different times in the Mass. Dan whispered objections. Then she clearly heard Grace tell Dan:

"Because it's respectful to God and Clare, that's why!"

Clare was with family now. She thought about that fact, smiled a little, and then a lot.

Here was Willie, still her husband, who almost wasn't. *We still don't know about that, do we?* On the other side of her, Silvia, her half-brother Tony's wife, and then Tony himself. Tony, who'd once been a perfect stranger and who she felt closer to now than to most anyone. Helene and her sister were just behind her in second pew, not far from Grace and Dan. And Frankie, lying in the casket? She was gone, but Clare felt her spirit still present. She *was* her mother. Lucia, the birth mother, the one who actually conceived her by sinning with her father, and then giving her up to be raised by her father's wife, Frankie, was almost a fantasy person. And Frankie did it without ever telling what her sister had done, as far as Clare knew.

Father Doran was speaking from the pulpit now about her mother and about what she was enjoying in heaven. Clare had attended a few funerals over the years, and she'd begun to see that in Christian burials, anyway, there was a lot of emphasis on what the person's life could teach those in the pews about Christ's messages to all. So there weren't any endearing episodes from Father about Frankie personally, even though she'd given him a few at his request at the funeral home. Rather, Frankie's life showed "The fruit of the Spirit."

"The fruit of the Spirit is love, joy, peace, patience, kindness, generosity, faithfulness, gentleness, self-control," Father intoned, quoting from St. Paul to the Galatians.

If Frankie had not had self-control, Clare did not know what she had. Love, joy, peace, patience—she had those, too, in spades. What power there was in Frankie that she could have all those qualities!

As the Mass continued and focused on the consecration and Communion, Clare began feeling a warming again, much like when she'd left the mountain to come to her mother's bedside. It was an intense zing all over her body that did not seem to let up. And with it a realization of the gift of her mother to her: an example of how she, Clare, could be. Not laundering and ironing the linens every Sunday like Frankie, but in her everyday life. Patient, loving, joyful, gentle.

The irony was that if Willie had never kicked her out, she'd never have known the truth about her mother's sacrifice in raising her as her own. She'd likely never met Tony, or at least not well enough for all the beans about her real mother to be spilled.

Throughout the Mass, Clare's mind bounced from Willie beside her to her mother's life and all it had meant. Then it ran over to Tony on her right whose damaged body spoke volumes about his patience and faith.

The graveside service was carried out with dignity, but it did not take long, as the light rain was continuing. Clare sat with Willie, Tony, Silvia, Helene and her sister next to the deep hole with Frankie's rose-bedecked casket hovering on a metal frame above. Fake grass covered the pile of dirt to the side, and more flowers from the church were laid atop that. Clare heard the priest's words:

> In sure and certain hope of the resurrection to eternal life through
> Our Lord Jesus Christ,
> we commend to Almighty God, Frankie Connor,
> and we commit her body to the ground.

This was what it was all about. Thou art dust and to dust thou shalt return. She was surprised how that passage from scripture jumped into her mind. It was as though her early education was just yesterday. The statement said that this life was so basic. Dirt. What we're made from. What we become. Except for our spirit continuing and that promise of resurrection. No, not promise, hope, the priest said. And the hope was dependent upon our right actions here on earth, she knew. She was trying her best to do the right thing for her mother.

The brilliant green of the carpet of artificial grass over the mound of dirt caught the light of the sun, now suddenly peeking from behind clouds.

Clare wondered what she would feel as the coffin was lowered in that big hole. But now it appeared there was no plan to lower it, at least right now. Father asked if anyone had any closing words before leaving. Clare was unable to speak. If she did, she might fall into that grave, so heavy were her many thoughts.

Clare felt a motion at her side. Willie was moving to the foot of the casket, turning to the group sitting and standing nearby. He wiped his eye with a handkerchief. He pulled himself erect and looked directly at Clare.

"I love my wife," he said. Then his gaze went to the casket, and he put his hand out to the foot of the metal vault. "And I loved my mother-in-law, Frankie."

He lifted his head.

"She had true beauty, though she did not enhance it or try to not look her age, as so many of us do. She made the best bread of anyone. All the wonderful things I think of when I think of Italy came from her—a love of flowers, a way with tomatoes in her small garden, pasta and sauce that would rival anything in Europe. A love of God that I don't think any of us could come close to. Everything I love about her daughter, I loved about Frankie."

Clare couldn't have been more shocked at the things he mentioned, especially her cooking. She'd wondered if it ever made a difference to him.

"Until we know we are about to lose something, we don't know its value. That is certainly true of me."

He paused. The handkerchief came up to his eye again. It wasn't a dramatic move, just an efficient one to give him time to speak further.

"I didn't get to spend time with Frankie at the end. I didn't get to tell her goodbye, and now I know the importance of doing that with someone. It's critical that we do that with each other. Tell each other how much they mean to us. Now. We don't know if we'll have tomorrow.

"I'm sorry Frankie has left us. But I know she will be looking down and watching over us as we go through our lives. At least that is my prayer. Thank you for coming today to help us celebrate her life."

Willie walked back to her side, looking sadly at Clare as he retook his seat. There was a strong heat again spreading over Clare's body. It was like that warming in the church, a suffusion all over her body, a blooming, with flashes of heat rapidly spreading to her arms, legs, trunk, fingers.

Willie had spoken honestly. From the heart. It was one of the few times she remembered him doing that. Maybe five times in their five years had he talked on such a deep emotional level. Like he did the night they first made love. It didn't happen often, but it did happen, as it did today. They would need to talk.

The funeral party adjourned, and they stood. Willie turned to her, put his arms around her, and pulled her to him. She felt his body shaking, as tears probably came. Her own tears were on the edge of her eyes. She put her arms around him. His smell and his touch and the way she fit in his shoulder, his body molded to hers, was familiar. She felt comforted.

Clare stepped back, moved to the frame holding Frankie's coffin, and put her fingernail in a rose that lay across the large box and snapped it off. She needed something for the journey.

Clare could see how uncomfortable Dan was at the bereavement dinner, which consisted of long tables laid out with cold cuts, casseroles, salads, and desserts. The church hall was filled with light, but with utilitarian folding chairs set at tables covered with cloths. The dinner seemed like it was something quite beneath his style. He didn't exactly have his nose in the air, but he held his plate a little above his waist, and, yes, he did look down at the chicken salad. And he turned some of the meats over with the serving fork as though looking for worms or dirt.

I wonder if he has any idea of what it takes to put together a dinner like this, Clare thought. *Probably not the first clue.*

But she found herself not trying to judge even Dan. If he was uncomfortable, that was that. She couldn't do anything to make it different.

Grace asked all those around Clare if they would like to adjourn after the dinner to DiMaggio's in Buckhead for a drink. Helene and Amanda, her sister, begged off. Tony and Silvia did also, leaving from the church for North Georgia, hoping to get ahead of heavy traffic up I-75. That left Dan and Grace and Willie and Clare.

Clare saw the choice of the elegant Italian restaurant and bar as another gesture from Grace toward her. Her mother-in-law was inserting her choices more vigorously than Clare could recall—at least in matters concerning her, Clare.

Willie drove in his car, Clare drove in her escape wagon, and Willie's parents arrived in their large white Mercedes. They gathered in the foyer, a large entry with white-and-black checked, polished stone floors. The waiters wore dark pants or skirts and white shirts open at the collar—very Italian looking. The bar was expansive and filled with sparkling bottles of an endless variety of liquor and other libations. They sat at a booth near the mirror-backed bar. It didn't take Dan long after they sat down to begin drinking heavily, running a long tab, while Willie nursed a single beer and his mother asked for a glass of white wine. Almost as soon as they'd gone into Dan's second round, Willie's cell phone rang, and he left to talk to the caller.

"You know, that's the first time I've been to a mackerel snapper church," Dan said, leaning toward Clare across the table of the booth. "That's what we called Cathlics when I was growing up. Did you know that?"

"Yes, that's the phrase a Baptist preacher from our neighborhood dropped on us every time he came in my mother's store," Clare said. *What was he trying to tell her?* She knew. She let it pass.

"Of course, I wasn't excited about Willie marrying a Cathlic. Felt like it was beneath him," Dan said, his words slurring slightly. "We were taught not to associate with em where I came from."

"I imagine South Georgia had its set of likes and dislikes," Clare said coolly.

"Naw, it wasn't from being from South Georgia. It was true of Atlanta, too."

"Yes, if I'm not mistaken, the modern-day Ku Klux Klan got its start here," Clare said, watching Dan flinch. "Actually, from their headquarters in an old Atlanta hotel, I understand that the KKK leaders pioneered the idea of a nationwide franchise, sending their robes and hoods all over the country so people from Portland, Maine to Portland, Oregon could be outfitted correctly and have all kinds of hate literature to draw from."

Clare heard Grace's intake of breath. She didn't care. She was not going to be bullied by Dan. She remembered her lessons from the nuns about KKK history. That and her own reading.

"They targeted blacks, Jews, Catholics, Italians, Syrians, anybody of a different hue," Clare continued, her skin warm.

Dan showed no awareness of her comment. Deep in his drink, he began talking again.

Blathering like his son had some days ago, Clare recognized.

"Of course, when all this credit card identity theft and this extra mortgage showed up, I encouraged him to ditch you quick. Bad for business!" Clare heard Grace gasp on the other side of Dan, but she looked at him, waiting for more. Her ears and her face burned. He was admitting trying to bust up her marriage.

"Yeah, and I put him in touch with my lawyer—"

"Dad, you need to shut up!" Willie came up, slid next to Clare and looked in his father's eyes as well.

"Well, she was likely going to go for everything you—and me—had, son," Dan said, unapologetic, his mouth slack.

"So just cool it, Dad. There's been enough trouble. We've been through a lot. We don't even have a good idea of what has happened and why. But I'm guessing it had less to do with Clare than you thought."

Clare watched, amazed that Willie faced his father down.

"I love Clare. She's my life. You need to get your own life. Leave me to mine."

Clare looked at Dan and Grace. Dan was looking down at his drink, now a chaser of bourbon whiskey after the beers he'd consumed. Grace had an angry look on her face, but she was controlling it, trying to keep it from showing.

"I need to go to the ladies," Clare said, lightly nudging Willie to move. Her body was foreign, like it didn't belong to her. When she stood, her legs were unsteady.

"Me, too," said Grace.

"I'm sorry Dan is drunk," Grace said as they walked.

"I've seen him tipsy, but not like this," Clare said.

Later, as Clare was washing her hands, Grace came up and put her hands on her shoulders. Her mother-in-law grabbed with strength Clare didn't recognize.

"I don't want you to be thrown off by what Dan said," she said, looking in Clare's eyes in the mirror. "Yet, I can't tell you that he didn't do the things he said he did. He does things he thinks are justified business-wise, and he often works in ways that don't show a lot of human compassion. That's the way he works. But he does love you, just as I do."

Clare's stomach churned. She found that hard to believe of Dan. She turned around and put her hands on Grace's upper arms.

"I would have to see some different ways of acting before I could believe that about your husband," Clare said.

"He treated Willie in ways I am ashamed of," Grace said. "But he would tell me how proud he was of him, not that Willie got a clue, from the way he acted. After a while, Willie figured it out, I think. He learned to wait for the compliments that finally came."

"The recent moves do not endear me to Dan," Clare said. "And I don't think Willie's as sure of his father's love as you think."

Grace's eyes dimmed, and her smile contracted.

"We live in an alcoholic home," she said slowly. "Things aren't normal. They're often unpredictable. But we're doing the best we can."

Her eyes lit up a little, and she squeezed Clare's shoulders. "Your mom's gone, and I'm sorry. I know you'll miss her. I hope you'll let us be your family. We love you, we really do."

Clare lightly squeezed her mother-in-law's upper arms. She liked Grace. "Thanks."

"You know, I came from a very rough background growing up. I never was sure we'd have a roof over our heads. My father was an awful drunk. My mother had to work extremely hard."

"Willie's told me. I know that was tough going for you."

"The one thing I told myself is that my life would be very different." She laughed softly. "Well, it was and it wasn't. Never have to worry about a roof, but I wonder about our sanity sometimes! Would my mother laugh if she saw me. Married to an alcoholic like my dad." She smiled.

"What helps me is if I remember what's really important. Dan will let me drive home from here. If he remembers anything of what he has said, tomorrow he'll be all apologetic. It may not be a very pretty apology, but there'll be shame about hurting you. He really does think you're good for Willie."

They walked back to the booth. Grace was smiling and her back was straight. Clare's thoughts flipped from anger at Dan to gratitude for his wife.

"We think you have a good wife, Willie. And we wish you both good luck," Grace said. Willie put his arm around Clare as she slid into her seat.

"If Clare wants me back, I want to be with her. And I want us to have kids." Clare leaned back from Willie and looked at him.

"First time I've heard you say that."

Willie looked in her eyes.

"I'm a deep guy. You just don't know that."

Clare smiled. This was getting interesting. The idea of having a baby seemed out of the question, given what had happened in the last two weeks. But this was the first positive move in that direction Willie had made. Clare looked at Grace. She had her head down a little bit, but she was smiling broadly. Dan continued to look at his drink. A man with a problem with one son who also had a big problem. And Willie had the tendencies, too. She still wasn't sure about their relationship, so decisions like a baby were way down the road. But she was glad to hear him looking toward the future.

Clare returned to Helene's to spend the night. She had told Willie she would meet him the next day at the police department. Helene and Clare talked late into the evening sitting on her couch.

"The lady we buried today—Frankie—was not my birth mother," Clare told her. "Frankie raised me from when I was a newborn. My father, Paul, was an alcoholic like his father for many years when they lived in Trenton. He and my aunt, Tony's mother, had a brief affair, and I was the result."

Helen looked at her with her mouth open.

"So Tony is your half-brother, not just your cousin."

"True. So you see we white people can get all messed up, too," she said with a wink. "That's funny," Helen laughed. "And all of you strong Catholics, too. At least you were at one time."

"Remember you asked once if there was bipolar disease in the family? I think I found it, big time, at least on the Irish side. And maybe Mom's family, too."

"Well, that certainly explains a lot," Helene said. "What do you do with that info now?"

"Might explain why I felt I had to leave Willie rather than sticking up for myself and staying with it. Turns out his father was pulling strings behind the scenes, making Willie feel he had to kick me out. Father's not too happy with a Cathlic daughter-in-law. Thought he had to protect the family assets." She stirred the herbal tea Helene served her.

"One by one, the mysteries are being solved," Clare told her friend. "The little speech at the gravesite was a shock, I must say. And his taking up for me with his father—an even bigger shock."

Helene looked at her with her one eyebrow up.

"So you're going back to him?"

"Not yet. But I am thinking of Tony's words. How long am I going to stay in this state of not knowing about my relationship?"

"You started out pretty upset about the credit card and mortgage identity theft. Those are still on your plate, right?"

"Yeah. I hope Willie and I can talk about that tomorrow. He wants to meet. At home. I suggested we meet at the police department and try to find Detective Scott. See what he's found out."

"Even if that can be solved, there's still the late nights."

"I'm just going to have to ask him. Find out why it happens. At least now I know he appreciates the cooking and what I do for him. And he wants a baby, he said."

"That's big. How do you feel about that?"

"For once, I want to take time to think things through. It's too soon to talk about that, but I really do want to have kids someday and sooner rather than later. I really like kids. I'll have to tell you sometime about the young girl who lived in the trailer before the family moved."

"I thought you said they'd moved out, weren't there," Helene said, a big question on her face.

"They did, but I kept imagining what she must have been like, just from little things that were left, including her picture."

"Look, Clare, I had imaginary playmates as a child, too, but I left that looong time ago!" Helene said. They both laughed.

Clare emerged from her car just as Willie was pulling up in the parking lot of the police department. He got out of the car, came over to her, and embraced her, pulling her by the waist to his body.

"God, I miss you," he said in her ear.

She disentangled herself and straightened her top. She was dressed much more casually than he, still dipping into her duffle bag of clothes, deciding against the funeral clothes for this visit to Detective Scott.

"I miss you, too. But we have things to discuss before we go in. You should know by now that I did nothing intentional to create this credit card and mortgage mess."

"Okay, I believe you. But we gotta find out what the police have uncovered."

"You need to assure me it was none of your or your father's doing either."

"You thought I did something? How could you think that?" He sounded hurt.

"There were a lot of things not adding up. The credit card mess, the loan fraud. Phone calls from a woman hanging up just before you came home. I did, however, find out that we had some neighborhood kids pranking us, making those suspicious calls just before you came home."

"In our neighborhood?"

"Kept an eye out for when I was coming in and calling soon after. I've talked to them, so hopefully that's the end of that."

Willie put his arms under her arms and looked at her.

"You thought I did something? I thought you did something. Are we a mess or what?"

When they went in the enclosed area of the police detectives' area, Scott was just beginning his afternoon shift.

"Three to twelve," he grinned. "That's me! Gotta be available to contact all the leads—at home or local hangout, at night," he said. He showed them to the conference table where Clare had sat before.

"I guess you want to know what's happened with your case." Willie was looking around the room, taking in the awards on the wall, the desks and cubicles ringing around the room. Scott observed him and spoke quickly, trying to give a good impression to both of them. "I did contact the mailbox location in Tustin you looked up on the internet." He opened a manila folder on the table.

"The renter's information was bogus, so nothing there. That's part of the pattern. These crooks have it all worked out after doing it so many times. Someone steals the identity and sells it to someone else. Then that party uses the info to carry out the ATM thefts. As you showed, they even made a payment with a certified check from a bank somewhere in the Midwest—counterfeit even though certified."

Willie spoke up. "Don't you think it's unusual that a crook could have both of our vitals to defraud—including Social Security numbers. How did they get that?"

"Didn't you tell me, Miss Connor, that you and your husband both had opened accounts at the same bank? The one that issued the credit card to you?"

"Yes," Clare said. "Could they have used data from his account and matched it to mine?

How could they do that if we have different last names?"

"Not hard," Scott said. "Small bank, not thousands of accounts, but hundreds. Something might have flagged him or her to look and find matching addresses. Maybe you gave information on next of kin."

"What about the loan theft," Willie asked. "How did all that tie in?"

"I told Ms. Connor when she first stopped by here about a politician whose travel arrangements gave his secretary access to his private information. She had a roommate who worked for a mortgage company, and they created several hundred thousand dollars of debt. Caught the thieves in that one."

"Good man," Willie said. "Does it happen that frequently?"

Scott exhaled loudly.

"Too often. It's likely in your case that the perp sold it to a ring creating false loans. The ring identifies a house sitting vacant for a long time and matches it to your identity. That happened a lot during the 2008 recession. Today, people posing as you two go to a mortgage company for a home equity loan, sit through a closing, walk out with money enough to live on for a good while. I mean it's somewhat the bank's fault, cause they should be checking the chain of title closely and watching for little inconsistencies to make sure this isn't happening!"

"So a couple posing as us walked with two hundred grand?"

He nodded. "Now you've got to get with the mortgage company after we make this police report about it. Tell them your identity was stolen so they won't come after you for payment."

"It's too late. They're already hounding us," Willie said. "We barely got Mom buried. Now we've got to call all these charge cards and other businesses that are yelling about our ruined credit."

Scott handed them a piece of paper with case numbers on it. "You'll need to pick up copies of the reports downstairs. It'll take you a while to get it all straightened out, but the police reports will help. My number's on there if they need any verification of who's responsible."

Scott tilted his head, gave them a questioning look.

"Hey, this didn't cause any domestic problems, did it?"

Willie snickered. "Who, us? Not a bit."

Clare laughed. "Just a few sleepless nights, that's all." A silence fell, both Clare and Willie unable or unwilling to talk about what they'd been going through.

"So where does that leave us?" Clare asked. Her stomach felt tight. Talking about these enormous thefts made her feel like they were happening all over again.

"I'll see what I can find out at the bank," Scott said. "Ask some questions, see who's left recently—or who needs to leave. Nine times out of ten these are short-term employees—trained enough to know the systems, passed their ninety-day probation before becoming regular employees, do a few thefts like this, then they're gone. But I have to say that the fraud takes a lot more players, and I haven't seen that since all the vacant houses in oh-eight and oh-nine."

"Seems like they'd be better off learning the systems, being a good banker, and not screwing up like this," Clare said.

"Some people just gotta steal, no matter what," the detective said, shaking his head.

Clare arrived at the Reidinger Drive house, saw Willie wasn't there yet, and went straight through the house to the backyard. Her tomatoes were leaning heavily with fruit. She returned to the kitchen and put on gloves and an apron to take care of the dead and wounded out back.

As she pulled the deflated fruit and put it in a pile to compost, she felt the return of her love for her garden. And her home. After circling over the half-dozen plants, now in the height of their growth and badly in need of rearranging inside their cages, she sat with a pile of usable orbs on her bench and gazed out over the hydrangeas, also in full bloom. What were the risks of reconciling? This garden and all she'd put into it was one of the bonuses, for sure.

She heard Willie come in the house, and she returned to the kitchen, took off her apron and gloves and guided him to the sofa in the den. She told him about the big revelation about her mother.

"Wow! So Frankie wasn't your real mom!" Willie exclaimed.

"And Tony Sands I introduced you to? He's not my cousin. He's my half-brother."

"What other surprises do you have for me? I can't believe all this stuff."

"The big deal was finding out my father had had a brief affair. He completely sobered up, they left the mountains with me in the care of my mother's sister, Frankie. Started a new life in Atlanta as a family of four, not three."

"I'm amazed. I know you had a really hard time with her as a kid, and you told me about that. But by the time I knew her, that wasn't going on so much. The two of you seemed to have an okay relationship. And every word I said at the burial was true. She and you were a lot alike."

"Blame it on the Italian family genes," Clare said, smiling. "I still think of her as my real mom. I don't know much about my birth mother, Lucia. I'm not sure how important that is."

She told him briefly about her place on the mountain top, meeting Tony, and tooling around the mountains getting to know about her ancestors, the coal mines, and the history of both sides in the valley. And then the great reveal on her way back to Atlanta.

Willie made a low whistle.

"Had no idea all that was going on."

"It was like a lightning bolt out of the blue."

He turned to her. "Okay, so when are you moving back in?"

"Whoa, wait a minute," she laughed. But she was serious. "We need to talk—about a lot of things."

"I'll say. I've got to get on the phone soon to convince the mortgage company again that we were not that couple sitting in the closing taking their money."

"Very important, but that's not what I'm talking about."

"So what are you talking about?"

"Your habit of coming in late without telling me. Over the last week before I left I'd held dinner for you at least twice while you had drinks with a coworker. I had dinner ready—a very nice dinner at that—and it was left for the fridge. How long do you need—should I just scrap dinner those nights? Can you give me a heads up when you'll be late?"

"I just get to drinking, I guess, and lose track."

"There's that, too," she said. She took his hand, afraid to say what she needed to, scared of his response.

"I'm concerned about your reaction to drink. I see your father and your brother, and I'm afraid you have the genes for being an alcoholic. I don't want that for our relationship."

Willie's eyes showed no surprise.

"You're right. It's a problem." He looked down at their joined hands. "I don't know what to say."

"I'd like to hear you say you'll never drink again," Clare said, her heart beating against her chest wall. She didn't want to frighten him away. "But I'm not unrealistic."

Willie continued to look at their hands, not at her.

"I am not my father, and I am certainly not my brother," he said, turning and looking at her. "I promise you that. I'll do better. I won't turn into them, even if it means I change the way I socialize."

Clare felt better, but things still were not settled between them.

"I think I'm bipolar." She said it for the first time out loud, with no qualifiers like "maybe" or "possibly."

He turned his head and his blue eyes looked sad.

"What does that mean?"

She pulled her hand from him and gave him a mock hit on the upper arm.

"You don't need to admit me to a hospital," she joked. "You need to just understand that sometimes I'll do things in a manic mode, like take off for the mountains without a job lined up. Or panic when my husband kicks me out of the house."

This time his head hung low.

"I'm sorry. I shouldn't have said you needed to leave. I was panicked, too, by my father's craziness. That was my fault." He grabbed her hand again. "Don't hold it against me forever, please!" She could see from his eyes, which had begun to water, that he was sorry. But she wanted him to know her better if they were going to get back together.

"I need to get some professional help. This identity theft stuff threw me into a tailspin like nothing I've ever experienced. I need your support, not your accusations. And I need your love."

He reached over, put his arms around her, and pulled her to him.

"You've got it. You're my wife, and I love you, and I want to have kids with you." He caught her questioning look. "Honest!"

She leaned against him, enjoying his arms about her.

"You know, I'm enjoying you more now, there's no question about it," she said, pulling back a little. "I'm freaked over what we've got to do to clear the mortgage identity thing."

"It'll be a pain for a while."

"There's something else you need to know," Clare said.

He pulled back in mock horror.

"I don't know if I can take any more surprises!"

"I need to go back up to Rising Fawn. That's where the trailer is."

"Why do you need to go back there?"

"It's my mom's property, and I need to clean it and advertise it and interview a new renter." She could tell this news wasn't going over well.

"And—I just want to spend time there. Not long, just as long as it takes to take care of business and maybe explore some opportunities for client companies in Chattanooga. It's just down the mountain from where the trailer is. I'll have a place to stay while waiting for new tenants to move in."

Willie cocked his head and looked at her closely.

"You're sure this isn't the bipolar thing kicking in."

She reflected for a moment. He could be right. Going that direction would be complicated. "Might be. I might not want to explore the business side after all.

"I just want to be where I feel at home now. Spend some time with Tony and his family. See if there are other relatives I didn't meet. I feel like I'm just getting to know a part of me." She shifted next to him on the couch.

"And it'll take a couple of days before Frankie's death certificates are ready. Once I come back, I can get to settling and closing her accounts."

"When are you planning to go?"

She checked her watch.

"In a few minutes. I'll just get some fresh clothes and go."

His face was dark.

"This doesn't feel right. I just got you back, and now you're leaving again."

She grabbed him around his love handles and hugged him, then lifted herself back, holding his arms.

"I'm sorry. Promise I'll be back in a few days. I just need to process some of this stuff. I hope we'll be able to go up there together soon. You'd love it. Lots of mountains, lots of creeks and waterfalls, too. Made for the kinds of things we used to do together."

"Yeah, just don't go getting no mountain lover. Don't think there's room for that here." Now he looked resigned.

"I'll miss you. I want you here, not there."

"I'll miss you, too. I'm not getting anything going up there. You can trust me."

She thought about the lack of trust of Willie that had so shattered her life. She wondered if it was possible to reassure the insecure holes that lay in each of them. They were like traps in the woods, placed to make them sink deep, throw them off their paths, wherever their paths were taking them.

Willie stood beside the driver's window of her car. Clare had checked her tire pressure, oil change record, and gas and sat in the car. She leaned out the window and stroked his arm.

"I want you to stay with me," he said.

"I know what you want, and I want it too," she said, winking. "There'll be time for that. Lots of time."

"I still feel shortchanged. I'm waiting for you."

She leaned farther through the window, and he drew near. He bent down and she kissed him hard on the lips.

"I love you, and I'll be back," she said.

She backed the school-bus-yellow SUV out of the driveway and turned on Reidinger Drive to leave their subdivision and head for the interstate. She made a mental note to call Lela Tremont, the mother of the girls with multi-colored hair.

Cumulous clouds hung above. Clare checked for any dark tinges that might mean rain. As she made her turns, she thought of the shifts in the earth's plates that forever changed the land surfaces above them and thrust into the universe the mountains she was bound for. Oceans of saltwater covered them, then receded. Then eons of ice melt and ravages of time wore them down, smoothed tops, carved that lightning bolt of a valley between two long mountains. Her body still carried the reverberation Willie's move-out demands sent through her, hurtling her on this same itinerary that seemed like months ago but was only a few days.

She didn't have to decide the course of their marriage right now. She had property to tend to. That aged single-wide perched there on Johnson's Crook represented a notch in her belt, a bit more armor for the balance she needed in her life to feel whole in the relationship. She needed to take care of it. Frankie would want her to take care of her little place on the mountain.

She now knew she didn't have to rush things, take a stand, build up the fortress of arguments pro and con. As the dense trees of the green-dressed street saluted her on the way out, she realized she could just let things flow, like the rivers cutting through the mountains to the north or the big one flowing nearby. Let things take their course. Not fight nature. If Willie was true, he would be there when she came back. And they could start sorting through their new life.

As she turned onto the interstate, Clare sensed a long line of people standing on her shoulder, some tall men and dark-haired women among them.

She owed it to herself not to hurry.

# Acknowledgments

From attending Plum Nelly Clothesline Art Show events in the late 50s and early 60s to visits with the very influential potter Charles Counts later, the Johnson's Crook area of Lookout Mountain has held fascination for me. The other side of Lookout Mountain, Lula Lake and Falls, were places my family and I visited as I was growing up. I thank my parents, Bill and Fannie Ford, for opening our eyes to the wonders around us in Tennessee and Georgia, and I thank the Lula Lake Land Trust for allowing access so that I could recall details of the rocks and crags of that amazing place. The Georgia Archives provided census data, journal articles, and pictures of the old mines on Lookout for my research. The archives of the Paulist Fathers in Washington, DC supplied correspondence about the Catholic mission at South Pittsburg.

*Rising Fawn* received early encouragement from Rosemary Daniell (myzonarosa.com), Phyllis Alesia Perry, Carol Lee Lorenzo, C. Michael Curtis, Susan Crawford, and Lauren Marino, in workshops at the Sandhills Writers Conference in Augusta, Callanwold Center for the Arts in Atlanta, the Appalachian Writers Workshop, and New Orleans' Words and Music Festival. Thanks to Susan Crawford from our Atlanta writing group, and to Laurie Reich for the manuscript finishing work. I appreciate the ongoing feedback I received from members of the South Carolina Writers Association Low Country Writers Group and assistance from writers Stephanie Austin Edwards and John Williams in particular. Writer Valerie Sayers, whom I met through the Pat Conroy Literary Center in Beaufort, SC was very helpful to me, as were Jonathan Haupt, Cassandra King Conroy, Kathleen Harvey, and Tim Conroy of this awesome Center and resource for writers. I have to give a shout-out also to my friends at the Wide Oak Writers of Beaufort, and to our short story instructor T.D. Johnston!

Thank you to my Italian heritage friends, especially Elizabeth Barr, Marie Jamison, Mary Monti, Beverly Morin, and longtime fellow opera lover Vivian Wolf Perasso Friend, for sharing so much of your culture. Professor Ennio Rao of University of North Carolina was a great assist on Italian research sources. A sequel to this book will detail more about the Irish in these mountain and valleys, so there's more to come on that. Kelleen Fitzgerald, MD, of The Atlanta Internists, provided valuable review of Frankie's medical condition.

Thanks to Lookout Mountain-based Jennifer Daniels and Jeff Neal of the Jennifer Daniels band (jenniferdaniels.com) for letting me use them as my model for Jill and Gene in the jam in Chapter 6. My husband and I follow Jennifer Daniels at live concerts in Atlanta and Decatur, and I often wrote with Jennifer's voice playing in the background. Thanks to my sister Katie Ford Sprouse for letting me be part of the farmhouse and riverhouse jams that took place during her and The Warblers' fabulous days in Athens, Atlanta and other locations.

I appreciate my husband, Richard Williamson, for his patience and encouragement of my work. Thanks, also, to his daughter, Tracy Gilbert, her husband, Derek Gilbert, all the kids, and to my friends and family for understanding my need for time for writing. The book finally got done!

Made in United States
Orlando, FL
29 January 2022

14198132R00104